1835—a bygone world of tyrants, lovers
and slaves. Peter Abdee, the master of
Dragonard Hill, his three daughters and his
young son David, become embroiled in a
bitter struggle for survival in the
wilderness of Louisiana. A shattering
climax rushes the whole family towards
total annihilation . . .

The Siege of Dragonard Hill is the fifth
and most sweeping novel in the best-
selling 'Dragonard' series.

D1439430

Also by Rupert Gilchrist

DRAGONARD
THE MASTER OF DRAGONARD HILL
DRAGONARD BLOOD
DRAGONARD RISING

and published by Corgi Books

The Siege of
Dragonard Hill

Rupert Gilchrist

CORGI BOOKS

A DIVISION OF TRANSWORLD PUBLISHERS LTD

THE SIEGE OF DRAGONARD HILL

A CORGI BOOK   0   552   11501   0

Originally published in Great Britain by Souvenir Press Ltd.

PUBLISHING HISTORY
Souvenir Press edition published 1979
Corgi edition published 1980

Copyright © 1979 Souvenir Press Ltd.

Conditions of sale
1. This book is sold subject to the condition that it shall not, by
way of trade *or otherwise*, be lent, re-sold, hired out or otherwise
circulated without the publisher's prior consent in any form of
binding or cover other than that in which it is published *and
without a similar condition* including this condition being imposed
on the subsequent purchaser.
2. This book is sold subject to the Standard Conditions of Sale of
Net Books and may not be re-sold in the U.K. below the net price
fixed by the publishers for the book.

This book is set in Highland 10 on 10½ pt.

Corgi Books are published by Transworld Publishers Ltd., Century
House, 61–63 Uxbridge Road, Ealing, London, W5 5SA

Made and printed in the United States of America by Arcata
Graphics, Inc., Depew, New York

All of the characters in this book are fictitious, and any resemblance to actual persons, living or dead, is purely coincidental

CONTENTS

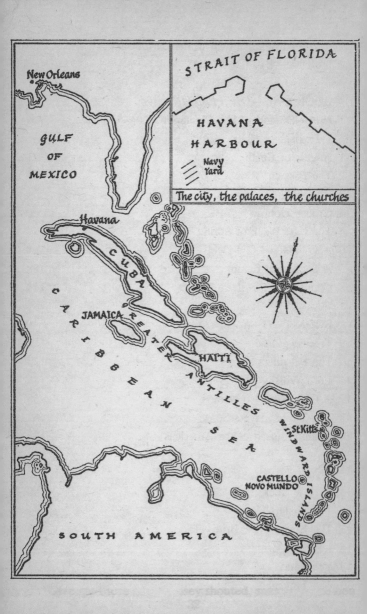

Prologue

BLACK SEEDS

Havana, Cuba
1836

The decanter of claret at supper successfully dulled Victoria's mind. The potency of the rich red wine enabled her to sit at the far end of the long teakwood table from her husband and glance occasionally through the flickering candles at his swarthy face without hating herself for having married him.

Conde Juan Carlos Veradaga was twice Victoria's age, a Spanish nobleman who owned one of the largest sugar plantations in Cuba as well as prospering from galleons which arrived regularly in the Havana harbour—slave ships from Africa brimming with Negroes to sell in New World marketplaces.

Wealthy. Influential amongst the Spanish aristocracy which ruled the island of Cuba. Devout in the Holy Catholic Church. Juan Carlos Veradaga also was crippled, a man confined to a wheelchair. His one joy was an infant son, the only child which Victoria had given him. But Juan Carlos no longer showed any love—not even affection—for his young American bride.

Tonight's supper passed without conversation. Juan Carlos picked fastidiously at his food; he continued to ignore Victoria when she finally beckoned a servant to pull back her chair from the table. She departed silently from the cavernous *comedor*; they did not exchange farewells.

The time was now past midnight. Victoria lay awake on her four-postered bed upstairs in *Palacio Veradaga*. The air was humid. She had pulled off her nightgown in a sudden fit of irritation and lay naked upon sheets encrested with the Veradaga coat-of-arms. She cursed Havana, the Caribbean's cloying humidity, her loneliness.

Having opened the bedroom door to create a cross breeze from the tall windows which overlooked the walled gardens, Victoria pressed her eyes shut as a further inducement for sleep. But the wine from supper was forsaking her: She was becoming increasingly alert. She again began counting the depressing facts of married life, moving from one complaint to another as a more religious woman would proceed through the *Ave Marias* on her rosary beads.

Juan Carlos was already insisting that their son be taught to speak Spanish before learning English. This infuriated Victoria. He also was beginning to make snide remarks about her inability to conduct herself as a loving mother to young Juanito. He wanted the child to be raised away from the city, on the Veradaga's vast *finca* where the sugar crops were grown and refined in the *central*. Juan Carlos had virtually told Victoria that she herself should return to her father's plantation in Louisiana.

Damn it! she cursed as she tossed again on the perspiration-soaked sheets. Why did I marry that swarthy rat? Was I really that desperate to leave my family? To escape New Orleans? Why could I have not merely let him indulge me and remained single? Retained my freedom?

The air in the stately bedroom was motionless but Victoria knew that she needed more than a breeze to satisfy her. She had passed too many tropical nights lately without a lover. She felt angry, betrayed, frustrated.

Despite his infirmity, Juan Carlos satisfied Victoria's specialized tastes in love-making. Or at least he once had. But Juan Carlos no longer desired to make love to her. He even refused to allow Victoria to kneel alongside his bed and satisfy his penis with her mouth—much less invite her to straddle him with crouched legs and clutching vaginal lips, a feminine expertise which she called her 'Jezebel's Grip' and had aided him in siring his heir.

Is this fair? Victoria asked herself as her hands pulled at the sheets in frustration. Is this fair that a son-of-a-bitch who is old enough to be my father should dictate my love life? I hate myself for even thinking that I might go to him now if he showed the slightest interest in me. Why can't I find a new man who enjoys the same sexual habits as I do?

Victoria rolled across the wide bed and asked herself another nagging question. Why was Juan Carlos becoming so critical of her? Was it because she had finally given him an heir and he no longer had any use for her? Or had he found a lover? If so, who was the sneaking bitch?

Thinking of her own need for physical satisfaction, Victoria lay on her back and opened her thighs. She inched the finger tips of one hand over the flatness of her milky white abdomen until she reached the furry brown delta between her legs. She brushed her other hand toward the nipple of one breast, gently coaxing the rosy bud into tautness.

She hesitated. The idea of masturbating repulsed her. She held her hand motionless between her bent legs, her middle finger lingering in the moistness of her vagina. She wondered if she should postpone this solitary act, if she might perhaps meet someone tomorrow who could give her true satisfaction.

Tomorrow! Victoria laughed at the idea of meeting someone tomorrow. She had postponed masturbation on previous nights and had met no one the next day to make love to her. Juan Carlos guarded her like a hawk-nosed *duenna*, she spent her days and nights in growing sexual frustration.

Curling her finger inside her furry slit, Victoria again reached to fondle her nipples. She pressed her eyes tightly shut but, now, she did not strain for sleep. She scanned her mind for the image of a man whom she could use in a sexual fantasy.

Victoria imagined a tall man. His legs were strong. He dressed in snug white breeches which hugged his muscled thighs like a second skin, handsome military clothing which betrayed his manly penis curling over the generous spread of his testicles.

As her breasts heaved with anticipation, Victoria envisioned herself falling to her knees in front of such a handsome man, of running her hands adoringly over that bulge of manhood encased in tight white breeches, of seeing his penis lengthen into a rod for her to lick through the fabric, to chew . . .

Victoria then became less aggressive, more romantic in her thoughts. She pictured the tall man embracing her, holding her tenderly in his arms, plunging his tongue into

4

her mouth, reaching to cup his hand around one breast, his fingers working . . .

A noise suddenly disturbed Victoria's thoughts, a sound which came from outside her bedroom door.

Was it whispering?

Lifting her head from the heap of pillows, Victoria quickly combed back her mane of auburn hair from one ear and strained to listen more closely.

Victoria's first thought was tinged with fantasy, a residue from her sexual wishes. She imagined that a lover was coming down the hallway toward her bedroom. A stranger who might have seen her this afternoon in the *Plaza de Armas*. The man was brave. He had climbed the walls surrounding *Palacio Veradaga* . . .

Quickly realizing that such a thought was absurd, Victoria considered a more likely possibility. Juan Carlos slept only three doors down the hallway from her room. He claimed to take laudanum each night to ease the pain of his withered legs but Victoria now wondered if he only used laudanum as an excuse to keep her from intruding on him. Juan Carlos might be awake himself at this late hour. He could very well be whispering for his new lover to join him.

Hearing the faint voice again, Victoria slowly moved to the edge of the bed. She lowered her bare feet to the low-heeled slippers setting on the marble floor and reached for the robe she had tossed to the foot of the bed. Cinching the cord around her waist, she next felt for the amber handle of the dagger which she kept buried in a deep china bowl filled with dried rose petals on her bedside table.

The luminescent Cuban moon lit Victoria's slim body as she stealthily moved from her bed toward the half-open door. She peered out into the darkness of the hallway vaulted with darkly stained beams. She listened for the sound of footsteps, a whisper from a female who might have replaced her in her husband's bed.

The call came again.

'*Malou . . . I am waiting for you . . .*'

Malou?

Victoria gripped the dagger tighter in her hand and stepped bravely out into the hallway. Malou was her Negress slave. A body servant. Was Juan Carlos secretly meeting Malou at night? Had he developed a taste for black women?

Proceeding down the hallway in the direction from which the whispering had come, Vicky wished that she carried a brace of pistols rather than this small amber-handled dagger. She imagined how she could shoot Juan Carlos. She envisioned herself pleading to the authorities that she had mistakenly shot her husband instead of a thief. She imagined how she would enter the necessary period of mourning observed here in Catholic Cuba and then emerge rich, free to marry a man who could satisfy her. She would become the belle of Cuban society! She could...

The voice called again.

'Cock feathers and sea shells ... yellow grass and a blue fish ...'

The sing-song words were soft, a call whispered in a Negroid drawl. Victoria quickly changed her opinion. The words were not coming from Juan Carlos. No. It was a Negro speaking. A slave whispering for Malou. Victoria also guessed that his words—*cock feathers, sea shells, grass, a fish*—were the ingredients for a voodoo charm or spell.

Knowing that her black servant, Malou, believed in the West African religion called Yoruba, Victoria's anger suddenly turned against the black woman. Like many other white people in Havana, Victoria considered the black religion of Yoruba to be nothing but witchcraft. The whites called it voodoo; the Negroes' absorption of Catholic saints and beliefs into the pagan religion only increased the fury of their critics.

Not believing in African *gris-gris* spells, charms, nor even the Holy Catholic Church, Victoria moved more swiftly down the hallway with the intent to punish the headstrong black woman. If she could not have sexual release tonight then at least she could inflict torture on a female who thought she could! Why else would a ... nigger bitch be meeting a man?

*   *   *

Victoria saw in the hallway's near darkness that the oaken door to her husband's room was firmly shut. She also saw that little Juanito's door was closed.

6

Tossing her hair back from her face, Victoria surveyed the other doors lining the stark white hall until she spotted a sheet of silver moonlight falling upon the carved panels of a door to a room used for guests.

'Malou . . .' the deep voice drawled again from inside the room, '. . . I am waiting for you.'

Pressing herself against a Castilian tapestry hanging in the hall, Victoria slowly edged her way closer toward the half-open door.

'Malou, I dones what you tells me to do . . .'

Stepping quickly in front of the door, Victoria pushed it open with her foot and hissed into the darkness, 'I am not "Malou"!'

'Condesa Veradaga!' the voice gasped.

'Who are you?' Victoria demanded as she stood in the doorway, looking at the outline of a broad-shouldered man framed by a tall window silvered by the moon. She could tell by the smooth contour of the man's shaved head that he was indeed a Negro.

The man backed further into the shadows and reached to cover his groin.

Victoria demanded, 'Who are you? What are you doing here?' She now saw that the black man was naked, that his clothes lay heaped in a white pile alongside him on the floor. He was trying to hide his groin from her eyes.

'It's me . . . Arturo . . .' the black man stammered, cupping both hands over his midsection. 'Arturo . . . your husband's criado!'

Victoria no longer was interested in the slave's identity. Nor the reason the black valet was here in this bedroom. She wanted to see what he was hiding from her.

Stepping toward him and swatting his hands away from his groin, Victoria demanded, 'Don't back away from me when I'm talking to you, boy!'

Shaking his head, Arturo pleaded, 'No, Condesa. You must not see . . .'

Victoria began to speak but the words caught in her throat. She stared at the Negro's crotch and saw—or thought that she saw—not one but two glistening black penises hanging between his legs. The twin organs were large, black, hardened to form blood-full crowns identical in roundness.

7

'Malou tells me to come here,' Arturo wailed, groping more frantically to cover his masculine equipment.

Victoria ignored his words. She knew that Negroes were often endowed more generously than white men but... two phallus? And both enormous?

'Don't tell your husband,' Arturo pleaded as his fingers worked nervously to move a thin black leather cord tied around his waist.

Jabbing her dagger at him, Victoria repeated in a louder whisper, 'What are you hiding from me, boy?'

Arturo struggled to work the leather thong around his naked waist. He faltered, 'Malou... she gives me this ... medicine to wear, Mistress. This be African medicine ... to make me ... strong.'

Victoria began to understand. She saw one penis now dangling over Arturo's bare hip. She also saw the leather cord to which the object was attached. Arturo wore a voodoo ceremonial phallus made to match his own penis and it was connected to a leather thong encircling his waist.

Grabbing for the shiny black phallus attached to the thong, Victoria held it by the crown and instantly felt that the object was hard, textured exactly like an erect penis.

Arturo tried to pull himself back from Victoria as she tightened her grip on the ceremonial penis still attached to the cord encircling his waist. Arturo's true penis now hung limp—lifeless—from his groin.

Jabbing her blade forward, Victoria quickly severed the leather cord and snatched the voodoo phallus from his hip. She stepped into a shaft of moonlight streaming through the window and saw that the organ had been made from wood and stretched leather, that the waist thong was still attached to the phallus by a peg carved into its base.

Nervously reaching for the object, Arturo pleaded, 'That be black people's medicine, Condesa Veradaga. That be nothing for a fine white lady like yourself to see...'

'Medicine!' Victoria shrieked, suddenly raising the voodoo phallus and lashing its leather thong at Arturo's face like a whip. 'How dare Malou meet you here! How dare you have this... obscene object in my house! Juanito is sleeping only two rooms away from here! My husband's room is at the end of this very hall! I could scream and you would...'

8

'No, mistress,' Arturo begged. 'Don't scream! Please don't scream for no one. The Conde Veradaga will have me whipped!'

'The Conde! What about me? I am the Condesa! I can also give orders for you to be whipped! But I won't! I will whip you myself! Like this! And this!' She said, lashing the phallus's leather thong at Arturo's face, repeating, '. . . and this . . . and this . . . and this!'

Arturo held one arm over his face to protect himself from the snapping cord as he reached with his other hand to gather his pile of tow clothing from the floor. Victoria continued to snap the leather cord at him, now hysterically striking at his arms and neck and back. She then hurled the phallus impulsively at Arturo when he turned to rush from the bedroom.

Halting to retrieve the phallus from the floor, Arturo wrapped it in the bulk of tow clothing and disappeared naked down the tile stairs which led to the servants' quarters in *Palacio Veradaga*.

*   *   *

The black woman, Malou, smiled to herself that same night as she stood near Havana's harbour with a child bundled in her arms. She hoped that her ruse to divert her mistress's attention had worked, that Arturo had gone to the guest room in *Palacio Veradaga* with the wooden phallus strapped to his waist. Malou had told Arturo to meet her in the bedroom but she had never intended to join him there. She had hoped, though, that her mistress would hear Arturo whispering. She knew that the Condesa greatly needed sexual attention from a male and, if the Condesa allowed Arturo to make love to her in the guest room tonight, she would be too embarrassed—and too pleased—tomorrow morning to chastise Malou for inviting Arturo there. If not . . .

Malou put aside the thought of the Condesa reprimanding her. She was not frightened of her mistress. Malou had the African gods to protect her, the deities called Obtala and Olorun.

Wrapping the cloak around the infant cradled in her arms, Malou proceeded down the narrow cobbled street

9

toward an iron gate which opened onto the courtyard of a large white-washed building. The street was the *Calle de Esclavos*—the Street of the Slaves—in the disreputable suburb of Havana called Regla. The building to which she was going was a slave house.

Remembering the instructions which the owner of the slave house had sent to her—along with money—by a messenger, Malou ignored the bell chain dangling alongside the iron grille which faced the street. She slipped into the courtyard and her bare feet quickly moved across the cobblestones toward a plank door.

Malou knew that the old man would be waiting to see her and the infant—an Englishman was paying her to bring him young Juanito Veradaga tonight.

Clutching the infant tightly in her arms, Malou climbed the narrow flight of stone stairs and mulled over the few facts she knew about the old man who had summoned her here to this district of robbers and thieves.

The old Englishman's name was Richard Abdee. He was one of Havana's richest slave dealers. The Conde Veradaga also dealt in slaves but Richard Abdee was more successful, a more ruthless merchant than Malou's crippled master. She admired ruthlessness, even in white people.

Malou reached the top of the stairs and knocked lightly—according to instructions—on the second plank door. She reached to knock again but her hand hesitated in mid-air when a man's voice within the room commanded her to enter.

Turning the iron handle, Malou pushed open the door and stared into total darkness. She saw no flame, no flicker of a candle or oil lamp.

A man asked, 'Are you the wench from *Palacio Veradaga?*'

'I am Malou,' she answered in a throaty voice, speaking with the assurance of a woman who had no concern about physical beauty, no plots to win over a male with her femininity. Malou was a plain-faced woman who wore simple clothes and a white kerchief knotted over her forehead.

She announced in a straightforward voice, 'I brought the child as I was paid to do.'

A sulphur match struck in the room's blackness. A tallow candle was soon lit and its flickering yellow flame glowed upon the slim figure of a man seated in a wicker chair placed alongside a table.

Although Malou had never before met Richard Abdee, she immediately guessed that this was the infamous old slave-dealer. He wore a white planter's suit and his white hair was tied at the nape of his neck in an out-moded style seldom seen anymore in Havana. His skin was leathery and, although lined with age, his face was handsome, strongly-featured, set with a look of determination. He had every appearance of a man who could control the slave trade of Cuba. Even his bright blue eyes had a malevolent glint as he studied Malou standing in the doorway holding the child bundled in her arms.

'Bring the child closer,' Abdee ordered, wiggling the fingers of a hand dotted with brown spots of age.

Malou padded toward the chair. She removed the cover from the sleeping child's face but did not relinquish him from her arm. She said, 'This is the son of the Conde Veradaga.'

Abdee peered into the bundle, asking, 'Does he look like his mother?'

'The Condesa has blue eyes,' Malou answered, turning the child for the candle's glow to catch his dark features. 'My mistress's hair is not black like . . .'

Abdee lifted his head and looked quizzically at Malou. He asked, 'Victoria is fair? My . . . granddaughter has blue eyes?'

Malou stared at the old man. His 'granddaughter?' She knew that the Condesa Veradaga came from America. That her family lived on a plantation in Louisiana. But Malou had not known that old Richard Abdee was related to her mistress. The rumours all said that he had gone many years ago from England to the West Indies.

Peering into the bundle, Abdee said, 'This child is the first of my bloodline I have ever seen.'

Malou blandly answered, 'You be like us black people, Master Sir. Black people taken from Africa don't see the children they plant in this new world neither.'

Abdee kept his eyes on the child. He showed no concern for the problems of black people. He likewise showed little affection for the child.

11

Malou studied Abdee's weathered face as she held the child closer toward him. She observed, 'You have a restless soul, Master. I see restlessness in your eyes.' Malou was a Yoruba priestess and understood people's dissatisfaction.

'I did not pay you to come here tonight to talk about me,' Abdee grumbled. 'I only wanted to see this child.'

Waving her away from his chair, he said, 'I have seen him. Go. You have papers to conduct you safely out of this district. Go back to your . . . mistress.'

Malou folded the covering over the child's face but she lingered in front of the old man's chair. The Englishman fascinated her. She asked, 'Is the boy what you expected to see?'

'I expect nothing,' Abdee answered in a clipped voice. 'I expect nothing from any man or woman. Black or white.' The corners of his thin lips raised into a smile. He added, 'And I expect the . . . worst from someone with *my* blood in their veins!'

Malou knew that he was serious. She warned, 'Do not die before you settle the problems in your soul, Master Sir, or you shall never rest. I can tell that you have spent many years wandering . . .'

'Damn my soul!' he suddenly thundered, 'And yours, too, you meddlesome bitch!'

Raising his hand toward the door, he ordered, 'Go! Get out of here! Never come back to this slave house or I'll have you seized as a runaway wench! I'll sell you downstairs on the auction block for a field worker!'

Malou left the old Englishman. She descended the narrow steps with the child in her arms and wondered if she would ever understand the workings of white people's minds.

Why would a man so rich, so powerful as this slavedealer not see his bloodline before tonight? Malou also mused why Richard Abdee would bribe her to bring him this child—his what? his great grandson?—to this slave house in Regla and then look so briefly at him?

No, Malou could not understand that manner of thinking. But she clearly understood the value of the gold coins which old Richard Abdee had sent her to bring the child tonight to his slave house. Malou told herself that she must now only concern herself with returning the child safely home—and prepare herself for any problems which might arise tomorrow morning in *Palacio Veradaga*. She had suspected that she had been followed tonight. That the Conde Veradaga had a trusted servant keep an eye on the traffic coming and going into his home. Malou knew that she had more to fear from her master than her mistress. *Aya*! Malou thought. Juan Carlos Veradaga is the one to watch out for! The Condesa is the mother of young Juanito but Conde Veradaga would kill for the little *muchacho*.

*   *   *

The city of Havana was built on a plain behind strong sea walls, a centuries old capital composed of white-and yellow-washed buildings decorated with a baroqueness which echoed the grandeur of Spain.

The *Palacio Veradaga* stood in the district of Havana called Jesus Maria, a princely residence given to the Ver adaga family by King Ferdinand VII of Spain. Little had changed on the exterior of *Palacio Veradaga*'s stone walls, its tall iron gates still protecting the inhabitants from hawking pedlars, strolling prostitutes, a wide variety of thieves ranging from pickpockets to pirates.

The Cuban sun was already bright at nine o'clock this morning; the louvred jalousies were tightly shut on the bedroom where the Condesa Veradaga still slept within the palace. The servants cautiously tiptoed past her closed door and threatened to pull the ears of any child who played beneath her windows.

Unlike his wife, Juan Carlos Veradaga had awoken early this morning. His servants shaved his face and dressed him in fresh linen, a blue silk stock, and a quilted robe. By nine o'clock, Juan Carlos had already paid his morning visit to the private chapel in *Palacio Veradaga* and now sat in his cane-sided wheel chair in the coolness of a shady courtyard adjoining the *sala* which served as his library.

A cup of strong black coffee and a chased silver plate of almond cakes set on a table nearby Juan Carlos's chair but he ignored this morning fare. The Conde was deep in thought. He had already received two visitors in the garden this morning.

Although the two bits of news which Juan Carlos had

learned from his morning visitors were ostensibly disconnected, he believed that he could find a way in which to use both of them to serve his purpose. Juan Carlos retained his hereditary power by being diverse in his resourcefulness.

The first visitor had come to the *Palacio Veradaga* from the harbour and had brought a sealed letter for the Condesa Veradaga. Juan Carlos had taken his wife's letter, broken the red wax seal, and promptly read its contents. He smiled to himself when he saw that it came from his wife's father in Louisiana. He believed that his prayers were finally being answered. Juan Carlos had once enjoyed his young wife's body and inventive bed games but, since she had given him a son, he had seen that he had to make a choice. Victoria was a deceitful and undependable woman. She did not love Juanito as he did but she could try to take the child as a way to spite him for distrusting her. Juan Carlos had been waiting for an opportunity to remove Victoria from his life. He chose his son rather than his wife. He was pleased that the Madonna had heard his petition for Juanito to be saved from the wickedness of his mother.

Juan Carlos's second interview this morning was with a Negro named Miguel, an old slave in the *Palacio Veradaga* who was a *coantado*, a slave saving money to buy his freedom. Old Miguel supplemented his earnings by spying for his master. He had brought Juan Carlos a vital piece of information this morning about Malou and his son.

Still maintaining his composure, Juan Carlos listened to Miguel report how Malou had taken young Juanito to a slave house last night on the *Calle de Esclavos*. Miguel assured Juan Carlos that his son had not been injured, that little Juanito had been brought back to the palace in the early hours of the morning and was now still sleeping soundly in the *almáciga*— his nursery.

Juan Carlos rewarded Miguel with a gold coin and told him not to tell Malou that he knew of her covert activities last night. He then sent the faithful slave to tell his wife about her maid taking their child to the slave house. He cautioned the old Negro, though, to withhold the identity of the man who owned the establishment on the *Calle de Esclavos*.

Juan Carlos also withheld the first bit of news from his

wife, the fact that a letter had arrived for her from America. He knew his fiery young wife too well. He knew what news would keep her locked in seclusion for the rest of the day, perhaps the entire week. He also knew what news would bring her immediately raging from her room.

True to his premonition, Victoria appeared in the garden only a few moments after old Miguel had gone to tell her about Malou taking Juanito to the *Calle de Esclavos* last night.

Dressed only in her *robe de chambre*, Victoria rushed past the drooping fronds of palm trees planted in earthen pots along the garden wall. Her auburn hair hung in a disarray around her face and shoulders as she moved angrily toward Juan Carlos, demanding, 'What is this report about Malou wandering the streets at night with my child? Where is the bitch now?'

Juan Carlos slowly raised one hand from the arm of his wheel chair. He pointed across the breakfast table and calmly said, 'Sit down, my dear.'

'Sit down? How can you remain so placid when Malou took our son to a . . . slave house?'

Juan Carlos noticed that Victoria had not even bothered to slip into her shoes. That she was barefoot like a slave wench. He hid his disapproval, saying, 'But Malou took Juanito to no ordinary slave, *costilla mia*!' He knew she loathed being called his 'little wife'.

'Do not try to irritate me at a moment like this!' Victoria shrilled. 'Malou took Juanito to the Street of the Slaves and I want her punished. Severely punished. Then you must sell her. I do not want the demented bitch in this house!'

Juan Carlos would have agreed with his wife on this matter in any other circumstances. But he now ignored her demands and asked, 'Do you know who owns that slave house, Victoria?'

'Why should I care?'

Turning his wheel chair around on the garden's blue-and-white tiled floor, Juan Carlos next asked, 'Have you ever thought that you might not be the only "Abdee" living here in Havana?'

Victoria furrowed her brow. 'Abdee'? What did her family name have to do with this? She muttered, 'What a stupid question. Especially at a time like this '

15

'*Estupido*?' Juan Carlos shrugged, saying, 'Perhaps. But does the name "Richard Abdee" mean anything to you, *costilla mia*?'

'Richard Abdee? That was the name of my grandfather. He was the disgrace of our family. He whipped slaves in public on the island of St Kitts. He did it for money. For the British government. But my grandfather is dead. He was killed on St Kitts when his plantation was destroyed by a slave rebellion.'

Juan Carlos had heard the story about Richard Abdee, that Victoria's grandfather had been the public whipmaster for the English colonials on the Leeward island of St Kitts, a mercenary position which had been called the 'Dragonard' by the English. But Juan Carlos had also heard other facts which were kept from his wife.

He said, 'Your grandfather was not killed as you believed. Your grandfather is still alive. He has been living in Havana even before you came here with me from New Orleans. He came to Cuba as a partner in business with a man named Ignatio Soto.'

'You lie!' she accused.

'No, I tell you the truth. *Por de dios*! I did not speak of it before because of your request. Did you yourself not beg me never to speak about your family when I married you?'

Victoria silently cursed her husband. She knew that she could not argue with him about that fact. There had been many facts that she had wanted to forget when she first came here. Her family, her disappointments, even her first husband, a marriage to a Yankee fop which Juan Carlos had arranged to be annulled. Incensed by the idea, though, that people knew facts about the Abdee family which were kept from her, that her grandfather might still be alive, she flared, 'I will find that wretched old man and confront him— if indeed that's who's living on the Street of the Slaves. I will see if any or all of this is true!'

Juan Carlos slowly shook his head.

'You can not stop me,' Victoria shrilled. 'I will go to *your* slave house. There will be somebody there who can take me to the Street of the Slaves. You cannot constrict me completely! Oh, no! I have some rights! Some freedom left!'

Juan Carlos now removed the folded letter from the

16

pocket of his quilted robe. He held it toward Victoria, saying, 'This arrived for you.'

Snatching the letter from his hand, Victoria saw that its red seal was broken. She said, 'You have already read it.'

'But of course.'

'You are . . . despicable! Have I no privacy?'

'If that is truly your opinion of me, that I am "despicable", then you will not feel sad to be parted from me for your long voyage.'

'Voyage? Long voyage? What do you mean?'

Nodding his head toward the folded letter, Juan Carlos explained, 'That is from your father in Louisiana. He pleads with you to come home. I am sorry to tell you that your step-mother was accidentally . . . killed.'

'Kate?' The image of the red-haired woman flashed through Vicky's mind.

'I believe that is the name your kind father mentions. Kate. *Verdad*. It is a woman named "Kate" who was thrown from a horse on your father's plantation.'

Victoria sank down to the chair across the breakfast table from Juan Carlos. She unfolded the page and slowly began to read the words scrawled in black ink. She soon saw for herself that it was true. Kate was dead. She had been thrown from a horse. Victoria finished the letter and immediately began to reread it, too stunned by the news to argue with Juan Carlos as he now proceeded to explain how she would sail from Havana for New Orleans, to comply with her father's wishes and go home. He proceeded to say that the black servant, Malou, would accompany her on the sea voyage to New Orleans, that Juanito would remain here in Cuba. He said, 'It is better to take Malou with you to Louisiana. Your love for our child does not match mine but if you have any concern for him—the slightest motherly care—you will agree that Juanito will be safer with Malou far away from Havana. You can sell her in New Orleans. You can leave her on your father's plantation.'

Looking at Victoria holding the letter crumpled in her fists, Juan Carlos paused to ask a question he had long waited to put to her. He said, 'Your father calls his plantation "Dragonard Hill". But if he was so ashamed of his own father being a public whipmaster named the "Dra-

17

gonard", why then . . .' He leaned forward in his wheel-chair, waiting for an explanation.

Victoria was not listening. Her blue eyes were dulled by the fact that her young stepmother, Kate, was dead. Only two thoughts cut through this shock. One was the question whether or not she did truly love her son. The second was her loathing for Juan Carlos.

'A rest will do you good,' Juan Carlos said in a soothing voice. 'Your two sisters are already at the plantation. You haven't seen them in years.' He remembered that fact from the letter.

Slowly raising her head, Victoria glared at him and said, 'I hate my sisters. I hate Veronica. I hate Imogen. And they hate me. The only person in this world whom I love—the only person—is my Papa. What do I have here? You? A son? No. I have been watching you turning Juanito against me. He is no more than an infant but you are building another one of your Spanish . . . walls between us. The only person I have left is my Papa. And I will go home—for his sake!'

Juan Carlos nodded his head. He was relieved to hear her utter this first hint of relinquishment of young Juanito. The words about her love for her father did not surprise him. He knew about the love. She had often tried to disguise it in the past seven years as hatred. But Juan Carlos knew it to be love, even a passion, an unnatural devotion which had driven her to marry him—a cripple, a man twice her age, an older male willing to indulge all her sexual fantasies . . . that is until even he had had enough of Victoria's appetite for perverse love. Juan Carlos was relieved that she was leaving. He hoped that she would stay forever on Dragonard Hill. He believed that every family should solve the problems they bred.

Book One

THE PLANTING

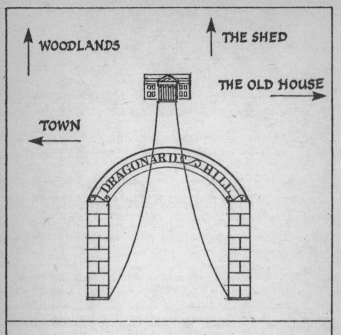

WOODLANDS

THE SHED

THE OLD HOUSE

TOWN

PUBLIC ROAD

CEMETERY

CARTERVILLE

TROY

GROUSE HOLLOW

GREENLEAF

TREETOP HOUSE

WITCHERLEY

NEW ORLEANS

Dragonard Hill Plantation, Louisiana, 1836

Chapter One

ANGELS OF DEATH

A pair of granite angels guarded two graves inside the family cemetery at Dragonard Hill, the two plots where the deceased wives of Peter Abdee now lay.

The stone angel standing sentinel over Melissa Selby Abdee's grave had weathered more that two scores of winter, the harsh Louisiana elements having worn down the monument's eyes, its hands reverently poised in prayer, the feathers chiselled into the spread granite wings.

The second angel erected in commemoration of Kate Breslin Abdee glittered white in the June sunlight as it stood fresh—almost alert—within the picket fence rising along the public road which ran between the small towns of Troy and Carterville.

Three weeks had already elapsed since Peter Abdee had buried Kate under this plot of freshly heaped dirt. Peter had visited Kate's grave every day since the funeral and, today, he had again walked down the hill from the main house and crossed the dirt road to the cemetery.

Kate's death fall from her lively roan mare still unnerved Peter Abdee. He struggled to assimilate the fact that Kate was dead, that she would not be curled alongside him in bed when he drifted to sleep each night, that she would no longer call homely questions to him from the library, that he was left alone to raise their six-year-old son. David.

Imogen Abdee stood a few paces behind her father in the family graveyard on this warm June afternoon; she was Peter's eldest daughter, a sober-faced young woman who wore her dark hair pulled severely back from her sharply featured face and was dressed in riding boots, deerskin breeches, and a man's nankeen shirt rolled above the elbows of her sunburnt arms.

Toying impatiently with a riding crop, Imogen looked at her father standing with his hand resting on the narrow shoulder of her small step-brother, David. Imogen had never shared the plantation's big house with her father, her step-mother, and their son. Nor would she move to the manorial white house now that Kate was dead. Imogen would remain living with her Negress companion in the ramshackle old house which the rest of the Abdee family had long-ago abandoned.

Looking from her father's immobile figure, Imogen glanced at her younger sister, Veronica, who had recently travelled South from Boston to comfort their father. Veronica had not changed in the seven years since she had gone North to live, at least not in Imogen's eyes. Veronica was still pretty, looking crisp and fresh in the black crêpe dress and bonnet of mourning she now wore in place of her usual pastel-hued cottons and dimities.

As Imogen studied her sister standing alongside their father, she suspected that her characteristic effervescence was only a façade. Veronica was married to a Negro who had once been a slave on Dragonard Hill. Imogen contemplated whether such a marriage, as well as being the mother to three half-caste children, was taking a toll on Veronica, a social strain which she refused to show to the world.

Wondering how long Veronica would remain a visitor at Dragonard Hill, Imogen thought of the precious hours she herself was losing each afternoon by visiting this grave with her father, young David, and Veronica. Imogen acted as the plantation's overseer. She was becoming increasingly nervous about the work she was neglecting on these balmy June days.

Imogen also had another concern. Her stomach turned into knots when she thought about her one sister yet to arrive home. Peter Abdee had also sent word to Cuba about Kate's fatal accident but, so far his other daughter—Victoria, but known at home only as Vicky—had yet to appear.

Veronica and Vicky were twins but, in Imogen's estimation, Veronica's gentle speech and considerate manners were highly preferable to the airs and lofty attitudes which Vicky exuded. Thinking about Vicky now being married to a titled Spaniard in the city of Havana, Imogen shuddered at the prospect of her fiery sister's latest affectations.

Imogen's unflattering thoughts about Vicky were interrupted by the sound of her father's voice. She looked to where he stood at the foot of an empty plot which lay between the two graves marked by the granite angels, a space where he himself would someday lie between his two wives.

'Melly didn't see much of life,' Peter said, speaking to no one in particular, staring blankly at the earth already green with summer grass. 'Melly longed for a big family but when she brought you and Vicky into the world, Veronica, the little thing's health gave way and . . .' He shook his head in bewilderment.

Peter Abdee was a tall man, built with wide shoulders and a body still firm for a man of forty-six-years. Although his black hair was flecked with silver at the temples, he had a youthful cast to his brilliant blue eyes and his lantern jaw gave him a handsome appearance which younger women found desirable. His recent moroseness was alien to his usual hearty manner.

Pulling his six-year-old son closer toward him, Peter said in a gentle tone, 'The people on this land called your mother "Matty Kate", David. That was the black people's and all our neighbours' term of affection for your mother. There was no woman more respected in this neighbourhood than Kate. She was always independent, spirited, enjoying the full bloom of life when the Lord suddenly . . . claimed her.'

Taking a deep breath, Peter said, 'I guess I don't bring much luck to a woman. First Melly died in childbirth. Now Katie killed like she was. I guess it's just a sign for me.'

Veronica moved closer to her father. She patted his forearm and said, 'Don't you be so pessimistic, Papa. You've got all the luck in the world.'

He answered soberly, 'You're right, Veronica. I do have some luck. A little bit at least. I'm lucky to have you come so far and so quickly to me.'

'Vicky will come, too, Papa,' Veronica assured him. Then trying to be light-hearted, she added, 'But we must remember that Vicky never makes it any place on time.'

Young David looked up at his father and, brushing a shank of dark silky hair from his eyes, he asked, 'Papa, when Aunt Vicky comes here will she bring my new little cousin with her?' The child's parents had taught him to call his stepsisters 'aunts' and their children, his 'cousins'—but refrained to tell young David about the Negroid colouring of Veronica's children.

23

Imogen interrupted in a stern voice from behind them. 'Your Aunt Vicky's kid is only a baby, Davey.'

'You have three cousins in Boston near your age, David,' Veronica said brightly. 'Why don't you write them a nice big long letter when we go back to the house and I'll include it in the envelope I'm sending to . . . Royal.'

David eagerly pressed, 'Can I go home with you, Aunt Veronica? Can I go to Boston and meet my cousins when you go?'

Veronica gently teased, 'David! If you keep pressing me about when I'm going home, I'll think you're trying to get rid of me!'

Imogen again interrupted. 'Maybe the boy's just wanting to know a little more about his . . . *Northern* cousins, Veronica.'

Veronica tried to ignore the sarcasm in Imogen's voice. She knew that her older sister disapproved of her marriage to a manumitted slave but she thought that a graveside was an inopportune place for Imogen to vent those feelings. Veronica reminded herself that Imogen had never possessed tact.

Peter said, 'I hope nobody leaves until Vicky gets home. I want all my family together.'

Imogen scoffed, 'If you want my opinion, Papa, we won't see hide nor hair of . . . Miss Priss!'

'Imogen!' Veronica scolded. 'How can you say such a thing? If Papa asked Vicky to come home you know that she will do everything possible to get here.'

Imogen said, 'It ain't as if Vicky and Kate were close friends, was it? Always together like two bugs in a rug!' She laughed at the idea.

Veronica glanced quickly at young David, wishing that Imogen would not speak so callously in front of a boy who had just lost his mother. She said, 'I was talking about Vicky and Papa, Imogen. I was implying that . . .'

She stopped. She knew that it was futile to argue with Imogen. She only hoped that she and Imogen would not have a confrontation during the ensuing days. There were too many ugly facts which could emerge. But if her older sister kept needling her in this way Veronica did not trust herself to behave like a lady.

Veronica had not expected to find either her father nor Imogen to be the same as they had been when she had left Dragonard Hill seven years ago. She knew that her father had built a new life with Kate, that the birth of a son had undoubtedly brought him and Kate closer together. Veronica also had been building her own life in the last seven years; she and Royal had their own children—six-year-old Lindy, five-year-old Peter Mark, and little Max.

The lack of changes in Imogen, though, distressed Veronica. Her older sister seemed to be only more settled in her disturbingly masculine ways. Although Veronica suspected what kind of sexual relationship Imogen pursued with her Negress companion, Belladonna, she did not want to point an accusing finger at them. She believed that every person found their own path through life. Nevertheless, Veronica wished that Imogen would be more generous toward her, less of a hypocrite about her marriage to a black man.

What does she have against Royal? Veronica wondered. Imogen herself is undoubtedly in love with a black person— surely this prolonged relationship with Belladonna cannot only be lust? And if she herself lives out all her days and sleeps every night with a black person why must she constantly make barbed remarks about me?

* * *

Veronica remembered back to conversations with her husband in Boston, of trying to keep Royal off the subject of Imogen's and Belladonna's relationship. She had told him that it was none of their business what anybody did on Dragonard Hill. But Royal persisted, asking Veronica if she truly thought that Imogen and Belladonna were female lovers. Lesbians. Veronica had to confess that, yes, she did believe so but she did not feel that it was her business to be curious.

Veronica and Royal had been in bed at the time, Veronica's head resting on Royal's cocoa-brown arm. It was a Sunday afternoon. The children were at a friend's house.

Veronica and Royal always seized such moments to make love.

Since Veronica and Royal first fell in love on Dragonard Hill, Veronica had treasured Royal's heart, his soul more than his body. She considered his firm, athletic frame to be a bonus to their marriage. He had grown lately to joke with her about the size of his penis; Royal was not boastful; Veronica knew he wanted to deflate the myth that white women went with black men for their manhood. But Royal's virility meant more to Veronica than the number of inches long and around which a penis measured. Royal was a strong, confident, trustworthy, responsible husband and father. That was virility for Veronica.

She had often rebuked him—although playfully during these love games—that she would love him regardless of how he was built. She knew that she would, too. She lay under him, alongside him, often raising one leg to let him lay between her legs to penetrate her vagina from behind. Regardless of what position they chose, despite the deep sensation which his penis gave her, she still considered his total self to be the man she called Royal Selby, her husband.

Veronica had often caught people in the street glancing at Royal's bulging crotch—equipment difficult to conceal—and then look up at her face. She knew what they were thinking when they saw she was a white woman. She tried to ignore their supposedly knowledgeable glances. And in that way, Royal's jokes about his penis did help her. He was deflating people's opinions about her.

Nevertheless, Veronica felt that it was unfair how so many white people disliked blacks for—she often felt—purely sexual reasons. Black men made white men feel sexually inferior. They often were threatening to white women . . . or, perhaps too sexually exciting.

Veronica wondered what caused Imogen's hatred for Royal. Was it only sexual? But Imogen is not interested in men, Veronica reminded herself. She then thought of the other answer, the more serious reason why Imogen might disapprove of Royal.

*   *   *

Does Imogen despise black people deep down inside

her like so many white people do here in the South? Veronica next asked herself. Is Imogen actually jealous that Papa freed Royal and secured a job for him in the Boston-New Brunswick Bank through his business connections? Is she angry that Papa allowed me to move North to marry Royal? To try to live a normal life with someone who should still be a slave, her property?

Veronica did not know the answers to these questions. But she did know for certain that her own opinion about black people—and slavery—had increasingly changed since she had been living in the North. The distance from Dragonard Hill had shown Veronica the indignities done to black people by keeping them in shackles, even enslaved in the most humane manner as her father did here in the Louisiana wilderness.

Royal still worked at the Boston-New Brunswick bank. Having diligently applied himself to his job, he had risen in position at the bank and now was the chief clerk. Veronica and Royal chose not to socialize with business colleagues from the bank but the New England atmosphere was not harsh on them, not intolerable as Southern critics would be of a white woman who loved a black man and gave birth to his children.

Veronica felt indebted to her father. He had shown kindness to her and Royal when he had finally learned of their love. His decision to approve of their marriage had been painful for him to make, Veronica realized, but he had risen above prejudices and not only granted them his permission to marry but assisted them in escaping to a new life.

Considering these facts as she now stood inside the picket fence of the graveyard, Veronica wondered how she could assist her father now that he needed help. She could see that he was clinging onto gloom. He kept talking about bringing bad luck to a woman. That Kate's death was a sign for him to obey in the future. How could she help her father to free himself from such harmful thoughts?

Closing her eyes, Veronica lowered her head and next thought about her husband. She had to help Royal, too. As she did not yet understand how she might be of assistance to her father neither did Veronica know in what way Royal wanted her to help him.

27

Before Veronica had left Boston, Royal had suggested a plan to her, a way in which they both could assist the black people still living in slavery in the South. Royal had not explained his intentions to Veronica, only promising her that a man would contact her during her stay at Dragonard Hill, that she must not leave Louisiana until the man made himself known to her. Veronica longed to know the exact date on which she could return home to Boston but she had to wait patiently for the letter of instruction from Royal to arrive.

* * *

The main centre of domestic activity during the daytime hours at Dragonard Hill was the kitchen. This bustling whitewashed annex was connected to the main house by a breezeway, a colonnade of white columns which were small replicas of the large white pillars flanking the house's front veranda.

Unlike most prosperous planting families in the American South, Peter Abdee had appointed a male Negro to be the head cook for the main house, bestowing the responsibility upon a tall and angular Negro named Posey whose only claim to his male gender was hidden beneath a voluminous apron and the starched white skirts of a woman's dress.

Posey—or 'Miss Posey' as the shrill black man insisted upon being called by the other Negroes on the plantation—ruled the kitchen with an authority which he had learned from his predecessor, an imperious woman named Storky.

Storky was now dead and Posey had assumed all the characteristics which had made her a domestic power in her lifetime. Apart from copying her starched white uniform, Posey also slept each night behind the cook stove in the kitchen annex as Storky had done, and kept a meat cleaver under his pillow as protection against possible intruders.

Posey's choice to attire himself and to live according to the sex into which he had not been born did not trouble the Abdee family. They had come to accept Posey's increasingly idiosyncratic ways as they had also grown to enjoy his honey-cured hams, delicious yam pies, pickled melon rinds, as well as becoming totally dependent upon the rigid schedule by which he kept the meals flowing from the kitchen to the dining-room of the main house.

Posey was assisted by two black children in the kitchen, the older subordinate being a girl called Lulu who fetched eggs from the chicken coop, carried milk, butter, and cream from the springhouse, and arranged the covered bowls and platters of food on the silver trays which the house servants hurried piping hot down the columned colonnade to the Abdee's table.

The second kitchen-helper was a corpulent black youth whom Posey had nicknamed Fat Boy. The black people on the plantation whispered amongst themselves—and joked openly—that Miss Posey kept Fat Boy in the kitchen for reasons other than assistance in domestic chores. The black girls on the plantation giggled about the prematurely large proportions of Fat Boy's penis; the young black field-workers gossiped that Miss Posey appreciated this physical hugeness. But, so far, no one had seen—nor heard prurient noises—which would have proved that a sexual relationship was consummated between Posey and Fat Boy behind the cookstove in the kitchen annex at night.

*   *   *

On this warm June afternoon, when Master Peter Abdee, Veronica, Imogen, and young David Abdee stood down at the roadside cemetery paying respects at the grave of the woman whom the black people had lovingly called 'Matty Kate', Posey hurried around the white-washed kitchen in a frenzy to prepare tonight's supper. Lulu had been sent to the chicken coop to bring back two hens for frying; Fat Boy perched on a stool next to a kitchen table where he had been ordered to shell fresh garden peas.

Posey's lanky legs kicked against the crisply starched folds of his skirt as he bustled about the kitchen, ranting, 'Fat Boy, I swears you gots earth slugs for fingers! Look!' He stopped by the table where Fat Boy sat. 'Do it like this!'

Snatching a green pod from the boy's chubby hands, Posey nimbly cracked it with his long delicate brown fingers and the peas tumbled out into an earthenware bowl. Posey tossed the broken pod into another bowl and shrilled,

29

'Don't just sit there staring at them peas! You keeps staring like that, Fat Boy, and I takes my fingers and I pops out your eyes from their sockets just like . . . this!' Posey menacingly pressed the pink tips of two forefingers in front of Fat Boy's bulging eyes to illustrate his threat.

Turning away from the table, Posey readjusted the white kerchief on his head—knotted at the nape of his neck exactly as Miss Storky had worn her kerchief—and he surveyed the black iron pots, bright copper pans, speckled blue bowls, and bleached wooden spoons surrounding him on the scrubbed pine tabletops.

Although having grieved for Matty Kate, Posey had not joined the other plantation slaves in singing religious songs at her burial within the picket-fenced cemetery which the Negroes called 'the boneyard'. Posey considered himself to be superior to the other blacks on Dragonard Hill. He had insisted on paying his respects quietly to Matty Kate like a white person.

Kate had treated Posey with the utmost respect and kindness since the day she had come to be the mistress of Dragonard Hill. The red-haired woman had trusted Posey to run the kitchen according to his liking, only occasionally offering him advice, and then only on holidays or the special occasions on which a party was given at Dragonard Hill.

The shock of Matty Kate's death was eclipsed for Posey by Veronica's arrival from Boston and, now, the imminent visitation of her twin sister, Victoria, from Cuba.

Being a trusted household slave, Posey knew more about the Abdee family's private life than the black people who lived in the plantation's slave quarter called 'Town'. Posey knew that Veronica was married to the black man named Royal, that they lived in Boston with their three children and were known by the name 'Selby' which had been the maiden name of the three Abdee girls' mother—and the name of the family who had owned Dragonard Hill when the plantation had been known as 'The Star'.

Posey also knew that Veronica's twin sister, Victoria, lived on the faraway island of Cuba. He was further aware that Miss Vicky was a countess. This elevated her in Posey's eye above all other members of the Abdee family, living or dead.

The only member of the Abdee family with whom Posey

30

did not obsess himself was the eldest daughter, Imogen. Apart from living too close to his own world for her to be exotic, Posey believed that Imogen should not demean herself by acting as the plantation's overseer. He knew that such a job was usually held by a man, and a man from the class of white people whom Posey disapprovingly called 'trash'.

Fat Boy now called to Posey from the work table, drawling, 'That Lulu, she taking a long time getting you them fryers from the coop, Posey. You thinks maybe I should just sees—'

'What you call me?' Posey snapped from across the kitchen.

'Miss Posey,' the corpulent boy corrected himself, hanging his shaved head as he reluctantly reached for another pod from the earthenware bowl. The job of shelling peas bored Fat Boy. He envied Lulu the task of going to the chicken coop.

'You better watch yourself, Fat Boy, or I sends you to live down at the old house. You finds yourself slopping food for Miss Imogen and that Belladonna wench.'

Fat Boy slowly broke another pod, asking, 'Those two eats chickens up here tonight . . . Miss Posey?'

'Miss Imogen eats up here . . . maybe! But never that Belladonna wench. Belladonna's a nigger and no niggers allowed to sit in that red silk dining-room with white folks.'

'If Belladonna so awful nigger trash, Miss Posey, why then Miss Imogen lives with her all alone down in that old house?'

'Mind your business,' Posey snapped, unable to provide a correct answer to the boy's question. Posey could not comprehend the relationship between Imogen and the black woman named Belladonna. He suspected that their private life in the old house had something to do with that physical activity which had played such a minor role in his life—sex.

Fat Boy asked, 'When Miss Vicky comes home to visit her papa, Miss Posey?'

'I tells you, Fat Boy, minds your own business or I takes down your pants, puts you over my knee, and I spanks your naked fat bottom with the flat of my hand till you turns as raw as a freshly peeled peach!'

31

Suspecting that a spanking was only an idle threat, Fat Boy continued, 'I hears in Town that Miss Vicky is like some empress or queen where she lives on that island called—what's the name of that island where Miss Vicky lives, Miss Posey?'

Throwing up his hands, Posey airily said, 'Miss Vicky is a . . . countess! She lives in a . . . castle!'

'Miss Vicky married herself some king?'

The sound of the kitchen door opening attracted their attention. Posey spun around in a crackle of starched skirts and saw a scrawny black girl dressed in a ragged blue shift. She stood in the kitchen doorway, holding a fully feathered chicken in each hand, gripping each red hen by its limp neck.

'Lulu!' Posey shrieked as he stared at the chickens. 'What's you thinks I going to do with them hens looking like that? You thinks I plucks them feathers right here in my kitchen and makes me a pillow? Go on! Get! Shoo! Take yourself back to that chicken coop and gets them feathers plucked or I throws *you* in the pot!'

Lulu backed nervously toward the door, confessing, 'Croney ain't got no time today to plucks no feathers, Miss Posey. Croney gots to rush to some meeting in Town about trouble brewing for us black people.'

'Trouble? I'll give you and that Croney wench troubles, nigger brat. I ain't going to pluck no hens here in my kitchen. Not me!' he exclaimed, thumbing the bib of his apron, expanding his imaginary breasts.

'Croney ain't there in the coop no more, Miss Posey,' Lulu whined, now trying to hide the limp hens behind her back. 'Croney's gone to Town to Maybelle's house for that special meeting.'

'Meeting? Niggers having meetings? Who that Maybelle wench thinks she is? That Maybelle wench sees herself as big as Master Peter? The Master, he puts Maybelle in charge of raising piccaninnies in The Shed but he ain't gives her—nor no other nigger—no permission to go holding meetings in Town.'

'I only knows what I hears from Croney in the chicken coop, Miss Posey. And Croney gone to Town and she tells me to asks you . . .'

'Give me those hens!' Posey shouted, snatching one hen

32

from Lulu's hand. He gripped a handful of feathers from the dead fowl and, as the red feathers fluttered to the floor, he tossed the chicken onto the table where Fat Boy was working.

He shouted to the bewildered youth, 'You leave them peas and tends these hens for me, Fat Boy. You gots big hands! Use them!'

'What about...'

'You just do like I says,' Posey commanded, turning his back on the boy and continued grumbling about black people having meetings, complaining about lazy piccaninnies not knowing how to shell peas, deriding dumb black girls who brought fully-feathered chickens back to the kitchen for him to fry.

* * *

The slave quarter on Dragonard Hill called Town was a small community located to the southwest of the main house. The majority of dwellings in Town were small log cabins built on pole stilts to prevent dampness from creeping into the plank floors. Peter Abdee allowed no more than six people to inhabit one cabin and, to accommodate the steadily increasing number of black people born on the plantation, he had also erected long, low-pitched roofed dormitories.

The children born on Dragonard Hill—youngsters referred to as 'Saplings'—lived in the converted warehouse called The Shed. The Southern slave system disapproved of black parents being allowed to maintain ties with their offspring and, following this strict guideline set down by his predecessors and rigidly upheld by his peers, Peter Abdee dutifully removed every newly born child from its mother a short time after birthing, allowing the young blacks to mature under the supervision of Negresses selected from Town.

Maybelle was one of the black women from Town who was responsible for overseeing the welfare of the small children in The Shed. She lived with a field slave named Ham in one of the long-legged cabins in Town, a husky black man whom she had considered to be her rightful husband. Maybelle and Ham had birthed one child, a son who lived in The Shed with the other saplings but was approaching the age when maturing young boys were moved to the Dormitory.

Returning to Town this evening after her two-day stint at The Shed, Maybelle ran her fingers through her hair which fit like a woolly skullcap on her head. She had washed her one extra shift this morning and, after it had whipped dry in the breeze she had ironed it in The Shed whilst the children had been weeding the vegetable patch. Maybelle felt fresh, even pretty, as she hurried down the wide dirt street of Town on her way home to join her husband.

Climbing the pole ladder to their tall cabin, Maybelle wondered if the four other people who shared it with them would be home this evening. She hoped that their house-mates would be outside weeding the cabin's garden patch. She wanted this time to cook a supper only for herself and Ham, to speak privately with him, perhaps even to make love.

'Ham?' she called as she stood near the top of the ladder and reached to part the strings which hung in the doorway to prevent flies from buzzing into the cabin. 'You in there, Ham honey?'

Maybelle remained on the ladder and adjusted her eyes to the near darkness inside the small log house, a blackness lit only by a faint shaft of light pouring through the smoke hole cut into the centre of the roof.

'Who you?' she suddenly asked, seeing a group of black people sitting in a sober circle on the cabin's plank floor. She leaned her head farther into the cabin and eventually recognized the woman from the chicken coop, two women from the looming house, three men from the dairy barn, and a stabler.

Finally seeing Ham sitting cross-legged on the floor amongst these other Negro slaves, Maybelle asked guardedly, 'What's going on here? Some kind of . . . meeting?'

'Come in, Maybelle,' Ham softly called. His chiselled mahogany-brown face was sober as he beckoned Maybelle to climb from the top rungs of the pole ladder and join them.

'You crazy?' Maybelle whispered, looking anxiously around the small room. 'You know us black people ain't suppose to hold no meetings. If Miss Imogen finds out about you being here, she's bound to dig out that old whip and makes an example of you for other black folks here to see.'

'Maybelle, you come in here and hold your tongue,' Ham ordered. Although he loved his pretty wife he often thought that she was too authoritative in her ways. He also believed that Maybelle was too cautious of the punishment which white people might inflict on them as slaves. Maybelle had helped nurse young David Abdee in his infancy and, ever since those years she had spent visiting the main house, Ham felt that she showed too much concern for the Abdees.

Ham now assured her, 'We ain't breaking no laws.'

'Breaking no laws? You crazy?' Maybelle impatiently asked. 'Master Peter is danged good to us black folks but he makes us abide by rules laid down by other white planters. You knows that, Ham. You do, too, Croney. And you, Dido. Same goes for you, Curlew, and Topper. What's this secret meeting you having all about?'

'It's about Master Peter,' answered the white-haired woman named Croney from the chicken coop.

'The poor man, he's grieving,' Maybelle said as she crawled across the floor to crouch alongside Ham. 'Master Peter loved Matty Kate and—'

Curlew the stabler interrupted, 'Master Peter maybe ain't grieving as much as we all think, Maybelle. You know that Sara wench who lives with Topper and Dido?'

Maybelle certainly remembered the brown-skinned girl to whom Curlew referred, a statuesque young woman not yet twenty-years-old and who worked in the looming house.

She asked, 'What Sara got to do with Master Peter and this meeting?' Her eyes darted to the couple, Topper and Dido, who also lived together as husband and wife. She knew that they were looking for a respectable black man to pair-off with Sara.

Croney continued, 'You seen how Master Peter been roaming Town late at night since Matty Kate died? Well, last night Master Peter went strolling with young Sara. Master Peter didn't do nothing particular bad with young Sara but she says to Dido and Topper here that Master Peter stared a lot at her titties. That he actually hinted that he would be mighty pleased if she—'

35

'Sara's lying!' Maybelle quickly protested. 'What that Sara wench want to lie about our Master Peter for? The poor man's still grieving for Matty Kate!'

'That's what Topper and me first claimed,' Dido said, 'We thought that Sara was lying to us at first, too. But what reason Sara gots to lie? She says that Master Peter complains to her about bringing bad luck to white women. That in the future he ain't going to do no marrying again.'

Maybelle said, 'Maybe the death of Matty Kate makes Master Peter's mind take a funny turn. Maybe he just lonely and wants to have company on his walks. Maybe that's why he talks to Sara. Using her for company. And as for gawking at those titties of hers—who could miss them? They sticks out like milk buckets!'

The black people sitting on the floor all agreed with Maybelle that Sara was extremely buxom. But Curlew argued, 'Master Peter gots his daughters for talking if that's what he wants.'

Maybelle grunted. 'Miss Imogen? You call her good company?' She shook her head.

'There's his other daughter,' offered Topper. 'She comes home all the way from Boston just especially to be with her papa.'

'Miss Veronica?' Maybelle again shook her head. 'Miss Veronica gots worries of her own. Any fool can see that by the scared look in her eyes. She ain't going to be no good company to her Papa. No, like I says, maybe Master Peter's brain just took a turn and he wants somebody for company.'

Curlew leaned closer toward the circle of people, saying, 'We got to protect our own women, Maybelle. You hears what white men do to our girls. We seen it happens here before. We hears about it still happening in the neighbourhood.'

'"Our" girls? What for you talking about "our" girls, Curlew? You thinks we all free? You forgets we all slaves here? Master Peter, if he wants to . . . lay each and every one of us black women, he rightly can. Master Peter can rightly do just that. He's the master here on this land. We just his slaves. But let me also tells you this fact. Master Peter, he's a good man. He ain't going to do nothing you're fearing. He ain't done nothing bad in the past and he ain't going to be doing it now or in the future!'

'I just hope you're right, Maybelle, honey,' Dido generously offered as she leaned back on her arms placed behind her on the floor. 'I wish I could have the same trust in white folks as you do. But I just can't find that trust in my soul. The Lord helps me to look but I can't find it.'

'White people? Black people?' Maybelle asked. 'We're talking about folks we knows and lives with. Folks who treats us good. We ain't talking about . . . trash!'

Curlew muttered, 'You tells that to Miss Imogen.'

'Out!' Maybelle ordered, finally satiated with this arguing. She pointed one hand at the door, saying, 'Get out! All of you! I've been away from my man for over two days and nights. Now out! I wants to be alone with my own man before I hears any more complaints about Master Peter, Miss Imogen, the Lord knows who else. Now out! All of you!'

Croney, Dido, Curlew, the black visitors all agreed to leave Maybelle alone with Ham. They spanned their exits down the pole ladder, though, allowing a few minutes to elapse between their departure to avoid attracting the attention of other black people in Town.

The last person to leave was old Croney. She called into the cabin from the ladder, 'What us black people needs now is somebody to speak for us to the white folks. We need to have a speaker. We used to have Nero but he's dead. And you, Maybelle, you know the Master good but you're too hot-headed. We need us a person who has a sharp mind and can speak for us.'

'Then pray!' Maybelle said flippantly. 'Pray to the Good Lord to send us such a black leader to appear out of nowhere like the Mother of Jesus!' She waved Croney to leave.

Chapter Two

THE PASSION

The Louisiana sun was sinking below the hilly western perimeter of Dragonard Hill when Veronica and Imogen walked together that evening toward the old house. The palatial proportions of the main house were silhouetted behind them against a scrim of golden light, sitting high on a promontory which commanded a view over the front fields of green cotton, the cypress-lined drive, and the public road which separated this property from the picket-fenced cemetery.

The supper hour was nearing; activity crested in the kitchen annex of the main house whilst the servants painstakingly arranged plates, goblets, and cutlery on the highly waxed mahogany table in the dining-room. Posey had taken a brief respite from his cooking to arrange daffodils and pussy-willow stalks in a cut glass vase for a centrepiece.

Imogen had again refrained from accepting an invitation to sit at the family table in the main house, opting to eat her supper instead with Belladonna in the privacy of the old house.

Veronica insisted that she accompany Imogen through the copse of trees which connected the two homes. She suspected that Imogen did not welcome her companionship on this walk but she wrapped a black shawl around the shoulders of her mourning dress and tagged along anyway.

Ferns drooped across the narrow path which led to the shadowy section of Dragonard Hill where the old clapboard house set in a small clearing. Evening dew already glistened on the lacy green foliage; the air was becoming noticeably colder as the sun inched down beyond the spires of the distant pine forest.

Veronica drew the shawl more tightly around her shoulders and began to ask Imogen idle questions about the potential of this year's cotton crop, the plantation's new arrangement with the cotton gin in Troy, even praising Imogen for her dedication to overseeing fieldwork here, for accomplishing a task which would be difficult for some men.

Finally, Veronica manipulated the conversation to the subject of their father. She asked, 'Have you noticed anything strange about Papa?'

Imogen swatted her riding crop at the prickly branches of a wild rose bush as she answered, 'I don't get involved much in life over at the big house. They have their ways. I have mine.'

Veronica persevered, 'I know Papa and Katie were happy but I'm talking about what is going to happen now. Papa seems to have changed so much since I've last seen him. I don't ever remember him being this morose. I'm worried about him, Imogen. I'm worried about things like . . . like the way he talks about the bad luck he brings to women—'

Pausing, Veronica shook her head and said, 'He keeps repeating that he brings bad luck to women. Did you notice how he said it again this afternoon in the cemetery?'

Imogen showed no concern. She answered, 'Talk like that just means he ain't planning to get himself hitched again.'

Veronica looked at her.

'Married,' Imogen explained.

Veronica considered this fact. She began, 'I can understand why Papa wouldn't be thinking about marriage. Look how long he waited to remarry after *our* Mama died—'

Imogen said, 'I don't see him ever marrying again. I'll give you odds that he's just going to plant a few . . . wild oats!'

Veronica stopped on the path. She looked at her older sister.

Imogen's voice had become more gravelly, more masculine over the years. She now sounded like a mimic of a man when she said, 'The guy's still got some fire in his blood, girl. You can't deny a man that!'

'I wouldn't deny Papa anything!' Veronica blurted. 'But if he's got "fire" in his blood then who is the object of his . . . affections?'

Laughing, Imogen said, 'I don't think "affections" are involved. I was talking about wild oats. I suspect he's about ready to start hunting for some black poontang.'

'Imogen! Please!'

'Please what? Please don't say our Papa's a healthy, robust man and needs his—' She groped at the crotch of her riding breeches.

Veronica dropped the black shawl from her shoulders. She walked rigidly down the path, saying in a cool voice, 'You were always too blunt for my liking, Imogen.'

'Bluntness saves a lot of time, little sister. But if you're so damned worried about Papa, why don't you have this talk with him?'

'I have never interfered with Papa's private life. But that does not deny me the right to have concern for him. Papa always struggled to understand my problems. To understand all our problems. Papa was always there, standing nearby to help us when we needed him.'

'He stood by you all right,' Imogen said, swatting her riding crop at rose bushes again.

Veronica flared, 'Papa granted you a few wishes, too, Imogen Abdee!'

Shrugging, she said, 'True. But it's one thing letting me work this land for him. And it's another thing for him to let you—'

Veronica quickly finished the sentence for her sister. And using the vernacular which she suspected Imogen intended to say. '—to let me marry a . . . *nigger!*'

Imogen nodded. 'Call it what you want.'

'What else would I call it? Knowing who it's coming from!' Veronica felt her face suddenly tighten with anger. She said, 'I love Royal. He is a true, considerate husband to me. We have three children. They are no geniuses but they are healthy, Imogen. Royal and I have three very healthy children. Lindy and Peter Mark are both in school now. Little Max will be starting before I know it. They all

40

have friends. They have food. Clothing. We have a nice house to live in...'

'Then you're damned lucky, ain't you.'

'Lucky? Why am I lucky, Imogen? Because my black husband—a Negro who used to be a slave on Dragonard Hill—managed to escape to the North and live like a... white person? Well, I don't believe that black people should have to escape, Imogen. I do not think that it is fair of us white people to lay down those rules!'

'Now, now, girl. Don't go getting het up about slavery,' Imogen said as they emerged in the clearing where the old clapboard house stood like a vine-covered spectre in the fading daylight of early summer.

'I get "het up", Imogen, when I see you misunderstanding a situation. And when I hear you constantly taking... jabs at me. Hurtful, snide verbal jabs. Oh, yes, you've been doing it ever since I've got home. You've made sarcastic remarks about Royal. You've said cruel things about little David meeting his "Northern cousins". And I don't like your attitude, Imogen. I do not like it one bit.'

A smile formed on Imogen's thin lips. She turned to appraise Veronica's neat black clothing and said, 'Maybe you're the one who has changed, Veronica.'

Veronica held herself upright. She said icily, 'Maybe I have. And if I have changed since I've been away from here it is only because I have to defend what I believe in. I cannot stand by and listen to you—my very own sister—making malicious remarks about my family.'

Arching one eyebrow, Imogen mocked, 'So little Veronica still doesn't approve of her red-neck sister!'

'There you go jumping to conclusions again, Imogen! Approval has nothing to do with it. The word you mean to say is "support". That is what Papa gave you by allowing you to be the overseer on this land, letting you take a job which rightfully should have gone to a ... man!'

Imogen shrugged. 'I guess I'm the closest thing Papa ever got to having a son.'

Veronica reached to rest her hand on Imogen's shoulder. She said in a softer voice, 'I don't want us to argue and fight, Imogen. I don't know how long I'll stay here. Please let us not spend these days saying hurtful words to one

41

another. Let us promise each other that. And let us promise not to argue with Vicky when she comes.'

'You still think she's coming?'

'Of course I do.'

'Let's just hope you're wrong,' Imogen said and turned toward the rickety steps which led up to the porch slanted with age. She called over her shoulder, 'Do you want to come inside or do you have to rush home? It gets dark fast here.'

Veronica was touched by Imogen's small gesture of politeness. She recognized that the invitation to come inside the house was insincere but she eagerly answered, 'Oh, I would love to come in for a minute or two. I haven't been in the old house for years. Also, I haven't had a chance yet to talk to Belladonna.'

Imogen turned on the top of the weathered steps and said to her younger sister, 'Let's you and me get another thing straight, Veronica. If you want me to slobber and make some kind of fuss over your brood, that's fine. I ain't promising I can do it but I'll try my damnedest to be civil if I ever do see them. But I don't want you going cock-a-hoop over me and Belladonna just because we eat at the same table and sleep in the same bed. Can you understand that?'

Veronica stared dumb-foundedly at her Imogen. She gasped, 'How can you say cruel things like that? I can understand that you might want to be protective about yourself but don't you think that Belladonna has feelings?'

'You worry about your feelings and I'll take care of ours.'

But Veronica was not looking at Imogen now. She stared at the slim figure of a black girl standing on the other side of a rusted screen door which faced onto the porch. She immediately recognized the girl as Belladonna, a pretty but shabbily dressed young black woman whose hair fell in a gnarled tumble to her shoulders.

Veronica moved toward the steps to speak to Belladonna. Imogen saw where she was going, though, and stepped in her way. And behind them Belladonna disappeared from the screen door, vanishing into the darkness of the old house.

Realizing that she was not wanted here, Veronica turned from the steps and murmured to Imogen, 'I'm sorry if I've made a nuisance of myself. I'll try never to bother you again.' She hurried toward the path which wound through the woods.

*   *   *

Imogen sat in the shadowy kitchen of the old house later that night, the yellow glow from the gas-lamp illuminating the furrowed expression on her hard face as she held a jug of corn whisky on the knee of her doeskin breeches and a half-filled glass of whisky set in front of her on the table. Imogen and Belladonna had finished their supper of porkside stew and fritters. Belladonna now busied herself washing the tin plates and black iron stew pot whilst Imogen remained seated at the table like the husband of the household. They had lived together here for the last seven years.

Recalling Veronica's castigation about the manner in which she callously referred to Royal and their half-caste children, Imogen first bristled about her younger sister's impudence. But, next, Imogen began to consider another fact, wondering if she might be ignoring a certain situation which could possibly arise here on Dragonard Hill.

The Abdee family was changing. Imogen realized this. She also suspected that Kate's death might make further changes. But momentarily forgetting about Veronica's plea for moral support, she remembered her sister's question about their father, the concern she had shown for his new restlessness.

'You ready for some coffee?' Belladonna called from behind her.

Imogen stiffened. Whenever Belladonna mentioned coffee after supper it meant that she thought Imogen was drinking too much. She waited for Belladonna to start complaining again about the jug of corn whisky.

But no criticism followed. And Imogen returned to her thoughts about her father, remembering how she had specifically answered Veronica's question about his loneliness.

Imogen considered the statement that she had impulsively made about her father becoming promiscuous, that he would probably take to wenching. She next thought about her step-brother, David Abdee, the one male heir to Dragonard Hill. She wondered if her father would indeed

43

resign himself to a life of self-indulgence knowing that he had a son to inherit this land.

Reconsidering the fact that her father might indeed seek companionship amongst the black wenches living in the slave quarter, Imogen's whisky-fuelled mind reviewed the implications of the rest of the conversation she had had with Veronica—the subject of Peter Abdee's attitude toward Negroes' rights as people.

What if Papa does start chasing darkies? Imogen asked herself. And what if he knocks up a wench? And what if that child is a boy? What will happen then? Papa allowed Veronica—his own precious daughter—to marry a nigger. He even allowed Royal to take our own Mama's name as his own. Royal Selby!

Pushing back her chair from the table with sudden anger about this plantation being divided between step-brothers and slaves, Imogen wondered what would happen to her? How would she fare in the future? Would old age see her at the mercy of charity from Goody Two-Shoes and . . . niggers? People talked about slavery coming to an end in the South someday, of black people being treated like whites, of niggers even being allowed to inherit and own land!

'You restless?' Belladonna called as Imogen began to pace the kitchen's bare board floor. She lifted the wash basin from a table covered with oilskin and said, 'I've got coffee on the stove.'

Imogen ignored Belladonna, thinking about how she could deal with a father who gave equal rights to black people, a philosophy which maddened her as well as threatened her hold on this rich land.

Whilst Imogen paced the board floor, Belladonna scuffed toward the kitchen door with the basin of dirty dish water in her hands. She tossed out the water into the back yard with a loud splash. She gave the basin a few wipes with a rag and hung it on a nail by the door.

Next, Belladonna moved toward the table and began wiping off the crumbs and grease stains with the dish rag. The gas lamp lit her high cheekbones, her generously formed lips, and almond-shaped eyes which gave her an almost Oriental appearance.

Imogen stood in a far corner of the shadowy kitchen and

44

surveyed Belladonna's pendulous breasts as she leaned over the table. Imogen tried to see Belladonna through objective eyes, to study her as a white man would see this black girl. A plan was quickly forming in her brain.

Belladonna was a woman but, like many black females, she wore her age well: Belladonna looked scarcely older than a girl. Imogen enjoyed Belladonna's slim body in bed at night; she acted as the aggressor to the Negress's passive femininity, using her mouth, fingers, often even home-crafted tools to exert the dominant role of a husband in their unnatural relationship.

Surveying Belladonna with new eyes, though, Imogen tried to imagine how a man—a born male—would respond to Belladonna's sexual attractiveness. The black woman—or girl—was sullen. That was good. Men liked sullenness in females. It made them feel victorious when they conquered them. Also, Belladonna had large breasts. She knew from field talk that men loved to chew on ample breasts, bury their faces between them, nibble taut nipples like babies nursing mothers. Belladonna could supply all that for a man.

Imogen suddenly held out her arm to stop Belladonna as she moved from the kitchen table. She had decided to prepare the groundwork for her plan.

Momentarily studying the instant fright flickering in Belladonna's eyes, Imogen realized how devoted the black girl was to her. The slightest harsh word, only a hint of a physical reprimand made the black girl quiver.

But Imogen was not interested in punishing Belladonna now. She wanted the girl to help her. And leaning forward, she brushed her lips against Belladonna's mouth and said, 'I've been neglecting you, Honey. I'm going to change that. I'm going to start by getting you a few yards of pretty cloth to make yourself some new dresses. How does that sound?'

Belladonna stared quizzically at Imogen. She had not owned a new dress in years. She could not remember the last time that Imogen had given her goods to make a new dress.

'What's the matter?' Imogen asked. 'You don't look too happy with the news?'

Lowering her head and resting it on Imogen's shoulder,

Belladonna said, 'Whatever makes you happy, that's what I wants.'

Imogen stood stroking Belladonna's thin back, her hand soon lowering to her full buttocks. She smiled to herself. Yes, it was a good plan.

Belladonna asked, 'You work hard today?' She kept her head resting devotedly on Imogen's shoulder.

'I always work hard,' Imogen answered, moving her hand around to Belladonna's midsection and, reaching under her skirt, she probed one finger into the wiry vaginal slit between the girl's thighs.

Removing the finger from under the flimsy skirt, Imogen held it to Belladonna's nose and asked, 'What's that?'

Belladonna coyly pushed away the finger, whispering, 'Don't . . .'

Imogen asked louder, 'What's that smell?'

'You know what it is . . . it's my . . .'

'Your what?'

Belladonna softly uttered the word which she knew Imogen liked her to say. 'My . . . pussy.'

'Your what?'

'My . . . pussy.'

'That's right,' Imogen said, pulling the girl closer to her as a reward for saying the word. 'Your little black sheep of a pussy. And what do you like done to it?'

'I likes you to make love to me.'

'Love? Just love? Don't you like to feel some . . . hurt, too?'

Belladonna dipped her head. She said, 'When you makes love to me I feel no hurt. Not when I know you really . . . love me.'

'How do you know . . . pussy? Because you adore me?'

Belladonna nodded.

'You like to kneel between my legs and push your tongue into me?'

Again, Belladonna nodded.

'Or do you like to feel me push into you? Push into you with my tongue? My fingers? Push that leather . . . pecker into you? You like the pecker I made for you? Do you like when I plays the man.'

'I likes that,' Belladonna confessed.

Imogen asked, 'You like it when I play the man, do you? You like . . . pecker?'

'I likes the pecker.'

'Your pussy likes it.'

'My pussy likes it.'

'Deep? Your pussy likes it deep?'

'My pussy likes it deep.'

'What does your pussy like deep?' Imogen pursued, wanting to hear Belladonna repeat her words.

'The . . . pecker.'

'That's right,' Imogen said. 'You like the pecker. That's good. You keep on liking the pecker. You get to love it even more will you, my little black sheep of a . . . pussy?'

Belladonna nodded.

Imogen stood holding Belladonna against her, thinking how she was going to use her and that wiry black femininity, use her as a sacrificial lamb to achieve what she herself wanted here on Dragonard Hill. Yes, it's a damned good idea to get this pussy to want a man. But I must pursue it slowly, carefully, step-by-step like some military general plotting against an enemy's camp. And I'll start by dressing up this nigger wench like a real pretty little pussy, too.

* * *

Veronica retired with her father to the library after supper; young David joined them dressed in a nightshirt and flannel robe. He kissed them both good night and, after he slid shut the walnut doors behind him, Peter was left alone with Veronica. He poured them both a crystal balloon of French brandy and settled himself in a buttoned brown leather chair by the Carrara marble mantelpiece. A fire crackled on the hearth; the atmosphere was homey, a gentle extension from the relaxed mood of the conversation at tonight's supper table—a light-hearted discussion about Posey's cooking, a quandary about the future success of the small café called The FireFly Tea Rooms which had recently opened in the nearby town of Troy, and harmless gossip about a handsome young Creole lawyer travelling from New Orleans two days a week to practise law in the small country town.

Veronica sat across the fire from her father and sniffed appreciatively at the fragrance of the imported spirits. She felt relaxed, even pampered in the luxury of Dragonard Hill. She thought about the future of the home and asked, "Papa, will you feel alone here?'

Peter was also enjoying this restful hour. He answered matter-of-factly, 'No, not really. Not after I become adjusted. I have a lot of friends in the neighbourhood. There's Kate's nephew, Barry. The Daniels. The Popoffs. The Schneiders. We have—I have my friends.'

'I mean will you be lonely in this big house? Living here only with David?'

Peter rested one tall black boot on the other in front of his chair and stared at the crystal brandy balloon catching the glint of the fire. He said, 'I'm thinking of sending David away to school.'

Momentarily pausing, Veronica asked, 'Papa? Would you like me to post you a prospectus from one or two schools when I get back to Boston?' She wanted to help in any way she could. She knew her father now had no one close to depend upon.

'I've pretty well decided on the school. Katie and I had actually been discussing in the last few months about sending David to Pearson's Military Academy in Charleston.'

'Not North?'

Peter shook his head. 'Charleston is closer. David can visit home more often. I can go see him. No, Boston served its purpose for you and Vicky. But . . .' He shook his head. 'David is a very young boy. I think he should stay in the South.'

Veronica saw that her father's eyelids were suddenly heavy, that he most likely felt sleepy after eating such a delicious supper and now being lulled by the crackling fire.

Deciding that she would leave him to rest in the library alone and seize these last few moments before her own bedtime to write a letter home to Royal, Veronica rose from her chair. She set her untouched glass of brandy on a table and moved toward her father's chair. She bent over him and, kissing him on the forehead, she murmured, 'Papa, thank you for the wonderful company.'

'I think I'll retire myself pretty soon.'

'Aren't you going to have a little stroll tonight?' Veronica had noticed that since her arrival her father had gone for a walk every night after supper. She did not know where he went, guessing that he walked to ease his mind.

Peter did not answer the question. He gently squeezed Veronica's hand and said, 'I'll see you at breakfast.'

Veronica moved across the library's Aubusson carpet; she slid the heavy door shut behind her, leaving her father alone in his chair by the fire. She was already thinking about what she would write in the letter to Royal. She did not want to press Royal for the name of the man who would call upon her here at Dragonard Hill but she was beginning to grow more uneasy with each passing day, wondering how long she would have to stay here. She loved these quiet evenings with her father but, also, she loved her own family and missed them.

* * *

The idea of freedom terrified Peter Abdee. He was not thinking of freedom in terms of slavery but in regard to the sudden freedom to choose a new sexual partner. He had been happy with Kate for the last seven years—even longer if he counted the days in which they had met for love-making before their marriage. He had never been promiscuous; he had felt complete when he had found one woman who had satisfied his physical needs. But now Kate was gone. And he asked himself, Do I have to start all over again? Begin that desperate search for a compatible woman?

These thoughts tumbled into his mind only a few moments after Veronica had left the library. He did not want to slip into deep introspection after spending such an enjoyable evening with her and David but, yet, he had to solve this problem. This sudden craving for sexuality was symbolic of other sudden losses in his life. He recognized that fact.

Peter Abdee had a strong mind but since Kate's accident he had had fleeting doubts about his sanity. He only now realized how much he had depended on her. He finally saw the reason why people paired-off; he desperately missed the reassurance of having a wife, a constant companion, a lover, a helpmate.

Gulping down the brandy, he set the glass on the table

49

in front of him and reached for the glass which Veronica had not finished. He repositioned himself in the chair and considered the alternatives to a monogamous way of life.

Promiscuity. Some men swore by it. Many Southern men even kept bed wenches in their houses, black concubines who slept on pallets on the floor in their master's bedroom. Their wives turned a blind eye to this practise.

Peter Abdee was not such a Southern gentleman. But why not? he asked himself. Why not now? He was free. And if he did not go to the extremes of bringing a black mistress into the house why not at least sample a wench or two in one of the out-buildings?

Trying to be brutally honest with himself, Peter forced himself to review the sex life he had had with Kate in the last few years. Had it been as passionate, as bold as their love had been when they had first met, in the days when he had sneaked over to visit Kate at Greenleaf Plantation, when Kate had made excuses to send her nephew, Barry, from the house so the young man would not hear her screaming at the crest of her orgasm?

Peter smiled to himself when he remembered how Kate used to shout, literally shriek when she crested with him sexually. This memory led to another thought: When was the last time he had heard that? Not for months. Even years. Yes, sex had evidently even become stale for dear, lovable Kate. He did not blame himself, though. Nor did he blame her. He was only trying to review the matter with honesty.

Love between husbands and wives often grew stale. That was an established fact. Peter also recognized the fact that he was having a resurgence of sexuality. He had noticed that recently.

Sara. He thought of the young black girl from the looming house whom he had talked to last night near Town. He remembered the protrusion of her breasts beneath the thin cotton shift. He remembered talking to her—about what? Kate's death?—but glancing all the while at her waist, her hips, her legs.

Remembering the response which Sara had awakened in him last night, and recalling similar responses from other young Negresses on Dragonard Hill, Peter now looked down at his crotch and saw that his penis had formed a stiff rod beneath his breeches.

He closed his eyes. He took a deep breath. He leaned back in the chair and jutted his groin upwards, fleetingly imagining that he was driving the crown of his stiff penis into the wetness between a pair of thighs—she had no name, no face, no identity. She was virtually a vessel for his masculinity. Nothing more.

Sitting upright in the chair, he opened his eyes and told himself that he must stop torturing himself like this. He was a mature man. He must not tease himself with fantasies. They would lead to masturbation. He did not want that.

Next, he asked himself the other troubling question: Was it disrespectful to Kate if he suddenly took to wenching? Gossip was rife on a plantation, he knew, and stories quickly spread to other plantations and farms in the neighbourhood. Kate had not been buried for a month. He could not blaspheme their marriage. And, so, should he only indulge in fantasies? Madness might well lay in that direction but . . .

Peter again closed his eyes and, leaning his head back on the chair, he stretched his long legs in front of him. He felt his penis hardening inch-by-inch down his thigh. He was imagining a naked wench sitting astride his riding boots. Her skin was only a few shades lighter—richer—than the boots' shiny black leather. She was rubbing her furry patch against the leather boots as she gazed at his erect manhood and tongued her lips to tease him. The seed heatened inside Peter's straining phallus with these thoughts. His breath quickened as he wondered if—and when—he could fulfil them. He was determined, though, to keep his hand in control, not to form a fist around his manhood to satisfy himself.

*   *   *

Ham's body, hard from fieldwork, straddled Maybelle's nakedness; she curled her bare legs around him, moving her feet with the rhythm of his tensed buttocks as he drove faster and faster between her opened thighs; she clenched her arms in desperation around his neck, holding herself up from the straw pallet by this clinging grasp, allowing her entire body to move with Ham's quickening excitement. Their tongues intertwined with one another; Ham encircled Maybelle's teeth with his tongue as he stirred his phallus deeper inside her heated wetness. She chewed his lower lip, quickly traced his upper lip with her tongue, then began to bite his strong chin as he lengthened the strokes of his penis to probe her warmth from the slit to the depth. He slicked in and out of this tightening and contracting course, gauging Maybelle's excitement by the fastness of her breathing. He did not want to speak to her, to ask the important question, the question about orgasms which would debase this act of love. Then, finally feeling her responding in the ultimate manner to his masculine pressure, he quickly ejected his penis from her and—frantically gasping himself—his phallus shot a jet of white sperm across her stomach, creating a trace of warm white seed across her black skin instead of planting it inside her womb.

Ham and Maybelle had already produced one child. The boy lived in slavery. He would grow up in slavery. They did not want to give another life to Peter Abdee regardless of how good he was to them. The idea of withholding life from the world repelled them; they did not speak about the matter as they now lay locked—limp, wet with perspiration, blotched with sperm—on the straw pallet in the darkness of their long-legged hut in Town. Their housemates had left them alone here for a few hours.

Maybelle made the first move to cleanse themselves, to prepare for the others' return. Ham stopped her. He put a hand on her shoulder and cautioned, 'Shhh—' He listened.

'What is it?' Maybelle whispered.

'I thought I heard a noise. A rumble. Like a wagon coming up the road. A coach mayhaps.'

Maybelle lay still in the warm clutch of Ham's naked arm and listened for the distant sound. She finally said, 'I hears it, too. A coach bumping up the drive to the big house.'

Ham grunted. He moved to grab the rag waiting on the floor alongside the pallet. He said, 'It's no business of ours, woman. Only white folks go by coaches. Here—' He wiped the puddle from Maybelle's skin, gently dabbing the rivulets which had grown cold and meaningless.

*　　*　　*

A loud pounding on the library door brought Peter Abdee from a distant world of passion where his mind had been travelling. He sat upright in the chair. He saw that his penis formed a hard rod under the fabric of his trousers. He had not touched his penis during the erotic thoughts but he felt as if it were about to explode. He now heard Posey frantically calling from outside the door, 'Master Peter, Master Peter, Sir! It's Miss Vicky! Miss Vicky's finally come home from Cuba, Master Peter, Sir!' His first reaction was to reach and shove the erect shaft of manhood down between his legs. The thought that he was loath to interrupt his fireside dreams passed quickly through his mind before he was able to check it. He had thought about himself—his own passions—before he had rejoiced that Vicky had finally arrived home. Such selfishness was new to Peter Abdee.

Chapter Three

VOODOO

Victoria—or Vicky as she kept reminding herself that she must now accustom herself to being called—claimed four rooms in the main house at Dragonard Hill. One room was for sleeping, one for her sitting-room, one to accommodate the unpacking of her seven trunks of gowns—plus the innumerable smaller cases, bandboxes, and valises filled with hats, gloves, scarves, slippers—and one room for her African attendant, Malou, to be constantly nearby her to attend the upkeep of her wardrobe.

Pleading exhaustion from travel on the morning following her arrival at Dragonard Hill, Vicky begged to be excused from joining her father, Veronica, and David for both breakfast and the midday meal in the dining-room. Veronica quickly assumed the sisterly duty of seeing that a food tray was prepared in the kitchen for Vicky; she carried it herself up the wide staircase to the room where Vicky lay propped-up by a bank of lace-edged pillows in a canopy bed draped in pink-and-yellow striped chintz.

'I'm afraid you are going to find life rather dull here compared to the life you must lead in Havana,' Veronica said as she pulled a chair alongside the bed.

'A rest will do me good,' Vicky assured her, softly stroking a silver-backed brush down her long auburn hair. She wore a mauve silk bed jacket over a nightdress of Chantilly lace. She had not touched the breakfast tray which set alongside her on the wide bed.

'Life here is certainly restful,' Veronica said, hating herself for acting so proper, almost mouselike in front of her self-assured, worldly sister. She twisted her hands in the lap of her black crêpe dress, saying 'I imagine you are going to miss—you do call your little boy "Juanito" don't you?'

Vicky sniffed. 'That's his father's name for him. Juan Carlos is so determinedly . . . Spanish.'

Veronica immediately noticed that the tone in Vicky's reply did not encourage further questions about her family life in Cuba. She said, 'You must make yourself enjoy this visit. I myself have forgotten how comfortable this house is.' She looked around the ornately decorated bedroom.

Vicky lowered the brush to the bed and, also appraising the silk-lined walls and gilt French chairs, said, "I keep forgetting, my dear, that you do not have slaves in Boston. That you must do all the work yourself!'

'I *do* have a woman who comes in to help me.'

Resuming her brushing, Vicky said, 'Royal? Is he happy?'

'Very happy,' Veronica answered with renewed eagerness. She was pleased that Vicky inquired about her husband.

'What colour are your children?'

The question stunned Veronica.

'I mean are they . . . black? *Black* black? Or are they—' She looked around the bedroom for a shade of wood or the covering of a cushion which a half-caste child might resemble in colour.

'Why, I never thought of their colouring, not specifically . . .' Veronica was flustered. She hated herself for being at a loss for words.

'Considering your fairness, dearheart, they must be a lovely light brown! Like little chocolate soldier boys and girls!' She worked the silver-backed brush down the other side of her head, saying, 'How charming!'

Veronica glared at Vicky, momentarily loathing her for speaking about Lindy, Peter Mark, and little Max as if they were candy.

Now holding her head forward to brush the back of her hair, Vicky said, 'I hope I didn't say anything to offend you, dearheart. You've suddenly gone all quiet.'

'To be perfectly honest, Vicky, I am upset.'

'Oh, my dear, I *am* sorry! Do forgive me!' She flicked back her hair and affected a look of apology.

'It is not only what you said just now, Vicky. It is the general attitude in this house about Royal, myself, and our children. Imogen says hurtful things. Papa has not once visited us—'

'Has he come to Cuba to visit me, dearheart?' Shaking her head, Vicky said, 'No, you must not be censorious about that.'

'Please let me continue, Vicky. We might as well discuss this matter now rather than later.' Veronica moved to the edge of her chair and explained, 'I knew that I would be isolating myself by marrying Royal. He and I discussed that very matter many years ago. But things still trouble me and I would like this opportunity to talk about them.'

'Then you must, dearheart. You must.'

Vicky's superior attitude irritated Veronica. But she continued, 'For instance, Vicky, *I* can travel home. Oh, yes. But if I bring my children here to visit their grandfather, they could very well be stolen from this house and sold at a slave auction! Be literally auctioned off in a slave house as "fancies"!'

Vicky soberly studied the hairbrush now resting in the palm of one hand. She reached toward the bristles and pulled out a few long strands of hair. She dropped them into a jug of hot milk setting on the breakfast tray and said, 'Then you simply must never bring your babies south!'

The flippant remark told Veronica that she must not pursue this subject with her sister. She knew that Vicky had always had a strange view of reality. She realized now that her life in Havana had obviously only worsened this, had removed Vicky yet farther away from the problems of everyday life.

Rising from her chair, Veronica moved to the window and looked out at a field which lay to the west of the main house. She saw a gang of black people working on the far slope. She saw Negro drivers moving down the rows of bent slaves. She saw Imogen riding her stallion toward the slope. She continued gazing out the window at this morning work scene, saying, 'I wonder what we would be like today,

Vicky, if we had stayed here. If we had stayed on Dragonard Hill like Imogen chose to do?'

'Imogen?' Vicky sank back onto the bed pillows and laughed. 'Imogen! And who's that black girl she lives with?'

'Belladonna.'

'Yes. Belladonna. She's the "woman" of that household I believe. Oh, well, it takes all kinds to make-up the world.'

Veronica murmured, 'And all kinds to make-up a . . . family.'

Vicky lay in bed and fleetingly thought now about telling Veronica that their grandfather, Richard Abdee, was still alive. That the fabled old 'Dragonard' now owned a slave-house in Cuba.

Deciding that Veronica was too fragile this morning to deal with such a revelation, she decided to withhold the matter for some future date.

She instead said, 'Tell me about father, Veronica. Is he upset that I haven't rushed immediately downstairs this morning?'

'Papa is changing.' Veronica moved back to the bedside chair.

'That doesn't answer my question. But do tell me what you mean.'

'I don't know exactly what I mean, Vicky. Papa has been so quiet, so different from—' She shook her head, saying, 'You'll see for yourself.'

'And Posey?' Vicky asked, again looking at the breakfast tray. 'Does Posey still think he's a woman?'

Throwing back her head on the pillow, she sighed, 'Good Lord, I hope so! I wanted to bring presents for everyone and, knowing how uppity house niggers are, I knew that Posey must get something very, very special from me. But the only thing that I could think of to give him was one of my parasols. There's a case of them in the next room, dear-heart. Why don't you dig through them and choose one which you think might suit Posey and give it to him for me. Will you be a dear and do that? And tell him that I'm *dying* to see him. All that nonsense. I don't want him poisoning my food!'

'You choose the parasol, Vicky,' Veronica firmly but

sweetly replied. She did not want to become her sister's errand girl again.

Vicky said, 'I brought a little gift for you, too, dearheart. I did intend to give you something for your home in Boston but I didn't know exactly—'

'No gifts are necessary, Vicky. It is nice enough to see you.' Veronica bent over her sister's bed. She kissed her forehead and said, 'I'm only sorry that such a sad occasion has brought us all together. In all this commotion of unpacking and gift giving, you must not forget that Papa has just lost the most important person in his life.'

Turning from the bed, Veronica called, 'I will leave you alone now. I know you must want to get dressed. Father would like to see you soon and, by that, I think he means sometime . . . today.' She gently closed the door.

* * *

Vicky lay in bed long after Veronica departed from the room. She ignored her sister's parting words of sarcasm. She thought instead about her father. The thought of facing him unnerved her. She wondered what he would think of her after these passing years, if he would approve of her appearance, if he would ask personal questions about her married life with Juan Carlos. There were so many facts in Vicky's past life which she wished to leave unmentioned. She longed to keep herself buried in this bedroom for the present. She needed time alone to sort out other answers, an opportunity to assemble the facts about her own future— as a wife, a mother to Juanito, the mistress in charge of that sneaky Negress, Malou!

But life was generous to Vicky. Anyway, so she believed. She had always prided herself in being resilient. And she now lounged in the canopied bed thinking about the latest favour which fate had dealt to her: She lay back on the bank of lacy pillows and remembered the man who had ridden with her and Malou in the public coach from New Orleans.

Jerome Poliguet! Vicky could not remember having met such a handsome man for a long time. Apart from being dark complexioned—a physical trait in men which attracted her—Jerome Poliguet had also been charming and attentive to her like a true gentleman. Jerome Poliguet was a Creole,

58

one of the old French families of New Orleans who were aristocrats amongst the rough pioneers who were slowly taking over that delta city.

The day-long journey from New Orleans to Dragonard Hill had passed quickly with Poliguet as a travelling companion. He had entertained Vicky with amusing stories about the Louisiana countryside, telling her how he came to the small town of Troy two days a week to offer his legal services—Poliguet was totally modest in Vicky's opinion, withholding nothing about the state to which he had been reduced by a father who had squandered a vast fortune. Poliguet had unequivocally stated how he must learn to support himself. That his Creole background was now only a luxury, a luxury which would not put bread on his table.

Creoles! Those aloof, haughty people had always intrigued Vicky. She had seen them in their carriages in New Orleans as a girl; their grand manners and strict etiquette made her feel like a bumpkin from the country.

The Abdee family *was* rustic compared to the Creole families living in New Orleans, the descendants of the original French who had settled there. The Creoles saw themselves as the aristocrats of New Orleans.

Luxuriating in the softness of the feather pillows and remembering how courtly handsome Jerome Poliguet had been to her in the coach, Vicky became certain that he had been attracted to her for reasons other than the Veradaga crests stamped in gold on her luggage. She knew when a man found her sexually attractive and Jerome Poliguet had left no doubts in her mind that he was as surprised to find her—a Condesa!—on the Troy-Carterville coach as she herself had been surprised to discover him as a travelling companion.

Quickly throwing back the coverlets and hopping out of bed, Vicky rushed to the cheval mirror standing in the corner of her bedroom. She leaned toward the glass and closely examined her face for any sign of fatigue, wrinkles, or puffiness. She told herself that she must not sleep too much. She did not know when she might see Monsieur Poliguet again. Would he come calling here at Dragonard Hill?

Thrilled by the idea of having a visitor so soon after her arrival home, Vicky next wondered if Poliguet would make advances toward her on his first visit. She knew that the Creoles were gallant but also that the blood ran hot in their veins.

Throwing open her gown, Vicky looked at her naked body in the mirror, seeing that her breasts stood firm, bulbous on her slim body. That her waist curved neatly to her smooth hips. That the dark hair between her legs covered a tempting mound. And looking at her mound, she quickly dipped to the floor in front of the mirror and imagined that she was squatting down on a bed to encase Poliguet's phallus with her squeezing vagina, using her favourite method . . . the Jezebel's Grip.

Throwing back her head and laughing about all the pending excitement, Vicky arose to a standing position, cinched the robe around her body, and thought of more practical matters. She must look very alluring for Monsieur Poliguet when he came calling on her.

Remembering the face creams she had packed to protect her complexion from the harsh Louisiana air, she called, 'Malou! Bring my cosmetic case! And a bath! I want a hot bath brought to my room! Immediately, Malou! Immediately!'

Silence greeted her demand.

Glancing angrily toward the window, she looked down to the yard and saw Malou standing on the edge of the colonnade which led to the kitchen annex. The black woman stood alone, staring at the fieldhands working on the nearby slope.

Vicky rapped furiously on the window pane with her knuckle to attract Malou's attention. Damn that black bitch! she thought. I might be having callers today and there she is staring at . . . niggers! I'll sell her yet!

'Malou!' She rapped again.

Then, turning from the window, she realized her first problem. She had come back to Dragonard Hill to mourn Kate's death. Mourning meant black. What did she have black to wear? What black gown did she have with her which would show her to her best advantage to a visitor?

* * *

Jerome Poliguet did not pay a call at Dragonard Hill that

afternoon. Nor did he come the next day. But Vicky did not give up hope. She spent these first days at home distributing gifts to the family and house-servants, regaling everyone with stories about Cuba and—everyday—painstakingly tending her toilette in preparation for a visit from the Creole lawyer. She was certain that she would see the dark, handsome gentleman again.

By the end of the first week of Vicky's arrival at Dragonard Hill, the parasol which she had given to Posey had replaced the meat-cleaver under his pillow; he covetously clutched the ivory stick decorated with rose-coloured silk in his arms as he lay on his pallet behind the cookstove.

The frilled parasol grew in importance to Posey over the passing days but, then, so did the black woman, Malou, become an increasing annoyance to him as she walked silently around the main house in her bare feet and visited every far corner of the plantation.

Posey had harboured misgivings about Malou from the first time he had seen the sober-faced black woman who wore a white kerchief knotted over her tall forehead. And the longer he observed her from a distance, the more fertile his suspicions became.

Malou struck Posey as an incongruous figure compared to her finely-dressed mistress; he knew that Vicky was rich—and a countess!—which further confused him why her body servant should not even wear shoes! He knew that bare feet were commonplace here in Louisiana but he suspected that everyone—even sullen niggers!—wore slippers in castles in Cuba.

Posey questioned the house servants about Malou's activities, trying to glean the slightest bits of information about her. He learned that her duties were only to keep Miss Vicky's wardrobe in fine repair. He also learned that the Cuban slave woman had originally come from the valley of the River Niger in Africa, by the land of the Dahomey tribe, a people who believed in the Yoruba religion. Most American slaves had forgotten—had been forced to forget—about the religion of their African forefathers. Southern masters imbued Christian religions into their slaves. But Posey learned that this slave woman from Cuba not only clung onto the forbidden gods of Yoruba but likened them to the apostles, saints, and beliefs of the white people.

Apart from miracles, Malou also believed in spells, hexes, and curses!

'Voodoo!' Posey shrieked to Lulu and Fat Boy at the end of the first week of Vicky's return home, a time by which he had at last assembled all the facts about Malou. He accused, 'Malou is a Voodoo witch!'

Lulu cowered behind a kitchen table as Posey proceeded to denounce Malou. As he explained that Malou believed in a religion which honoured witches and devils, Lulu curled the fists of her small brown hands in front of her mouth. She shuddered at the thought that a witch was here at Dragonard Hill.

Fat Boy was likewise frightened by Posey's opinion of Malou. He anxiously looked toward the cookstove where Posey kept the parasol under the pillow. He asked, 'That Malou witch, she done put a hex on that sunshade Miss Vicky done gives you, Miss Posey?'

Posey felt bolstered by the effect which his words were having on the two children. He beckoned them to come closer as he said, 'She tries! That black Voodoo bitch probably tries to cast hexes but Miss Vicky has her magic, too! She's a countess!'

'Miss Vicky's a . . . witch!'

'Not only witches have magic! But countesses, too,' Posey explained. 'And princesses. And saints. And . . .'

'Strong enough magic to fight bad witches like Malou?'

'Pooh' Posey said. 'African magic ain't so strong. I come from Africa once, too, didn't I? Least the woman who mothered me did. I gots my own magic, too. I gets some more from Storky who's now in Heaven with the White Lord God.'

'Storky's a saint?'

'One of the highest!' Posey bragged. 'And she gives me the power to protect us. You don't see that Malou coming into this kitchen, do you?'

The two children shook their heads.

Posey shrugged. The matter seemed to be settled by their agreement.

Fat Boy said, 'I sure feels safe now, Miss Posey. I scared thinking about a witch being here. But if you says that Miss Storky is a saint sitting in Heaven, and that Miss Storky gives you powers to protect us here in the kitchen—then

I sure feels safe, Miss Posey.' The boy leaned his shaved head forward to rest it against Posey's shoulder.

'Shoo!' Posey said, pushing Fat Boy away. 'What do you think I am? Some mother hen? Shoo!'

Lulu tattled, 'Fat Boy just trying to gets on the good side of you, Miss Posey. Fat Boy wants you to give him a piece of your fresh raisin bread with strawberry jam on it.'

'That true?' Posey said, eyeing the youth.

Fat Boy lowered his head and slowly began to shake it from side-to-side.

'*That true?*' Posey repeated louder, yanking for Fat Boy's ear.

'No, Miss Posey—' he began. 'Lulu done fibs.'

'Don't argue with me, Fat Boy. I has enough of you arguing in the kitchen. I has so much of you arguing lately that—'

Posey released his hold on Fat Boy's ear and, grabbing him by the shoulder, he slapped him across the face with the flat of his hand. He slapped him again, demanding, 'You lies to me, Fat Boy? You lies?'

Jerking away from Posey's grasp, Fat Boy dashed across the kitchen, shrieking with pain as he ran behind the cookstove.

'Ha! Don't think I'm going to chase you around the kitchen like a dog, Fat Boy! I don't need to act like no dog because when I wants you I gets you like . . . *that!*' Posey snapped his fingers. He turned to Lulu, saying, 'We got our own work to get on with, nigger girl. We ain't got all day to be chasing fat boys around. But I'll get him. I'll get him if he lies to me.'

Cowering behind the stove, Fat Boy no longer was listening to Posey's threats. He was thinking about seeking his own revenge. He spotted the silk unbrella which Miss Vicky had brought Posey from Cuba. Fat Boy wondered what terrible thing he could do with the silk umbrella, how he could destroy it and truly punish Posey for pulling his ears, slapping his face, being so proud of himself. Fat Boy hated Miss Posey.

*   *   *

A chapel set at the intersection of the two main dirt roads of Town, a small greyboard building with jalousies which had been hinged to swing open for Sunday services in the hot months of summer. But since the black man, Nero, had died there was no one to conduct religious meetings on Dragonard Hill and the chapel was used for storing corn for the chickens, nails for the carpenters, odds and ends of equipment and supplies which went wanting for a proper storage hut or shed on the plantation.

The black woman, Croney, walked from the chicken coop this morning with two empty buckets to fill with corn feed for her hens. Her mind was occupied with matters of the main house as she pushed open the door on this weathered building which had once been a chapel. Croney was thinking about the productivity of her hens, worrying if they could supply the vast quantity of eggs which Posey was suddenly demanding for the kitchen. She worried about Posey boiling too many chickens only for their stock. She was thinking about the sudden drain on her coop.

The door squeaked on its leather hinges as Croney adjusted her eyes from the brightness of the June sun to the darkness here inside the old chapel. Knowing where the gunny sacks of corn feed were kept in a far corner, she turned toward that direction when she suddenly stopped. She saw a figure standing in the middle of the peak-ceilinged room, a black woman with a white kerchief knotted over her forehead.

The black woman's voice was not warm and friendly when she spoke to Croney. But neither was she hostile. She said, 'Good morning, sister.'

'Who you?'

'Malou.'

Croney immediately recognized the name. She remembered the stories which the kitchen girl, Lulu, had brought from the main house, the tales that the black woman, Malou, from the island of Cuba was a voodoo witch.

'Don't look so scared, sister,' Malou said as she lifted her head to survey the rafters. "I'm just standing here feeling the spirits.'

Backing toward the door, Croney said, 'This be a house of the Lord. This be a *good* place of . . . worship.'

'All worship is good,' Malou answered as her eyes studied

the timber rafters, looking at the closed jalousies slanting light through the dust motes, glancing to the benches piled in the corner.

She asked, 'When was the last time a meeting was held here, sister?'

'A good while back,' Croney said, feeling more confident now. Malou's questions did not sound like the words of a witch. 'We ain't had a meeting here since Nero done died. He was once overseer here. Then he caught the deep shivers one winter. He died a hard death and—'

'Now you got no one.'

'We hears a preacher when Matty Kate was buried a short while back. He comes from Troy.'

Malou nodded. She said, 'But the black people got no one.'

'We got our songs. Our beliefs.'

'The master here, he lets you sing, sister?'

'We sings. Sure we sings. Master Peter is a good master to us.'

'And dance? He lets you dance till the spirit takes over your soul and you . . . *feel* the spirit making you dance?'

Croney shook her head. 'There ain't no dancing on this place. Not that kind of dancing. We do reels and jigs on Saturday nights sometimes but—'

'But not in church.' Malou shook her head, saying as she again raised her eyes to appraise the old chapel, 'I don't see no pictures hanging here, sister. I don't see no statues. No crosses. What happened to them?'

'This chapel never had no decoration,' Croney said. 'Nothing except cedar boughs on the floor to give it a nice perfume on Sundays.'

Feeling much more confident now, Croney stepped farther into the chapel and said, 'You Malou woman. I hear stories about you. I hears that you a voodoo gal.'

'What that word mean to you, sister? Voodoo?'

'Voodoo means blood sacrifices and black magic and stuff that gives niggers bad names.'

'That's white people talk!'

'Well, it's white folks who owns this land. And owns us.'

'Owns our bodies!' Malou corrected her. 'Owns our bodies but not our souls. But because they can't ever own our souls they tries to destroy them. They try to say that if we

65

believe in spirits those spirits is bad. But all spirits be the same, sister. They only have different names. And the names of our spirits are the names of our people. The black people who come before us on this earth. That's why white people don't want us to believe. They don't want us to believe in . . . ourselves!'

Croney stood staring at the sober-faced black woman. She could not argue with her. The words did not sound like the words of a witch. She said, 'I guess there are some people on this place who might agree with you.'

'Then you must take me to meet them, sister.'

Croney mumbled, 'I got to get feed for my chickens now. I done wasted enough time.'

Malou smiled. She had suspected that she had come to this distant land for a reason. Now she understood what that reason was. The white people had their missionaries spreading their religions. She herself now was carrying the words of the African gods to Dragonard Hill.

*   *   *

The activity at the main house escaped Belladonna's attention as she busily worked sewing three new dresses from the yardage which Imogen had purchased for her in Troy. Belladonna now had a dress length of yellow calico, a length of brown cotton sprigged with dainty pink roses, and a length of glazed blue cotton the colour of cornflowers.

Imogen returned tired in the evenings to the old house, often too exhausted from field work to speak to Belladonna. She never referred to her family's affairs in the main house. Nor did Belladonna press Imogen for facts. Not these days. She was too content deciding on what kind of sleeves—how long the sashes would be—for her three new dresses.

Belladonna also did not question Imogen about the reason she had been prompted to buy her such extravagant gifts. She remained ignorant of any ulterior plans until one night when Imogen announced that she was going to retire early to her bedroom upstairs. She informed Belladonna that she wanted her to accompany her upstairs, not to stay late again in the kitchen tonight but to come to bed now.

The corn husk mattress crunched on its leather straps as Belladonna climbed obediently into bed.

'Blow out the candle,' Imogen ordered. She was already under the flannel sheeting and quilt. Her bare arm lay outstretched on a pillow.

Belladonna obediently complied with her wishes.

'You ever been laid by a man, girl?' Imogen's voice was hard, not soft and loving.

Belladonna snuggled against Imogen's naked body, whispering, 'I tell you always I don't wants nobody but you.'

Imogen pushed her away. She said, 'I asked you a question, girl!'

Raising herself on the corn husk mattress, Belladonna said, 'You knows the answer to that! You knows a man tried to pester me. And you knows I would kills the next man who tries it!'

Imogen was silent.

Belladonna lowered herself to the mattress. She could not smell liquor on Imogen's breath but she knew that whisky often made her say crazy things like this.

Imogen spoke in the darkness. 'I wants you to make love to a man, girl.'

'You want me to—' Belladonna sat bolt upright in bed again.

'I don't have to explain myself to you, girl. I want you to make love to a man! I'll tell you who it is when the time's ready. For the moment I want you to . . . pretend.'

'Pretend?'

'I want you to be ready. I want you to act like you enjoy him when it's happening.'

'Who is he? Who do you plan to have pester me?'

'Damnit, wench!' Imogen shouted, shoving Belladonna down onto the mattress. 'Bitches like you don't ask questions. They just . . . obey.'

Belladonna held one arm across her shut eyes, trying not to let Imogen see—nor hear—her sobbing. She felt the mattress crunch with the weight of Imogen's body leaning to one side. She knew that Imogen was reaching for the object she kept on the floor under the bed. Belladonna had learned to enjoy Imogen protruding the object into her femininity. But that was when they made love together, using the phallus-shaped object as if it were part of Imogen's body. Belladonna next heard the sound of Imogen's hand slushing in a tin can next to the bed. Then she felt the coldness of the phallus move between her legs. She heard Imogen issuing orders. She knew she must obey. She had no choice. And as Belladonna slowly opened her slim thighs, she whispered, 'I love you, Imogen. I does anything for you. But please let me pretend that this be . . . you.'

'Shut up, bitch,' Imogen hissed. 'You'll understand soon enough. Now stick up your pussy for him . . . stick up your pussy.'

The crown of the wooden phallus was moist with goose grease from the tin can. Imogen slowly inched it between Belladonna's legs, whispering, 'Take the man in your pussy, wench. Open your pussy for him . . . That's right . . . take him into your pussy and tell him you love it.'

Choking back her tears, Belladonna whispered, '. . . I loves it.'

'Do you feel the man pushing inside you?' Imogen asked as she inched the blunt crown of the greased instrument deeper between Belladonna's legs.

'I feels—' Belladonna wanted to speak as she had done in the past, that she was enjoying Imogen as a man.

'You feels . . . what?'

'The pecker . . .' She began to move, to shift herself on the mattress.

'Don't squirm!' Imogen ordered, slapping her against one leg. 'Lay still. Be obedient. You're taking a . . . man. A man's pecker. Not me but . . . a man.'

The instrument's crown had passed beyond the lips of Belladonna's vagina; she could feel the cold greasiness gliding deeper inside her. The sensation was impersonal, debasing, not similar in any way to the movements when Imogen used the instrument on her during their love-making in the past. This was not love. It was torture.

'Take him . . . deeper,' Imogen said, smiling as she now knelt between Belladonna's naked legs and thrust the instrument farther into the black girl. 'Close your eyes. Think that a man is mounting you. Raise up your legs to take him deeper. Raise up your legs, bitch.'

Slowly, Belladonna lifted her slim legs. She kept her eyes firmly shut.

'You feel him?'

'I feels him . . .'

'You feel the man?'

Belladonna knew that Imogen wanted her to perform a complete scene for her and, fearing the consequences if she did not, Belladonna obediently raised her legs as if she were wrapping them around a man. She lifted her arms to hug the imaginary lover. She pushed her midsection higher in the air, stretching to take the wooden-and-leather phallus. She whispered, 'I feels you . . . I feels you . . . Oh, I feels you.' She began tossing her head back and forth on the pillow as Imogen worked the phallus faster in the greased vaginal course. Imogen smiled to herself as she saw what a good actress Belladonna was becoming under her guidance, that the black girl would soon be ready to confront a real male, to receive a real phallus.

Chapter Four

GROUSE HOLLOW

The farms and plantations in the northern Louisiana wilderness received news about important local events—births, deaths, reports of runaway slaves—from pedlars who travelled through the countryside, at church or social gatherings, or around the potbelly stoves at the mercantile stores of small towns such as Carterville and Troy.

Newspapers were a rarity in upcountry Louisiana; the nearest newspaper was printed in New Orleans. The largest publication was the 'New Orleans Bee'—printed in French as *L'Abeille de la Nouvelle Orleans*—and the second largest was the 'Louisiana Courier', also known as *Le Courier de Louisiane*. A smaller, more conservative paper called the "Louisiana Whig' seldom travelled from the city; a new weekly was rumoured soon to be appearing but the 'Times-Picayune' had yet to be published in the year, 1836.

The popularity of the 'New Orleans Bee' was due to the fact that it included both stories about the city and the upcountry plantations. Circulation outside the city depended entirely on travellers taking copies in wagons or coaches, though, and the stories in the 'New Orleans Bee' were often out-dated by the time that a copy reached the hinderlands. Thus, the most effective method of keeping well-informed in the countryside was still by the various word-of-mouth circuits.

A strict social caste amongst the white country people prevented much of the populace from learning about events in their vicinity from neighbours. The excluded parties were often small farmers—settlers who owned only a modicum of land and a few slaves, people who were referred to by both Negroes and their more affluent neighbours as 'white trash.'

The widow, Claudia Goss, was considered by many people to be 'white trash', a label reinforced by her occupation as a travelling slave-pedlar. But Mrs Goss was a vindictive woman; she seldom repeated any of the news gleaned in her travels to those people who refused to impart any news to her.

During the month of June in the year, 1836, Claudia Goss again was suffering from an old recurring illness to which she referred as her 'ague'. The mysterious malady kept the woman confined to a cabin on her farm, Grouse Hollow, a small patch of acreage which she had inherited from her last husband.

Claudia Goss received no callers at Grouse Hollow. Nor did her two slaves, Jack and Mary, travel to other plantations and bring news home to their mistress. Claudia Goss could not depend on them either to learn what was happening in the outside world.

Consequently, Claudia Goss welcomed the old copy of the 'New Orleans Bee' which the young lawyer, Jerome Poliguet, had sent to her by a messenger from Troy. She was the foundation for the practise which Poliguet was now conducting two days a week in this vicinity.

Claudia Goss had first met the young Creole lawyer after her last husband had died. She had decided after Mister Grouse's demise to change her surname from 'Grouse' to 'Goss'. She had also heard at that time about a young Creole opening a professional office in New Orleans for legal advice. She knew the Creole people to be crafty—as well as influential citizens of New Orleans—and immediately recognized the benefits of having one as her lawyer.

Being realistic, Claudia also suspected that a Creole who opened an office which would take her for a client must badly be in need of money, that such a man might even be as unscrupulous as herself.

Claudia's suspicions proved to be correct. She had visited Poliguet's offices on Canal Street, had entered as Claudia Grouse and emerged as Claudia Goss. The normally long procedure of legally changing a name had been accomplished in minutes. She was totally convinced about the handsome young Creole's integrity—or lack of it. She visited him again, suffering the day's journey to New Orleans to learn how to deal with loans, mortgages, the ways she could insure her own money whilst exacting a high rate of interest from people who did not qualify to borrow money from a bank. Poliguet told her about compounded interests, taking slaves as collateral against risky loans, how she could sell the slaves as interest against the interest outstanding and, above all, he instructed her to have all agreements—however shady—committed to a binding written contract. Claudia gladly paid Poliguet's fee, acquiring a store of knowledge which began increasing her small fortune.

Four years after she had first consulted Poliguet in New Orleans, Claudia now considered him to be more than a financial advisor. He had an impressive background but also understood the burning drive of revenge. Being a Creole ostracized from his own peer group, Poliguet understood Claudia's complaint of being slighted by people who considered themselves to be her social superiors. Poliguet had become a colleague in Claudia's long-term plan for total revenge against certain leading families in northern Louisiana. She would not have a good night's rest until she saw one specific plantation—Dragonard Hill—razed to the ground and its fields planted with salt.

*　　*　　*

Claudia Goss sat wrapped this chilly June morning in a patchwork quilt. The back copy of the 'New Orleans Bee' which Jerome Poliguet had sent to her now lay opened on a deal table in front of her, its yellowing pages turned to the obituary columns.

'Jack!' she shrieked, throwing back her head. 'Mary! You lazy wench! One of you thieving niggers around this house someplace?'

The sound of shuffling feet moved in a small lean-to adjoining the one-room cabin, a makeshift space serving as a kitchen. A Negress soon appeared in the doorway, a young but weary-looking black woman who wore a badly patched
72

cotton shirt and her hair frizzed in a cloud around her haggard face.

Claudia demanded, 'Fetch me that no good coon! Tell Jack I wants him to hitch-up my mules! I aim to start travelling again.'

'Travelling? Mrs Goss?' Mary asked. 'Your ague done passed?'

'My ague passed from my body this very morning,' Claudia announced as she threw back the patchwork quilt from her shoulders and grabbed for the newspaper. 'The ague done passed from my body like a fart after eating too many butter beans!'

Mary had suspected recently that her mistress's strange illness was brought on by slow periods in her trade, that the malady was a camouflage for the fact that none of her usual customers were buying—or had the money to buy—the sad-looking Negroes whom Claudia trailed around the country roads tied to the back of her wagon.

The hut where Claudia kept her supply of slaves was empty; her stock of toothless old men and barren women was depleted. This knowledge made Mary wonder about the reason why her mistress should suddenly announce that she was going travelling.

Mary asked, 'You plan to go . . . selling, Mrs Goss?'

'Don't go snooping into what I plans or don't plans to do. Just you tells that coon I wants him to hitch up my mules. And then you fetches me something clean to wear.'

'Clean?' Mary repeated. The word—in all its connotations—was unknown in this household.

'I didn't say dirty, did I, you dumb cluck? I needs a clean dress to wear. I sees here in this newspaper that a neighbour of mine done died.'

'A neighbour . . . died?'

'That's right! Killed! Threw from her horse! And almost a month ago by now! So make sure the dress you finds for me to wear is black. Black for mourning. Dig around and see if you can finds the mourning clothes I wore for my last husband.'

'Mister Grouse done died five years ago, Mistress.' Mary cautiously reminded the white woman. 'You tells me to use those togs to scrubs the floors with! That be nearly three years ago now you gives me those orders. I done already used-up and throwed-away that black dress you mourned Mister Grouse with.'

'Not Grouse, damnit! *Goss*! Won't you ever learn to get that name right? Who wants to go through life as a "grouse". A grouse is a bird! A simpering timid little bird that done gets chased and hunted and pecked by other birds. I hate Grouse! I'm Goss now. And soon this place is going to be called something different than Grouse Hollow. I'm going to change the name of this place to something fine as soon as I can think of it. But if you don't start remembering to stop saying, "Grouse", missy, I'll tie you up to my wagon and drags you down to the crossroads the next time I takes a string of niggers there to sell!'

Mary knew that her mistress's threat to sell her was not idle. She had seen her sell off other slaves from Grouse Hollow since her reign of terror had begun here. Hanging her head, Mary said, 'I looks and sees what black dresses we gots for you to wear, Mistress Mam.'

'Make it snappy,' Claudia ordered. 'I wants to start my trip this afternoon. I plan to rest the night away from home. I heads to Dragonard Hill bright tomorrow morning.'

'You going to sleep tonight in the wagon?'

'Whores and thieves sleep in wagons,' Claudia ranted. 'I plans to go as far as Troy today. I got business there with my . . . lawyer! I also got a few friends in Troy who finds it to their advantage to put me up in their homes.' Claudia smiled at the prospect of wringing hospitality from the white families who still owed her money. Yes, she needed this trip to revitalize her spirits. She already felt like a new woman.

* * *

The name of the plantation, Dragonard Hill, meant little to the black woman, Mary, but the Negro, Jack, immediately recognized it when Claudia Goss explained her intentions to him a short while later.

Jack drawled, 'Dragonard Hill . . . that's be the plantation where your first husband was the overseer of, Mistress Goss?'

Claudia sat by the old table and said, 'My first husband was Mister Chad Tucker, the overseer of that plantation when it was still called The Star. In the days before uppity Peter Abdee took control of that land. Mister Tucker and me were living on The Star when Peter Abdee was bought from a nigger house in New Orleans as a . . . slave!' Her eyes gleamed in their sockets as she announced this long-forgotten fact, then continuing, she said, 'Mister Tucker and me were still living on The Star when it was proven that young Abdee was actually a white person and then allowed to marry that sickly Selby girl. The Selbys used to own The Star but when they allowed Abdee to take control of the land, Mister Tucker and myself did not approve of the treatment which we saw certain people receiving on the plantation—that's when we decided to . . . depart! It was not until many years later that Abdee married Kate Breslin of Greenleaf Plantation.'

Claudia puckered her small lips, saying, 'I could tell plenty of stories about that Irish filly but, being she met such an unfortunate death, I shall keep my peace like a . . . white lady. I plan to travel to Dragonard Hill to pay neighbourly respects to the grieving family. That's the least any white lady of my position can do.'

Jack knew that his mistress was not what polite Southerners referred to as a 'lady', nor did she perform any generous acts without having an ulterior motive. He knew better than to question his mistress, though, and lifting his cap toward his head, he mumbled, 'I better gets going so you can take advantage of driving those mules in as much daylight as you can catch.'

'Me? Drive? What rubbish you talking, coon? You'll be handling the team! Same as usual!'

He stared at her. He had expected to be left here at Grouse Hollow with Mary. They had few moments together as husband and wife.

Claudia asked, 'You don't expect me to go calling on neighbours driving my own wagon, do you? A white lady is always driven by her darkie!'

Jack lowered his head. She had shattered all his hopes of spending time with his wife. He slowly left the room.

* * *

The road leading from Grouse Hollow was barely more

than a path worn down into the quack grass which grew between the water oaks and scrub willow trees. Once the slave, Jack, drove the mules of Claudia's wagon to the public road, the wooden wheels rolled smoothly over the dirt thoroughfare and a blue sky was visible beyond the spires of pine trees. Claudia Goss and Jack reached the small town of Troy before sundown. Claudia told Jack to leave her by the mercantile store where Jerome Poliguet rented office space in the upper floor.

She said, 'You take the wagon over to Willy Browne's place. Tell Willy to stable these critters and find a place for you to roost in the barn. Tell him to have his missus prepare their room for me. Say "Mrs Goss don't know how long she's staying." Say "Mrs Goss done gone visiting her attorney and does not know how long her business will keep her in town." If Willy Browne or his missus give you any back talk, say that "Mrs Goss also got the deed to their house and she's thinking that she might need her money pretty soon owing on the house". And then say "Mrs Goss has been considering lately of moving into town. That she finds their little house very pleasing".'

Satisfied with the message she was sending to the Browne family who had little choice in offering her hospitality, Claudia Goss turned and mounted the wooden steps to the mercantile store.

A bell tinkled over the door as she entered the glass-fronted building. The pungent smell of coffee beans, cloves, and tobacco filled her nostrils as she surveyed a group of men seated near the window.

The men were mostly small farmers or town people who had nothing to do other than to idle in this store. Many served as patrollers on the public roads, self-appointed militia men who watched for runaway slaves. Claudia recognized a few faces amongst them, men who had debts outstanding to her for slaves they had bought from her, or from loans which she had extended to them with usurious rates of interest, loans—and interest—they had difficulty paying.

Adjusting the straw bonnet on her head, Claudia surveyed the collection of sober faces and asked, 'Don't a man stand up no more when he sees a white lady?'

Chairs creaked. Shoes shuffled. The men moved to rise.

They murmured, 'Afternoon, Mrs. Goss.' 'You looking fine, Mrs Goss.' 'That a new bonnet you wearing today, Mrs Goss?'

Claudia now ignored them. She had their attention. She had received the homage she expected. She waddled past a line of wooden kegs filled with nails and withered apples, calling to the store clerk behind the counter, 'Ralph? Mister Poliguet upstairs in his office?'

'Yes, Mrs Goss,' the clerk quickly answered. 'Good to see you again, Mrs Goss.'

'Good to be out and about again,' she mumbled and headed for the board stairs which led up the side of the mercantile to its upper floor.

The door at the top of the narrow stairway was opened before Claudia reached the landing. A tall man dressed in a black frock coat and grey-striped breeches stood with his arms folded across his chest. He was a young man, no older than thirty-years, and his black wavy hair was brushed back from his cleanly-shaven face. His dapper appearance made a sharp contrast to the slovenly group of men seated in front of the store's window.

'Claudia Goss! You old hellion! What brings you into town?' His eyes twinkled as brightly as the diamonds set in the gold stickpin decorating his burgundy silk cravat. 'I bet you've been reading the newspapers!'

Puffing for breath, holding onto the banister for support, Claudia panted, 'Poliguet, if I don't get more respect from you, I'll—I'll—I'll do something awful to you!'

Moving now to give a hand to his best client, Jerome Poliguet teased, 'You don't have anything awful enough for me! Come on in! Take a load off your feet! Tell me what you're plotting now, you . . . queen of the backwoods!'

Claudia dropped the shawl from the shoulders of her linsey-woolsey dress and looked past Poliguet into his office. She remarked, 'Business don't seem to be booming here for you, Poliguet.'

'And I haven't seen you parading niggers around the countryside lately.' He stepped aside and, extending one arm to a chair placed alongside his desk, he said, 'Come in. Tell me what you've been reading in the newspapers. All about local society, have you? Oh, you always were the fancy one!'

'Damnit! Stop sweet-talking me! You know what I've been reading in the newspapers. The obituaries, that's what! Why else did you send it to me? And you also know there is something I can do. *I* know there is something I can do. There's no better time to take advantage of people than when they've had a death in the family now is there? So you and me only has to decide what that something is going to be. I've had a few ideas but—' She stopped to wipe the beads of perspiration from her brow.

'I never forget old friends, Mrs Goss. Nor old feuds. That's exactly why I sent you the newspaper. But there's also been a development since I sent you the *Bee*. I happened to meet someone last week on the coach travelling here from New Orleans. Now come into my office and let me tell you all about it. Who knows, old girl? Who knows but we might both be richer by the end of this planting season. Richer than we ever thought we would be.' Jerome Poliguet closed the office door behind them.

Chapter Five

THE LAST WEEK OF SPRING

The last week of spring, the first days of summer in the month of June, was a fertile time at Dragonard Hill; the rich soil began its abundant yield in the fields and the gardens; the orchards blossomed with promise of a full harvest; the deer, wild fowl, the possum trailed the woodlands and pine forests with their young, predicting that there would be fine hunting and trapping before the cold months of winter arrived.

Peter Abdee welcomed these seasonal auspices; they helped turn his attention from the recent loss of his wife. He also enjoyed having his four children on this land and, although he had not so far established a reunion which would join them at one table, he hoped soon to achieve this wish.

True to his considerate spirit, Peter noticed that the presence of Vicky and Veronica in the main house at Dragonard Hill took its toll on his son. Young David Abdee became overly excited at the supper table and had difficulty falling asleep these nights. He also began asking questions about his mother and repeatedly described days from their life together to his step-sisters. David Abdee was proving to be a highly-strung boy. To avoid any disturbances now in the young boy's mind, Peter decided in the last week of June that David should spend a few days visiting his cousin—Kate's nephew, Barry Breslin—who was the master of nearby Greenleaf Plantation.

Peter Abdee himself had been waiting for the opportune moment to visit Greenleaf himself. He knew that Barry Breslin's cotton crops had repeatedly failed in recent years. The young man did not know how to manage his land nor lay aside profit for the next season and lean years. Peter had decided to extend the financial assistance he and Kate had previously given to Barry. He spent his time considering all these facts in the last week of June, planning visits and considering loans rather than to concentrate on the sexual appetite growing in his groin.

Vicky and Veronica still had not said when they were going to leave. Peter did not press them. He wanted his daughters to enjoy themselves for however long they remained home and decided that a brief visit to Greenleaf Plantation would benefit everyone. They would leave on Sunday morning to take young David to stay at the neighbouring plantation.

* * *

Although smaller than Dragonard Hill, the main house at Greenleaf Plantation was painted white and proportioned in a similar classical style; its parlours and bedrooms were tastefully furnished; the food which came from the kitchen was plentiful, tasty, and varied—all attributes associated with this small but pleasing house since the days when Kate Breslin had first been its mistress.

Barry Breslin kept the appearance of Greenleaf as the house had looked at the time Kate had transferred its title to him when she had married Peter Abdee and moved to Dragonard Hill. He kept the same house servants, same furniture, same English silver cutlery and Sevres china, the same schedule for meals, morning rising, even whiskys-at-sundown as his aunt had enjoyed during her days as the mistress of Greenleaf.

As the passage of time seemed not to have touched the jewel-like quality of Greenleaf so did years leave Barry Breslin visibly unmarked by age and wear. The sandy-haired man appeared to be no older—but, also, no more responsible—than he had been when he used to travel to Dragonard Hill years ago and make bumbling efforts, first, to court Imogen and, next, to make seductive attempts toward Vicky. Barry had discovered his masculinity in those formative years, but, even now when he pursued veneries only amongst the plantation slave women on Greenleaf, he still exuded a clumsiness.

The discussion of finances also still embarrassed Barry Breslin. He now tried to divert the subject of conversation from money when Peter mentioned his present situation at the bank. Peter and Barry were walking together, strolling from the main house in the gentle warmth on this Sunday afternoon after a midday meal of roast chicken, steamed vegetables, spiced rice, and a tingly white French wine still chilled from the coolness of the springhouse.

Barry held his large red hands behind his back and, kicking at a stone with the toes of his outsize boots, he confessed, 'I guess I'm going to miss Aunt Katie more than you.'

Peter knew that Kate had done the financial accounts for Greenleaf long after she had moved from here. That she had even spent time discussing crops with the overseer, menus with the cook, taking care of Barry and this plantation long after she had become known as 'Mrs Abdee.'

'We both have to try harder now,' Peter said, disliking this new responsibility of goading a mature male into becoming the master of his own land. He said, 'Perhaps it's time you considered getting married.'

Barry did not reply to the suggestion.

Peter glanced sideways and saw Barry's cheeks flushing brightly red. He remembered seeing the same blush on Barry's face when he had met him, Veronica, Vicky, and young David on the front gallery of the white house. Although Vicky had long forgotten—or, at least, made no reference to their past assignations—Barry still was obviously embarrassed by his conduct as her erstwhile paramour. He also stayed away from Dragonard Hill in fear of seeing Imogen—who was once supposed to become his wife.

Hoping to put him at ease, Peter said, 'There are plenty of pretty young girls in the neighbourhood. What about Polly Sinclair? Or Wilhelmina Schneider?' He elbowed Barry in the ribs, saying 'They say that the young Schneider girl is filling out very nicely. And she's German. That's good stock. You'll get strong, hearty sons—some German blood mixed in with your Irish!'

Barry shook his head. He kept staring at the tips of his boots as they now reached the crest of a hillock. He said, 'I feel I'd be cheating my wife—whoever I married. The real kind of woman I want to live with I can't. And . . .' He shook his head saying, 'No, I guess I'm not cut out to be the marrying kind . . .'

Peter did not have to press Barry to understand his dilemma. He knew that Barry enjoyed bedding Negresses, that if he were to settle happily with one female that she would have to be black, and he could not do that here— not a choice he could make and still remain the master of Greenleaf. White planters had to keep their involvements with black women away from the public eye, not to allow love to tease them into thinking about marriage.

'You're planting well again this year,' Peter said in a brighter voice, looking to the fields furrowed into neat rows.

Barry remained maudlin. He said, 'Nothing in my life seems to be going according to how it's supposed to. Not the planting. Not who I want . . .'

'The planting looks fine.'

'I had to borrow more money to do this much. More of Kate's money. Least money Kate signed for.' He knew that Peter was aware of this arrangement for Kate providing money or collateral for the loans from the bank. She had done it this year as well as the year before. She had insisted that Barry use formal banking procedures rather than to use her as a bottomless purse to finance his way in the world. She had felt that such a practise would bring him closer to the realities of the business world.

'Don't let me burden you with my problems,' Barry said, turning to glance back toward the yellow roof of Greenleaf dotted with four dormer windows. 'Let's talk about David. I'm glad to have him here for a few days. How long you want him to visit?'

'I appreciate your hospitality. A change of scenery will do the boy good. The mood at home now is—' Peter paused, struggling for the right words. He did not really know how to describe the atmosphere at Dragonard Hill. He secretly feared a rift was coming between his three daughters but he did not want to admit that, not even to himself.

'A nice handsome young boy,' Barry said. 'Before long he'll be chasing poontang himself.'

Peter jerked his head and looked at his step-nephew. He knew that Barry was joking. He nevertheless resented the fact of him speaking about the sexuality of someone who was still a young innocent lad. Must Barry talk about nothing but sex?

'I was only making a josh!' Barry quickly apologized, sloping down the hill in long easy gaits. 'You don't have to worry. I won't be mating him up. But there *is* a real beauty here. Old Milly and Abe's young one. She's blossomed into a right piece. I hear from Gigi, though—she's still my honey, Gigi—that this young Georgiabelle gal ain't interested in me one bit. Oh, no. She says that a certain gent in this neighbourhood is who she's got her eye on. A certain gent who—'

Barry looked mischievously at Peter out of the corner of his eye. 'You know what I'm saying . . . Uncle Peter?'

Peter's answer was cold and abrupt. 'I understand your meaning perfectly, Barry. And I not only think it's impudent but in mighty bad taste. You should show more respect to your aunt's memory.'

Thinking of a young black girl brimming with the first ripeness of womanhood, and making the fact known in the slave quarter at Greenleaf that she was desirous to give herself to him, excited Peter but he tried to push it from his mind. He told himself that he could not take a bed wench from Greenleaf, not a Negress from the same place where he had once sneaked to meet Kate.

*   *   *

The red-and-yellow spokes of the Abdee buggy revolved like bright carnival pinwheels over the public road as Peter, Veronica, and Vicky returned home to Dragonard Hill from Greenleaf late that Sunday afternoon.

Vicky tried to amuse her father and Veronica with reminiscences about Barry Breslin's physical defect, the fact that he had only one testicle, a deficiency which had no effect on his prodigious appetite for love-making.

The stories were met with silence. Peter snapped the whip over the jerking heads of his pair of chestnut mares;

Veronica held one hand on the wide brim of her straw hat which was catching the breeze; the cloud of dust billowed behind the buggy as they now moved along the poplar-lined road to the steady clip-clop, clip-clop of the smartly stepping horses.

Two stone pillars stood along the roadside supporting a black wrought-iron rainbow which announced in classical lettering 'Dragonard Hill', an entrance to this land which had replaced the rough timber posts planted further down the road, the old gate supporting a cross-beam from which had long-ago hung a wooden star to signify the former name of this plantation.

Peter cracked the tip of the buggy whip again over the horses' heads as they turned from the public road to enter this land; neither he, Veronica, nor Vicky glanced back toward the cemetery on the far side of the road; the buggy bounced across the open field flanked by cotton furrows and began climbing the gentle slope to the white pillared house commanding the crest.

The driveway turned into a circle in front of the Doric columns lining the front gallery; no other buggies, carriages, nor horses were in sight; Peter reined the horses to allow Veronica and Vicky to alight from the buggy before he drove to the stable. As it was Sunday, he had given the groom permission to spend this free day in Town and expected no one to take the buggy-and-team from him here.

A figure came running toward them from the stable setting in the distance. Peter strained his eyes to see who was trying to attract their attention. It was Vicky who first recognized the person.

She said, 'What's Posey doing coming from the stable? Silly nigger! I thought he was frightened of horses. Doesn't he know he'll get manure on his . . . skirts!'

Running toward the buggy and waving his arms, Posey panted, 'Don't go in the house, Master Peter! Don't go in the house!'

Posey stopped and, catching his breath in deep gulps, he pointed toward the side of the main house, saying, 'I didn't let her come in the front door! I made her nigger driver take that old wagon out back. I didn't want no trash littering up the front of the place, Master Peter.'

'Posey, catch your breath!' Veronica urged and walked
84

toward him to give him an arm to lean on.

'Oh, Miss Veronica, you're so good to me. You've always been so good and understanding to me, Miss Veronica. But, oh, do be careful—there's trouble here today. There's trouble—'

'Trouble?' Peter asked still seated in the buggy.

'Posey, I do declare you've been in the peach brandy!' Vicky accused, turning to mount the steps of the house. She had not yet been home for a fortnight and she was already bored with rural life.

'Don't!' Posey shrieked, breaking away from Veronica to keep Vicky from moving one step closer toward the front doors. 'Don't go inside that house! Not while that mean awful old Tucker woman's in there!'

'Tucker?' Peter asked.

'*Goss!*' a voice called from behind them. 'Claudia Goss!'

Peter, Veronica, Vicky, and Posey turned at the sound of the firm announcement. Claudia Goss emerged from around the side of the house, saying, 'I stopped by today to pay my condolences for the late . . . Mrs Abdee. I ain't been feeling up to snuff lately myself and took to keeping indoors. I just received word at my place about the sad news here. I was planning to come calling on you yesterday but business kept me . . . in Troy longer that I expected.'

Surveying the surprised expression on Peter's, Veronica's and Vicky's faces as they still gaped at her, Claudia continued, 'I came today to pay neighbourly respects but that silly nigger woman there took such a fright when she seen me that . . .'

Posey held his head in sudden triumph. He was pleased that not only had Claudia Goss not recognized him but had mistaken his gender.

Peter said from the buggy, 'You can go now, Posey. It's very nice of Mrs . . . Goss to come here and—'

'Posey?' Claudia repeated, staring at Posey attired in his white dress, stiffly starched white apron, and a kerchief knotted at the nape of his neck. 'You mean to tell me that this nigger is . . . Posey? That little nigger pansy who used to pick all them field flowers on this place? Hell's bells! I remember you, Posey! But I remember you as a . . . boy! My memory also seems to tell me that my late husband, Mister Chad Tucker, had some sport with you, nigger priss.

Yes, I do seem to recall that the Good Lord didn't bless you with much between your legs. In fact, the Good Lord hardly blessed you at all!'

Appraising his feminine attire, Claudia clucked, 'My, my, my. So now you've taken to getting yourself up like some . . . woman. Ain't that rich! If that ain't just the richest one I've heard yet!'

Peter intervened on Posey's behalf, again saying, 'Posey, why don't you go quietly to the kitchen.' He saw Posey glaring hatred at the white woman, that Posey's long black fingers were curling with rage at the sides of his skirts as if he were about to fly at Claudia Goss and rip her apart with his talon-like hands.

'I said, go now, Posey!' Peter commanded in a more authoritative tone.

Glancing from Claudia Goss to his master, Posey threw up his head and loftily said, 'I've got more important business to do anyway, Master, Sir. I've got a letter to give to Miss Veronica here. A letter dones arrives this morning from Carterville for Miss Veronica whilst you were all visiting at Greenleaf.'

Posey glanced hatefully back at Claudia Goss, adding, 'It's Sunday today but some gentleman in this district are willing to ride all this distance from Carterville to bring a letter to *fine* white ladies. The rider tolds me personally that he would've gots here much sooner but seems some big old white trash woman was blocking the road with her . . . mules! Mules! No white woman I never sees in this world lets herself be pulled around the countryside by . . . mules!'

He turned and swept majestically away from Claudia Goss while Veronica hurried after him. She asked, 'A letter came for me, Posey? A letter from the steamboat landing in Carterville?'

Claudia Goss said after they disappeared around the corner of the main house, 'Excuse me for saying so, Mister Abdee, but you always did allow your niggers to carry on around here too much. No good will come from that. No good at all.'

Peter quietly smouldered when his mind quickly flooded with the troubles which Claudia and her husband, Chad Tucker, had caused amongst the black people on this land years ago when Tucker had been the overseer here. He did not want to dig-out old animosities but neither did he want to extend hospitality to a woman who had brought nothing but trouble and grief.

He said, 'I thank you for dropping by today to pay your respects, Mrs Goss. It was doubly considerate of you to do so considering how poorly you felt. The girls and I have just come back from Greenleaf and, so, I hope you won't think us too rude if we don't invite you into the house. You will understand—'

'Greenleaf?' Claudia said, tilting her head to one side. She had not really expected to be given hospitality at Dragonard Hill. But a snub was a snub in her eyes just the same and she slyly asked, 'Greenleaf? I hears that Breslin boy ain't too well with that property.'

'Barry's doing just fine,' Peter said but wondering if word was out amongst the farmers and businessmen about Greenleaf's precarious financial position. 'Barry was close to his aunt and you can imagine what he's going through.'

'That I can imagine!' she sniffed. 'Especially without her signing all his notes.'

Peter strained not to order Claudia Goss immediately from his land. He said, 'You will understand, Mrs Goss, that it would be both disrespectful and unethical to discuss my nephew's affairs.'

'And what about your daughter here?' Claudia said, turning her attention now toward Vicky. 'This must be the one who went off to New Orleans or someplace and then comes home now a countess. You bring your family with you, honey?'

Claudia's direct question caught Vicky uncharacteristically off guard. She faltered, 'Why . . . no . . . my husband and son . . . stayed . . . , in Cuba.'

'Better for you that way, ain't it, honey? Much better for a pretty thing like you to be travelling alone.' Studying Vicky's slim figure dressed in a smartly cut gown of black chintz, she said, 'Yes, you're a pretty little gad-a-bout even in your mourning clothes.'

Gathering the skirt of her rusty black dress in one pudgy hand, Claudia said, 'I won't be troubling you no longer.

Not today. I just wanted to pay my condolences like I said. Pay my condolences and—'

Claudia Goss paused to gaze over the sloping vista of Dragonard Hill. She said, '—and have myself a look at this place. Have myself a real good look.' She remembered Poliguet's words about them being richer at the end of this planting season, of their plan to seize, first, Greenleaf, and, then, Dragonard Hill.

* * *

Veronica sat alone in the library and reread the letter which Royal had written to her from Boston. She had hoped to learn the date when the mysterious man was going to contact her at Dragonard Hill and, thus, when she would finally be able to go home to Royal and the children. But Royal did not mention the man in the letter. He did not say when she could leave the plantation. Royal's letter contained nothing except what appeared to be idle facts. He had written about the welfare of their three children, that Lindy had won the spelling bee at school by correctly spelling the word 'picturesque' when her ancient rival in the Chadwick Elementary School, Bethesda Collins, had inserted a 'k' instead of a 'q'. Royal proceeded to explain how he was spending his evenings at home but he urged Veronica to use her free time in Louisiana by socializing with neighbours.

Then came the most puzzling part of the letter. Royal mentioned the names of families and clerics who meant nothing to Veronica, and he mentioned the towns they lived in or the farms which they tilled—places which were not even close to Dragonard Hill.

Jake and Miranda Dupres. Celia Breakwater . . . Reverend and Mrs Reginald Lewis in Haddleytown . . . The Sell family who lived even farther north. . . .

Who are these people? Veronica wondered. Why is Royal mentioning them? Has he taken leave of his senses?

Veronica then reread the conclusion of the letter, the lines which totally baffled her. '*I always find it is best to keep the names of my friends written on my heart, better than scribbled on paper like this for any stranger to see . . .*'

'Written on his heart'? 'Strangers'? What was he doing?

88

Asking her to remember the names and then destroy this—

Veronica slowly lowered the letter to her lap and realized that Royal might possibly be asking her to destroy this letter. Yes, perhaps he *did* want her to visit the homes of these people he mentioned but leave no hint as to whom she had gone visiting.

Royal furthermore urged her to begin immediately, to take advantages of time to 'reestablish old friendships.'

Knowing that she must get to the bottom of this mystery, Veronica folded the letter and put it into the pocket of her dress. She would destroy it in due time but not until she consulted a map to see exactly where she must visit. She also realized that she must invent some credible story for her father as to why she had to visit . . . old friends? Would he ever believe it?

Although Veronica desperately wanted to return to Boston, she realized that she must stay here. That Royal—for some curious reason—wanted her here. She also told herself that for once in her life she had to be artful in inventing an excuse to go visiting the people whose names Royal had sent to her. She intuitively knew that her future with Royal depended upon it.

*   *   *

That Sunday evening on Dragonard Hill was the first time in years that a service was held in the chapel in Town. The meeting in no way resembled the services which the late overseer, Nero, had once conducted here in the full brightness of a sabbath's morning. Dark night now enshrouded the sky but the jalousies were kept closed to allow not even moonlight to enter the chapel. The only light came from a wick immersed in a cup of bear fat. The flame sputtered. Maybelle and Ham sat crouched near the makeshift candle on the dirt floor. They crouched near Croney, the Negress from the chicken coop who had persuaded them to come to the chapel tonight and hear the Cuban slave woman, Malou, speak to them about the divine spirits, the souls of black people, and how slaves in America had a right to believe in their own gods as the white people had a right to believe in the gods they brought to this new world from Europe. Maybelle had originally protested about the meeting, adamantly refusing to join the few black people from Town invited here to hear Malou speak. But when Croney had insisted that there was nothing different between the religion which Malou preached compared to the religion preached by the white reverend in Troy, Maybelle finally relented to come. She now sat listening to Malou speaking about a woman whom the Christians called St Barbara. St Barbara? Maybelle knew that some white people believed in certain holy women and men they called saints but she had never before heard of that one, Saint Barbara. She listened avidly about the holy St Barbara's attributes and how she was like the African spirit, Man-o-the-River's-Wife. Neither had Maybelle heard before that name. She leaned forward and whispered to Ham, 'Maybe there is no difference between black gods and white because none of them mean nothing to me.' Ham answered, 'There's enough difference for us to learn which ones are ours. This woman is a good talker. You let her talk. I bet next meeting to be held here we see a lot more black faces inside this old church.' Maybelle secretly hoped that Ham's words would not prove to be true, fearing that there might be trouble if word spread in the neighbourhood that the blacks had their own special church services on Dragonard Hill. She knew it was against White Law for black people to hold secret meetings. She listened now as Malou was speaking about the old chapel itself, saying that its position here on the crossroads of two streets in Town was a good sign for black people here. Some divine force had guided the dead black man, Nero, to claim this site for building the chapel. Malou explained that a crossroads was a place of good luck in the belief of some African people, that an African spirit already was looking after the black people on this land. She asked the small convocation of slaves to pray to their gods. She said that some would learn the names of their gods. That some would only feel a spirit. That no one should feel abandoned, though, because every African—even slaves on Dragonard Hill—had a special spirit looking after them.

*   *   *

Like Veronica, Vicky also was troubled about the duration of her stay at home. She had not been here for two weeks but Dragonard Hill's isolated location—a full day's ride north from New Orleans—was already beginning to depress her.

She spent little time with her father; she did not seek out Imogen for companionship and, whenever she and Veronica met they seemed to quarrel about something.

There was no reason to remain here with her family but she did not know where to go. She felt that it was too soon to return to Cuba, dreading the prospect of being confined again to *Palacio Veradaga* by her demanding husband. The thought of going to New Orleans tempted her but she did not want to be alone in that city. She day-dreamed about using Jerome Poliguet to introduce her into a fashionable circle of friends there.

Realizing that all her hopes were dependent upon Poliguet, though, Vicky became more sexually frustrated whilst she waited for his visit to Dragonard Hill. She knew that there were many young black men on the plantation, even remembering how she had bedded with some of them seven years ago. Considering black males to be no more than sexual objects for a white woman to use, Vicky debated whether she should seek out a slave to enjoy as a temporary lover. Preferring the idea of making love to dashing Jerome Poliguet, though, she procrastinated her search for some one to satisfy her.

Finally, she could wait no longer. She decided that she at least had to discover for herself what young black men were available on Dragonard Hill. She decided that the best place to look was the men's dormitory which her father had built. She waited until nightfall, after the day's field work was done, to pay her visit to the dormitory which lay to the west of the main house. She dressed herself in a dark cloak, planning only an exploratory visit to study the dormitory from the woodland which surrounded it, to catch a glimpse of its masculine inhabitants.

* * *

The unmarried, and the romantically unattached, male fieldslaves on Dragonard Hill spent their evenings in front of the dormitory. Their talk included stories about the day's work, comparisons of opinions about the budding young

91

wenches in the women's dormitories, even gossip of what married black woman cheated on her husband.

The subject of sex dominated most of these robust young men's conversation. They worked hard each day; they received little reward except for the solid, rock-hard muscles produced on their bodies by manual labour. They were proud of their rippling bodies. They brimmed with youthful maleness like young bulls. They also respected a code long since followed on this land that a young slave must not sew his wild seeds—not to produce offspring—before he had chosen the one female with whom he would settle.

Vicky stood in the trees near the front of the dormitory, the woollen cape wrapped around her slim body as she watched the group of young men sitting around the fire in front of the dormitory. She caught a few of their words, knowing that they were talking about their sexual prowess; she stepped closer when she saw two young men rise from the logs and drop their tow trousers to the ground.

Vicky's throat went dry as she realized that the two field slaves were comparing the size of their penises. The firelight glowed against their muscled ebony skin as they protruded their midsections toward one another. One black man produced a stick to use as a measuring rod. Vicky listened to their laughing words.

'Do it soft first,' called one onlooker.

Another agreed, 'Measure soft, then measure hard.'

One of the two men standing with his pants lowered to his feet said, 'Me gets hard? How I'm going to shoot my load if I gets hard? What's the use of getting worked up hard?'

Vicky imagined herself calling from the woodland, or offering herself as an object for their pleasure. She envisioned both young men satisfying themselves with her. She had gone so long without sex that she even imagined allowing all the black slaves to have her—if they wanted.

Telling herself that she must not be rash, that she must not risk the slaves talking about her in Town, she struggled to keep her passions in control. She watched the second man lay his penis on the stick. She saw by its limpness that the penis was not even half erect but, even from her distance away from the fire she could see that the organ was long and bulky, a sight which made her move a few steps forward.

It was then that Vicky—as well as the young black slaves gathered around the fire—looked toward the woodland on the other side of the dormitory. A young black boy was emerging from the shadows. He held a parasol over his head.

Immediately recognizing the child as being the kitchen helper called Fat Boy, Vicky cursed to herself, 'Damn that brat! What's he doing here? And look! Where did he get that? It's my . . . parasol! The parasol I gave to Posey!'

The two young men standing near the fire quickly pulled their pants up to their waists as Fat Boy walked closer toward the dormitory. The men teased Fat Boy as he approached them, asking him where he got the pretty sun shade.

'I runs away from the kitchen!' Fat Boy smugly announced. 'I runs away from Miss Posey and I'm never going back there again because—' He threw the sunshade onto the ground, saying, 'I'm going to stay *here*!'

Vicky backed farther into the shadows as the men tried to convince Fat Boy that he was too young to live in the dormitory, that he must to The Shed if he did not want to live in the kitchen with Posey anymore. That he was still a young boy.

'*Damn nigger brat!*' Vicky muttered to herself, wondering how she was ever going to find someone to pleasure her. She walked angrily back to the main house deciding that she must do something very soon. That if she did not find some other lover she would definitely come back to the dormitory—would probably let all the young black men use her for their voracious sexual appetites.

Chapter Six

ACCOUNTS AND OLD DEBTS

Peter Abdee refused to allow Veronica to travel alone through the Louisiana countryside. She had informed him over a light Sunday night supper of cold beef, horseradish, and potato salad that she wished to seize the advantage of her visit here to revitalize old friendships with girlhood chums whom she had not seen for years and that she was also curious about seeing how planters differed here from the farmers who tilled the lands in the North.

An inquisitive mind pleased Peter and he did not discourage Veronica from wanting to satisfy her curiosity about differences between agricultural ways in the two sections of this country. He also believed in maintaining ties with old friends. His only objection about Veronica's trip involved her physical safety. But when she suggested that she take a black couple from Town with her on the travels, Peter finally relented to her brief foray into the surrounding countryside.

After presenting her father with maps of the houses and towns which she planned to visit, Veronica then named the slaves she wanted to accompany her. She suggested Maybelle, the Negress who had nursed David as a child, and the black man who lived with Maybelle in Town, the Negro named Ham.

Again, Peter was in agreement. Ham was both trustworthy, and strong of build. He could provide physical protection. Maybelle's presence would prevent any malicious gossip about a young white lady travelling alone and sleeping nights away from home with a black man in her company.

Peter promptly wrote the necessary papers which would serve as passes for the two slaves from Dragonard Hill—Maybelle and Ham—to present to patrollers in their absence from the plantation with Veronica. The public roads and riverways of this district were now rife with the volunteer patrollers who served as a constabulary force against runaway slaves and the white people who helped the black people escape to freedom in the North.

* * *

Veronica departed with one valise, a food hamper, and Maybelle and Ham on the Wednesday following the Sunday on which Royal's letter had arrived. Vicky at first feared being left alone in the plantation's main house with her father, that her increasing sexual frustrations might drive her into making an approach toward him, to consummate a girlhood fantasy about making love with her father. But looking for the new traits in him which Veronica had mentioned to her, Vicky saw that his mind did indeed seem to be aloof and that he took very little notice of her presence.

Consequently, Vicky remained virtually alone in the main house during the first days of her sister's absence. She made few demands on Malou, the house-servants, or Posey. She met her father only on those evenings when she chose to eat a meal in the dining-room. On all other occasions she remained in her bedroom, debating whether she should return to the dormitory or wait for Jerome Poliguet to arrive.

Vicky soon became obsessed with thoughts about Jerome Poliguet. She could not rid her mind of his image, nor the idea that he might soon visit her here on Dragonard Hill.

Remembering how Poliguet came upcountry from New Orleans only two days a week, and considering how work must keep him occupied in Troy regardless of how much he might want to visit her at Dragonard Hill, Vicky decided at the beginning of the following week to pay a call on him in Troy.

Vicky used the same excuse as her sister, that she desired to reacquaint herself with the background in which she had been born. Rather than visit old schoolday friends, though, Vicky pleaded that she wanted to see the physical changes in plantations and towns. Her main excuse for travelling to Troy was to visit the newly opened FireFly Tea Rooms. She took care to laugh appropriately about a tea shop opening in Troy, to scoff at local pretensions so as not to make her father suspicious that she was, in fact, visiting the nearby town for reasons other than to scorn the local attempts at gentility. That she had a lusty image of a young lawyer from New Orleans at the forefront of her devious mind.

*   *   *

The town of Troy immediately impressed Vicky as being decrepit, filthy, run-down—unchanged since she had last seen it twelve years ago. She immediately ordered Curlew, the black driver of her open carriage, to take her directly to the FireFly Tea Rooms. Curlew slowed the team of white horses in front of a small building with yellow gingham curtains criss-crossing the inside of its window. Vicky's heart sank as she thought how this small building—no bigger than a cabin—was the latest object of gossip in the countryside, that acceptance into the FireFly Tea Room meant social approval.

Curlew pulled the reins for the carriage to stop by the hitching post in front of the tea room. Vicky protested, 'No, I think I want to go there first—' She pointed her parasol at a larger building located a few doors down the boardwalk.

'But, Miss Vicky, mam. That be the mercantile store. They ain't got nothing in there . . .' Curlew followed the instructions which Peter Abdee had given all the house and stable slaves at Dragonard Hill who would be coming into contact with his daughter—to eschew her Spanish title 'Condesa' and address her only as they would address Veronica and Imogen.

'I want to go into that store,' Vicky persisted but, drawing her skirts around her, she said, 'There's no reason I can't walk these few yards, you argumentative nigger!'

Curlew soon stood alongside the carriage, holding his

hand to help Vicky step down to the boardwalk. She daintily held onto his forearm for assistance with one hand and held the voluminous-skirt of her black gown with the other. She had carefully chosen today's outfit, a black dress to mourn her stepmother, but a dazzlingly full-skirted black dress with both its neck and trumpet sleeves bordered with white organza. Vicky also had chosen a low-crowned, wide-brimmed straw hat for this outing, a hat worn by many ladies here in the Louisiana countryside. But she had draped a finely worked black lace Cuban *mantilla* over the hat, transforming it into an exotic headpiece which accentuated her period-of-mourning.

Vicky stood on the boardwalk and, opening her small black parasol, she exclaimed, 'Why look there! Look on that little window upstairs in the mercantile. I see—what does that gold lettering say?'

Curlew could not read but he had heard the story about a lawyer opening offices here in Troy. He answered, 'That done must be the place of that lawyer man who comes here from New Orleans.'

'A lawyer? Here in Troy?' Vicky clapped her hands in mirth at the idea. She pursued her charade even in front of Curlew. She knew that the faithful slave would undoubtedly repeat all about her activities in town to her father.

Reaching for her skirts, she called, 'You just wait in the carriage for me, Curlew, while I just... snoop around.' She ignored the FireFly Tea Rooms, moving directly toward the mercantile store.

The bell tinkled over the door as Vicky entered the establishment. The men collected in front of the windows had watched her arrival in town, had seen her descent from the carriage and her approach toward them down the boardwalk. They stared in amazement now that such a dazzling creature should be coming into this humble country store.

Their chairs quickly grated on the plank flooring. The men who wore hats doffed them from their heads. The men smoking pipes pulled them from their mouths. They all gaped at Victoria.

Nodding politely to the men, Vicky said, 'Good day, gentlemen.' Her eyes skimmed over them as she directed her attention toward the merchandise for sale in the store.

'Condesa!' a man's voice boomed from the foot of a narrow stairway at the back of the store. 'Condesa Veradaga! What brings you to town today?'

Vicky was prepared for this salutation. She had indeed preened herself, loitered and twirled on the front boardwalk long enough for everyone in town to see her.

She now moved graciously past the wooden kegs of nails and withered apples, holding out one black-mitted hand in front of her, saying, 'Monsieur Poliguet! What a surprise to see you here!'

'But these are my offices, Condesa. I told you on the public stage that I practise two days a week in this town.'

'So you did, Monsieur. So you did. I haven't been here for years. I heard that a new little tea-room had recently opened here which I greatly wanted to visit. But when I passed this store which I remember so warmly from my childhood, why I . . .'

'Of course! Of course! Regardless of how high one rises in the world one never forgets the charming places in one's past. Of course, Condesa. I understand very well. But why go to the tea rooms for refreshment? If you do not consider my proposal to be too impudent, why don't you accept my humble offer to take tea with me upstairs? I am certain that Mister Webster can help us . . .'

Jerome Poliguet turned to the store clerk who stood gaping at their encounter. He called, 'Mister Webster, do you think we could have some boiling water? And perhaps a pinch or two of your . . . better India tea?'

'Oh, no!' Vicky protested. 'I could not put you to such an inconvenience. You must have so much work to do, Monsieur Poliguet. I could not allow you to make space amongst your papers and ledgers for a . . . tea party! Not when there is a perfectly charming little place only a few doors down the street!'

'But I insist, Condesa Veradaga!' Poliguet said, standing to one side and extending his arm to assist Vicky in mounting the steps to his upstairs office.

The store clerk, Ralph Webster, soon brought hot water, tea, plus a selection of cakes and biscuits upstairs. He had arranged a white towel on a small table and set out two Blue Willow cups-and-saucers which he had taken from stock, dusted with his apron, and arranged on the makeshift tea-tray, feeling pleased—even proud—that such quality people were now stepping foot into his establishment.

*   *   *

Jerome Poliguet was more bold than Vicky had imagined. The store clerk had barely shut the office door when Poliguet grabbed her in his arms and, pulling her toward him, he whispered, 'You voluptuous little tart! I know what you want!'

His breath tickled her ear. He began kissing her neck, running his mouth toward her shoulder, placing one hand on her buttocks to bring her closer toward him to feel the phallus hardening inside his breeches.

Shoving her back from him, he held her by the shoulders and ordered, 'Look! See what you've done to me! Now you aren't going to leave me in such a condition are you?'

Vicky could not speak. His manner thrilled her. Although it was what she wanted, she whispered, 'What about the . . . people downstairs?'

'Them! To hell with them! What are they compared to what you have done to me? See! Look at it!'

Poliguet's breeches lowered and his phallus bobbed its nakedness in front of Vicky's startled eyes. She stared down transfixed, not even believing her own voice as she heard herself praise, 'It is . . . beautiful.'

'Then get down on your knees and . . . kiss it. Lick your tongue around the crown. Tell it what you want from it . . . Condesa Veradaga!' He laughed at her, a jeering, mocking laugh.

Poliguet's hands were firm on Vicky's shoulders as he pressed her to the floor in front of him. She tried to tell him that she wanted to lay with him, to make deep love together, to clutch him with her contracting vagina. He assured her that they would do everything in due time. That she would have no choice of the matter. That he was the master to her now. That he wanted nothing else from her except physical fulfilment.

'Keep your husband!' he chided. 'Come to me only for . . . lust!'

Vicky tasted the stretched skin of his phallus deepening in her throat. She longed for him to pull her up to him, to embrace her, to make love to her lying down. But he would not release her from her kneeling position. Not for the moment. But he assured her as she kept working on his manhood that they would do everything in the ensuing days, weeks. That he would drive into her so deeply that she would scream with delirium. That he would tease her with his phallus until she begged him to please, please let her possess it. That she would not stay one day here in this backwoods country without eagerly waiting for him to return from New Orleans, to treat her as his unworthy mistress, a slut who did not deserve his masculine magnificence. And he warned her that if he heard of her giving herself to some other man that he would punish her.

That was how Vicky had imagined their meeting would be, had hoped in her wildest dreams that events would progress. They did not. She and Poliguet talked about . . . Damnit! Greenleaf!

Conversation between Vicky and Jerome Poliguet was stilted at first, even formal; she asked him about the success of his country business; he enquired about her family's spirits after the loss of her stepmother.

It was the subject of Kate and Dragonard Hill that eventually brought Poliguet to lower his eyes and say, 'It is sad about Greenleaf.'

'What do you mean?'

'I would normally not mention anything. But as you are a member of the family, perhaps even their most illustrious, I can say to you—' He hesitated. He appeared to be embarrassed by the subject.

'Monsieur Poliguet! Please do tell me!'

'The present master of Greenleaf—' Poliguet again faltered, pitifully shaking his head.

'Barry? You are talking about Barry Breslin?'

Poliguet nodded. 'Mister Breslin is not the manager that his aunt was. This is a small neighbourhood, Condesa. Everyone knows everyone's business. That is unfortunate.' He shrugged, adding, 'There is also, you will appreciate, constant communication between the legal and banking communities in such small . . . towns.' He still appeared to be unprepared to disclose what troubled him.

'I implore you, Monsieur Poliguet. Do not hesitate in telling me anything.' She was still trying to be a supplicant, even in this tedious reality.

'Well . . . the truth of the matter is that Mrs Abdee—the late *Kate* Abdee—has been signing for her nephew's expenses. She signed notes at the bank which legally involves your father—' He again shrugged, adding in a voice of disconcern '—and which could endanger your family's plantation. Perhaps. What I am saying, Condesa . . .'

Vicky sat to the edge of her chair, gasping, 'No! She didn't! Kate couldn't have been so foolish!'

'See. I have distressed you. I am sorry.' He opened both arms toward her black clothing, saying, 'You have come home to mourn your stepmother and I have been very foolish. Hasty. Stupid. How stupid of me!' He slapped the side of his forehead with the palm of one hand.

But Vicky ignored his gestures of apologies. She sat immobile, silently cursing Kate. She was distressed, not so much distressed by the content of the news that Kate's actions might have placed Dragonard Hill in jeopardy but that the subject matter had cast an instant mood of gloom over this visit. Vicky's original intentions had been dashed by this accursed family business. She saw that Poliguet was more handsome than she had even remembered him.

Rising, she said, 'I hope the next time we meet, Monsieur, we will have more . . . pleasurable things to discuss.'

'Oh, dear. I have distressed you!' He rose to his feet, looking at her with his rich brown eyes, promising, 'If there is anything I can do for you, Condesa—anything—you know I would be only too willing to serve you . . . in any capacity.'

Patting his forearm, Vicky said, 'You look like a man on whom someone could lean. I will not forget your offer.' She allowed her hand to linger on his forearm, holding her head lowered in a remorseful pose. She was in fact studying the crotch of his breeches and seeing that he filled his clothing exactly as the man did in her sexual fantasies. She even thought that she saw his phallus move, to spread over the bulge of his testicles.

Taking a deep breath, she reached for the black lace mantilla and, lowering it over her face, she quickly moved toward the door, down the stairs, and past the wooden kegs of nails and withered apples.

* * *

Vicky sat glumly in the padded leather cushions of the open carriage on her return to Dragonard Hill, her mind skipping between the shocking news which Poliguet had told her about Kate, and the thought of making love to the Creole lawyer. There was something mysterious about his dark sexuality, some facet which intrigued, even puzzled Vicky. She knew that his clothes harboured a riddle and she yearned to discover the secret.

Nevertheless, the tantalizing image of Jerome Poliguet did nothing to satisfy Vicky's immediate desire for a man. She knew that she could wait no longer to consummate her fantasies—even if only in some small way.

Sexual frustrations often made Vicky lose all sense of decorum. She usually tried to guard herself against this but she no longer cared as the carriage moved along in the warm afternoon through the leafy countryside.

She called from the back of the carriage, 'Curlew, drive more slowly. I want to step-up over the seat and ride alongside you.'

He looked over his shoulder, thinking he had misunderstood her request.

'I want to ride alongside you,' Vicky said, taking off her hat and standing onto the seat of the carriage. She held her hand toward Curlew, ordering, 'Help me! Keep driving but help me step over the seat. And if you mention a word of this to anyone I'll see that you are punished. Believe me about that, nigger!'

Curlew still did not know what Vicky had in mind until she sat alongside him and started fondling his crotch. He had heard of white ladies making black men pleasure them, threatening to punish them if they refused. Curlew kept his eyes on the road, saying 'Don't you . . . think we should at least drive into . . . the trees, Miss Vicky?'

'No!' Vicky said, 'This makes it more exciting for me. Just keep driving if you see anyone coming. And—' She stopped. She had worked his penis from his trousers. She saw that it was thick, dark and that it was already thickening with excitement. She teased, 'You naughty thing! Look! You're getting hard already!'

Curlew kept his eyes on the road as Vicky's fingers pulled and squeezed on his penis; she worked his loose foreskin back and forth, attempting to increase the hardness of the organ. When one hand grew tired, she turned on the wooden seat and worked with the other.

Finally, feeling an iron firmness in the penis, Vicky lowered her head to his crotch. She pulled her head up-and-down, stretching her small mouth to accommodate the penis.

The carriage continued to bump over the road. Curlew kept his eyes directed in front of him as Vicky kept working her head up and down between his legs. Curlew's eyes never once lowered to Vicky. He gripped nervously onto the reins, his arms held out high in front of him.

Finally, Curlew felt a tingle in his groin. Then when Vicky greedily pursued the reward of her endeavours, mouthing the black phallus long after it had reached its exploding hardness, Curlew began to look behind them on the road, to see if anybody was following them. He was relieved when Vicky climbed silently back into the padded seat of the carriage.

* * *

Vicky rearranged the black *mantilla* over her straw hat as the carriage passed under the wrought iron gate and climbed the drive to the main house. She did not wait for Curlew to help her down from the carriage when he reached the front galley of the house. She quickly hopped to the gravel. The brief act of satisfying Curlew with her mouth had been the diversion she needed. Her mind now seemed more alert, better prepared to attend other problems. She virtually forgot about Curlew's existence, deciding that she would solve one of the questions which had been nagging her since her visit to Jerome Poliguet. She would find out about the rumour of Dragonard Hill being in jeopardy because of mismanagement at Greenleaf.

Rather than immediately confronting her father, Vicky decided to question Imogen. If anybody knew about this plantation, it would be her older sister. Vicky knew that Imogen held a miserly grasp on this land, as if it were almost her own and nobody else's.

Vicky did not bother to change into other garments but trailed her organza-trimmed black dress across the dirt fields of the nearby slope where Curlew had told her that Imogen was working today.

'Imogen!' Vicky called, waving the black lace *mantilla* to attract Imogen's attention. 'Imogen! I want to talk to you!'

The sight of Vicky traipsing across the dirt furrows amused Imogen. She sat on her horse and smiled at her snippety younger sister coming out of the fields. She called, 'Something pretty important must have brought you out here, little sister!'

Vicky shaded her eyes against the sun and called to Imogen mounted on her horse, 'How much do you know about Greenleaf? The money Barry owes to the bank and if Kate had been loaning money to Barry and getting Papa to sign for it?'

The impact of such a question stunned Imogen. She gaped at Vicky, asking, 'Who have you been talking to?'

'Never mind who I've been talking to. Answer my question. What do you know about Greenleaf? Is Barry likely to lose it to the bank if his crops fail this season? Did Papa give Kate any control or interest in our land?'

Imogen pondered the question. 'Kate would have her rights as a wife. But she's dead. They'd be null and void.'

'Not if she and Papa signed for Barry. Those signatures would not be null and void—' She hesitated, asking in a weaker voice, '—or would they? Would Papa have to honour promissory notes Kate signed?'

Imogen narrowed her eyes, considering the question.

Vicky proceeded, 'Papa would honour anything Kate signed. That's what I think. If the law demanded it or not. Papa would refuse to tarnish the image of his beloved . . . Kate in any way.'

'I think you and me better have a talk, Vicky. You know something I don't and I think you should tell me all about it.'

'If you haven't seen anything wrong the whole time you've been here, I don't see why I should tell you what *I* know!'

'Listen, don't you care if we lose this land?'

'So it *is* possible!' Vicky shrilled.

'Stop being so damned secretive. You tell me where you found this out or I'll hop off this horse and . . .'

Imogen's demand immediately convinced Vicky that she

would not divulge her source of information. She refused to give in to threats of physical violence. Also, she had kept many facts to herself so far since her arrival home. She did not see why she should start divulging information now about her visit to Troy. She did not trust Imogen nor did she want her to know any more about her private life than she already did.

Turning, Vicky lifted her skirts and said, 'Some overseer you've turned out to be! Ha! As dumb as the red-neck farmer who should've had the job in the first place. It's a good thing I came home while there's still a home to come to.' She turned toward the main house.

*   *   *

Imogen remained seated on her horse in the field. She watched Vicky disappearing—stumbling on stones, angrily kicking at clods of dirt—as she teetered and wobbled down the hill. She suspected that Vicky would consult the ledgers in the library in the main house. It was no secret that the ledgers were kept in the library. Kate had acted as both accountant and secretary at Dragonard Hill. What loans or notes they had made or signed would all be noted in the library. Imogen decided that she would let Vicky tear through the drawers of her father's desk in an attempt to make sense of Kate's book-keeping. Vicky could also have a confrontation with their father. Imogen decided that if Vicky's words were true—that a failure at Greenleaf would have an immediate effect at Dragonard Hill—it was best for her to remain silent at the moment. She would pursue her plan. She saw no reason not to put it into immediate effect. Imogen had primed Belladonna to make love to her father and . . .

The original reason to form a plot to keep her father from philandering—even producing possible heirs—with other black women on Dragonard Hill, though, now seemed less important to Imogen as she realized that the tantalizing moment of her ruse was near. She became excited by the prospect of watching it all . . . her father, Belladonna, their love-making.

105

Curlew knew that white women had more rights than black wenches but he had also seen—heard—that white women were supposed to conduct themselves in the manner which they themselves called 'ladies'. Curlew was not a worldly man, only a hard-working country slave devoted to the Abdee family who had owned him all his life. According to his rustic code of ethics, though, he believed that Miss Vicky had conducted herself in a manner which even the uneducated black women in Town would call shameless.

When Peter Abdee asked where Vicky had wanted to go on her excursion in Troy, Curlew muttered that they had stopped by the mercantile store, that Miss Vicky had wanted to look inside. He did not elaborate, He did not mention Miss Vicky's demands on him during their return ride home.

After leaving Peter Abdee, Curlew went to the kitchen annex to question Posey about Miss Vicky. He knew that Posey understood white people's ways. But he also was aware that Posey was very impressed with the finely-dressed young white woman from Cuba. Curlew asked his questions, as discreetly as possible, beginning by complimenting Miss Vicky, praising her beauty, then saying that she seemed more flighty, more-nervous-acting than her twin sister, Veronica.

Posey was still distressed about the theft of his umbrella which Miss Vicky had given him. At the mention of her name, he flew into a rage about Fat Boy stealing the umbrella, saying, 'If that picaninny shows his face in here I'll kill him. I hear he's living in the Shed and he better stay there. I don't know where I'll get another kitchen helper but I'll get one before I'll get another sun shade like that one Fat Boy done stole from here!'

Curlew reminded Posey that Miss Vicky had a full supply of fancy parasols, that she thought highly of Posey and would probably give him another one. These kind words induced Posey to begin speaking about Miss Vicky, to give Curlew some clue about why she conducted herself so differently from her sister, Veronica.

Posey did not have a knowledge of sexual matters but

he remembered stories about Vicky which the former cook, Storky, had told him in the kitchen. Posey explained to Curlew that he must be extra kind to Miss Vicky because, apart from being a countess, she had suffered a terrible accident as a girl, that a pedlar man had come to Dragonard Hill one afternoon and done something unspeakable to Miss Vicky when nobody was looking.

Curlew soon saw that Posey did not know any specific details about the matter and he did not press him for them. He complimented Posey on the cleanliness of his kitchen, promised to hitch a wagon for him whenever, if ever, he needed it, and to give him one of the road passes from the stables for travelling short distances. He also promised not to mention the fact about the pedlar man and Miss Vicky to anyone. Curlew called over his shoulder, saying that he would also keep his ears open for a new kitchen helper to replace Fat Boy.

Chapter Seven

THE SACRIFICIAL LAMB

Jerome Poliguet rented a horse from a stable in Troy and made arrangements to leave the animal at a stable in Carterville where he would catch the public coach later that evening to New Orleans. He required the mount to ride to Grouse Hollow.

Claudia Goss listened eagerly to Poliguet's report about Victoria Abdee's visit to his office this afternoon. She sat on one side of the deal table in her shadowy house, slowly assembling each detail of Poliguet's report. He next proceeded to repeat the points of the plan which he and Claudia Goss had discussed at their last meeting, how Claudia would buy the Greenleaf notes and force the immediate payment of them, a sale at a highly inflated price and with crippling—retroactive—interest rates which would force Peter Abdee to mortgage his own land to pay them, a mortgage which Claudia would finance in her last step to destroy Dragonard Hill.

A narrow shaft of fading daylight poured through the dingy rags hanging in the small window cut into Claudia Goss's log cabin. A yellow dog slept on the threshold which led to the porch, a mangy dog which only occasionally lifted his head to chew between his vermin-infested hind legs or listen to the clatter of the tin plates made by the black woman, Mary, as she worked in the lean-to which served as a kitchen at Grouse Hollow.

Claudia Goss was pleased that Poliguet had informed

her on his arrival that he would be catching tonight's late stage for New Orleans, that he would not be staying for supper. She did not press him to stay for a meal, preferring not to share even a scrap of bread with anyone.

The news which Poliguet had brought to Grouse Hollow even made Claudia Goss forget to offer him a cup of coffee. She listened closely as Poliguet now instructed her in the next step of their manoeuvres.

He said, 'It was no master stroke in telling a member of the Abdee family about the precarious position of Greenleaf. Everyone in the countryside knows about Breslin's mismanagement. The only benefits we enjoy are that—for one thing—that I was able to tell the fact to one of the most . . . excitable members of that family.'

Claudia repeated the word. ' "Excitable?" You find that filly . . . exciting?'

Poliguet often grew impatient with Claudia Goss. He knew she was a crafty woman—devious and cunning—but her base prurience often repulsed him. He also did not wish to divulge to anyone his interest in the woman whom he called the 'Condesa Veradaga'. He considered her to be very physically attractive. Jerome Poliguet required certain proclivities—sexual preferences—in the females with whom he made love. He still was not certain that Vicky could fulfil them.

He answered Claudia, 'I am talking about Victoria Abdee's ability to cause alarm in the household. She will fan embers into flames for us. Panic will only help us.'

Sitting forward on his chair, he said, 'Now this is what I want you to do. You told me about a black man who was killed many years back on Dragonard Hill. A black man named Monk. A half-brother to Peter Abdee sired on the island of St Kitts by one Richard Abdee.'

Claudia nodded. 'That's right. The coon's name was Monk. He and Peter was sold as young ones with that old crazy nigger wench, Ta-Ta, who died a long spell back. She was Monk's mother and a lady's maid to Peter's own ma back on that West Indian island. But Ta-Ta, she shot her own natural son, Monk, to keep him from killing . . . Peter Abdee.'

Nodding, Poliguet said, 'You also told me that this Monk

impregnated a black woman on Dragonard Hill. That Peter Abdee freed the girl after Monk was killed and sent her to live on the colony for freed slaves. That Monk's wife moved to Treetops and gave birth to a son there.'

'Lloy. That was the name of her git. Lloy. Sired by Monk. Lloy's still living at Treetops. A full grown coon now himself but he's there all right on that farm for free niggers.'

'I want you to get in contact with this . . . Lloy,' Poliguet said.

Claudia studied the nattily dressed Creole, saying, 'You remembers a hell of a lot of facts, don't you, Poliguet?'

'That's my business,' he answered breezily. 'That's why you're paying me.'

'Speaking of paying, what will you be expecting to see for yourself from all this?'

'We'll settle the money arrangement once we, first, get a hold on Greenleaf. But—'

'And what do you want me to do with this Lloy coon?'

'Don't concern yourself with that now. Just make contact with him. Make yourself known. Remind him of his past. Pay a visit to Treetops in the next couple of days. Use any excuse for going there. But do not, do *not*, I repeat, antagonize him. You have enough enemies amongst the white people around here. We'll need a good man shortly to help us. But your loan-sharking has eliminated all the white men. So do not antagonize this black man.'

Claudia repeated, 'Antagonize?'

'Make an enemy of yourself! Do not do that. Remember that this Lloy fellow is free. I know it will be difficult for you to do but try to show him some respect. I'll give you more news when I come back next week from New Orleans.'

Jerome Poliguet bade Claudia farewell, stepped over the yellow dog spread across the threshold, and hurried to his horse. He did not want to miss the night stage south. He hoped to be in New Orleans at the early hours of the morning, a time when a certain establishment was still open on Rampart Street. These visits to the Louisiana countryside always exhausted Poliguet, requiring a call upon his favourite spot of relaxation in New Orleans, the one place where he was truly understood and satisfied.

110

*　　*　　*

Peter Abdee respected other people's privacy; he expected the same honour to be paid to him. He did not like to remind people about the generosity he had shown to them in the past but neither did he like them to forget it. He had not extended his sympathy and understanding to his daughters in expectation for their return sentiments. Nevertheless, he was maddened by the fact that Vicky had confronted him at tonight's supper table about the financial arrangement which he and Kate had offered to Barry in an attempt to save Greenleaf. He did not believe that any arrangements existing between him and Kate—even Barry Breslin—concerned Vicky. He had not dragged out facts at supper about Vicky's past life, mistakes which she had made which he had chosen to forget but he had been tempted to tell her that everyone makes a few mistakes.

Had it been a mistake to help Barry? Peter asked himself this question as he walked along a path leading from the main house. The fact that he was even weighing Vicky's accusation maddened him. He was giving credence to her questions by brooding upon them. He was beginning to have negative thoughts about the future of Greenleaf, to consider the repercussions on Dragonard Hill if Barry Breslin failed to harvest a successful crop this season.

Peter next asked himself, why would Vicky be so inconsiderate, so crass as to press me with these demands? And to ask questions about ledgers and old accounts co-signed by Kate? Has she no respect for the dead? At least through a period of mourning? Kate's body is barely cold in the ground!

The night was still; the indigo sky brilliantly spotted with an array of twinkling stars. The ferns drooped in luscious rows over the woodland path which Peter now followed farther and farther away from the main house.

He wondered again how Vicky had learned of the notes which he and Kate had signed. Had she gone to the bank? He considered the idea of approaching William Tyndale, the banker in Troy, and to ask him if his daughter had paid a visit today to the bank. He instantly rejected the idea. He did not want to add to the problem by asking questions in Troy. He knew how the townspeople gossiped.

Thinking of townspeople, though, Peter next thought of Curlew reporting to him that Vicky had only visited the general store. He wondered who in there would know of the notes-of-payment. When he envisioned the mercantile store in Troy, he only thought about the men who idled in the chairs by the front window, the men who served as patrollers on the public roads, a local element for whom Peter had little respect.

Considering the fact that gossip was probably already rife in Troy that Barry Breslin was in financial difficulties and that Dragonard Hill was now legally responsible for standing the debts, Peter's stomach knotted with tension. He tried not to curse Vicky for worsening the situation. He also tried not to wonder what his other daughters might unwittingly do to him.

Veronica? Where was she tonight? Vicky had claimed that her foray into Troy was for old-time's sake. Look what she's come home with, he told himself.

So what about Veronica? Why did she suddenly announce that she wanted to go traipsing into the wilderness north of here? Would she be the instrument of more problems?

It was at that moment that Peter saw the slim silhouette of a young girl standing ahead of him on the path. He immediately thought of the slave girl, Sara, when he saw two brown arms folded demurely in front of her waist. He realized that if he needed any sexual release it was tonight. His resistance to making love with one of his slave-women was low. It was non-existent.

*　　*　　*

Imogen Abdee stood in the bushes alongside the path and watched her father's half-naked body pumping eagerly against Belladonna's naked thighs. Imogen had been amused at first when she had watched her father approaching Belladonna, knowing that he did not recognize the black girl dressed in such different, such alluring clothing.

Not knowing exactly how long it had taken her father to realize Belladonna's identity, Imogen had stood concealed by the thickly growing brush and watched them finally embrace—of her father wrapping his arms protectively around Belladonna as she moved closer to his body.

It was then that Imogen passed into her second stage of emotions. She next felt jealousy. She watched her female lover giving herself to her father—her father making love to her own concubine—and she felt hatred for both of them.

Reminding herself that this was all her own plan, Imogen controlled her raging jealousy and waited again to see if her father would abandon Belladonna once he discovered who she was.

He did not.

Perhaps, Imogen wondered, he still does not know who the bitch is.

Finally, Imogen knew for certain that there could be no doubt in her father's mind about whom he was giving his love. She watched him kneeling on the ground between Belladonna's spread legs. She watched him pulling the slim black girl up and down on this thickening phallus. She watched him spreading his hands over Belladonna's full breasts as she tossed her head from side to side as Imogen had instructed her to do to feign excitement for a man.

Yes, Belladonna's face was in full view. He could in no way not know to whom he was making love.

Imogen remained standing motionless in the brush and watched her father's penis dart in and out of the furry patch between Belladonna's legs. Imogen knew that she could never have the sexual equipment of her father, that a crude replica was the closest she could even hope to strap between her legs. But through Belladonna she could possess power. And she watched her father quickening his drives into Belladonna and she swore that she would have control, total control over Dragonard Hill.

Chapter Eight

CHANT SANS PAROLES

A narrow cobbled street spined by a gutter. Lacy iron verandas overhanging board sidewalks. Vendors crying a variety of streetcalls for oysters-on-the-half-shell, garlands of fresh tuberoses, sprigs of medicinal herbs. An aroma redolent with spices, perfumes, horse manure. A cacophony of noises ranging from lively Irish reels fiddled in saloons to the abandoned jangle of ass jawbones clattering to the steady beat of a Cajun's drum. This was Rampart Street at night, a popular thoroughfare in the French-flavoured section of New Orleans called *Vieux Carre*.

Black men dressed in satin waistcoats called to passersby to eat in cafes, to visit girls in upstairs parlours, to drink rum concoctions which would make you believe that Heaven existed upon this very earth. Other Negroes—and whites—promised celestial pastimes by the wink of an eye to passing strangers, by the flash of a bosom or the glitter of a coin. Snaggle-toothed old women leaned over iron verandas and called that they could tell fortunes from coffee grounds, read the future in Tarot cards, divine good luck by the casting of magic Indian stones.

Rampart Street was most enterprising after sundown; night-time brought out the hucksters, vendors, prostitutes, gamblers, thieves. The world was divided into two types of people at night on Rampart Street—the buyers and the sellers.

The least conspicuous of the business establishments on

114

Rampart Street set behind a pair of ornately wrought gates. The house was called *Petit Jour* but the only hint about the business which was conducted behind its wisteria-swagged walls was a fountain situated in the middle of the courtyard, a fountain centered with a statue of richly-carved cupids to depict that this was a house of love—prostitution.

The proprietor of *Petit Jour* was a black person, a freed Negress named Naomi who had long since established herself as a landmark on Rampart Street. In the passing years, Naomi still maintained her rule of offering only the finest—and most bizarre—sexual pleasures to a gentleman if he had the money to pay for it. No man dared enter *Petit Jour* without his pocket full of gold, or a reliable banker's note for credit. Naomi's brothel, *Petit Jour*, was unrivalled in New Orleans either for expense or lasciviousness. And for those men who gained entry, Naomi offered special theatrics staged in a small room at the top of her house, visual excitements staged to transform the most impotent man into a stallion, the most frigid female into a shameless nymphomaniac.

* * *

The theatrics at the bordello, *Petit Jour*, varied not only from night-to-night but also differed throughout the course of one evening. Those habituees who had enough money to afford the price of admission often viewed all three performances on one night—or commencing at night and culminating in the late hours of morning.

Jerome Poliguet arrived at *Petit Jour* before the last theatric was about to commence. He left his outercoat and hat at the door, telling a waiter to bring a bottle of champagne upstairs to the theatre as he anxiously took three red-carpeted steps at a time so as not to miss a single moment of tonight's presentation, *Chant Sans Paroles*.

Sinking into one of the black velvet chaise-longues encircling a small stage area, Poliguet saw an object—he guessed it was a new prop for the premiere of tonight's presentation—which set in the middle of the stage. He immediately detected that the shiny wooden object looked like a grand piano but no ordinary grand piano. It was too deep, too wide, too bulky. But, then, Poliguet knew that at *Petit Jour* many things were not what they appeared to be.

Other men lounged and visited amongst themselves around Poliguet as, slowly, more and more of the chaise-longues became occupied. The room was surrounded by a black curtain behind which were small niches where dignitaries—or females—could watch the theatrics without being seen.

The waiter brought the green bottle of champagne to a table setting alongside Poliguet's chaise-longue. He popped the cork with calm expertise whilst Poliguet talked to him about the impressive turnout at tonight's premiere, his travels to the upcountry wilderness, a rambling account of his business there—nervous chatter which betrayed that Poliguet became a completely different man from his usual confident self once he entered this sanctuary, *Petit Jour*.

The black waiter departed as the candles in the crystal wall candles were snuffed out, leaving only a dim lighting near the stage area. The room fell to a hush when a tall, broad-shouldered black man walked slowly to the middle of the stage. He wore a cutaway coat, tightly fitting white breeches, shiny black leather boots. He bowed to the audience like a concert pianist and then took a seat in front of the keyboard of the wooden object representing an outsize grand piano.

The black man extended his hands toward the piano's keyboards but no music filled the room. As he continued to mime the act of playing a piano, though, the piano began to revolve and, on the space in which would normally be keys lay a white girl who was totally naked.

The audience applauded as the black pianist began to twist the girl's nipples with one hand and finger her vagina with the other, occasionally running one hand down her legs like a pianist trilling the keys—but, then, giving the naked white girl a sharp slap on the thigh.

Although the black pianist continued his mild tortures on the girl lying where a keyboard would be, the piano again began to revolve and a Negress entered the stage, a voluptuous young black woman dressed in a red beaded gown which exposed both of her fulsome breasts. She stood facing the audience and, closing her eyes, she began to open and close her mouth—miming that she was a singer accompanied by a pianist. But the piano played no accompaniment: The song had no words.

The lid of the grand piano slowly opened behind the silent singer and the sudden crack of a whip pierced the theatre's silence. Then a second whip snapped from inside the piano. Next a third and a fourth whip echoed in the near-darkness, echoing like taut piano wires springing from inside a grand piano until, soon, six black girls slowly rose from the curved depths of the piano, flailing their long whips to the offstage accompaniment of a drumbeat slowly gaining momentum.

The black singer now turned to the six young Negresses behind her and, ripping off her beaded dress, she stood in nothing but a small beaded patch covering her vaginal delta. She then spun back around to face the audience of startled male onlookers and, as the six girls with the leather whips now backed her like a threatening chorus, the singer coldly began to scan the white men lying on their velvet chaise-longues.

Her eyes finally lingered on Jerome Poliguet. She slowly raised one arm and, pointing toward him, she motioned with her other hand for the Negro pianist to emerge from the darkness behind her to carry Poliguet to the stage where she stood.

Poliguet panicked as the black man reached to lift him from the chaise-longue. He knocked over his bottle of champagne. He shouted for assistance. But no one moved to help him. Nor was his own strength a match for the black man who now dropped him in front of the black singer's feet.

Poliguet began to tremble, to look nervously around him, but the six black girls closed their circle around him. They held the leather whips behind them with one hand and used their other to hold Poliguet into servitude, forcing him to remain kneeling in front of the singer who now ripped the beaded patch from between her legs, rubbed it against Poliguet's face and then spat upon him.

The audience finally began to applaud as the Negresses forced Poliguet to move his head forward; he opened his mouth; he extended his tongue; he began to lick, then to eat from the coarse wool between the black singer's legs.

Only Poliguet—and the performers—knew that he had paid for this public subjection. That he himself had previously arranged to be debased in front of this audience of white men, to be included in the premiere, of this theatric at *Petit Jour* as if he were a helpless party to it all.

But as Poliguet now knelt in front of the statuesque black woman, mouthing his tongue deeper and deeper into the sweetness of her vagina, he lifted his hands out behind him for the other Negress to clasp his wrists tightly together with iron manacles.

Poliguet no longer cared if any—or every—one in the room knew he had arranged for this humiliation. That he realized what was to follow this act of cunnilingus. The knowledge that the members of the audience might realize that he himself had asked to be subjected in such a public manner only increased the thrill for him.

Jerome Poliguet could not enjoy love-making unless it was forced upon him by a dominant female and the only place where he knew he could find it was on Rampart Street in New Orleans at the brothel called *Petit Jour*. That was the reason he went to Troy—to supplement his income and be able to afford the exorbitant prices at *Petit Jour*.

*   *   *

'Why do you bother me with details about that pervert?' asked Naomi, the madam of *Petit Jour*. She was seated behind her desk in the office located on the brothel's ground floor. 'Poliguet's paid well. He's upstairs enjoying it. Why do I care what he told you before the show started tonight?'

The Negro waiter stood in front of Naomi's desk, daring not even to raise his eyes. Although Naomi wore a black lace veil over her face—and had worn one since she had long-ago come to New Orleans as a free black woman from the island of St Kitts—the waiter also knew that she did not like even to be glanced at by anyone. He had heard how her constant veil hid vile wounds, scars from a fire.

Also knowing that the Negress, Naomi, was interested in any matter pertaining to the family called 'Abdee' who lived upcountry in Louisiana, the waiter awkwardly explained, 'Poliguet's a bit of a braggart, Mistress Naomi. A braggart and a snob. He was complaining whilst I was opening and pouring his expensive French champagne that he was all weary from dealing with people at someplace called . . . Dragonard Hill.'

Naomi jerked her head. She asked, 'Dragonard? Dragonard Hill?'

The black waiter nodded.

'Did he mention the Abdee family?' she demanded.

'Yes, Mistress Naomi. Not much. But he mentioned meeting a daughter. A young Abdee woman who's now calling herself a countess. A young woman at Dragonard Hill who's come home from Cuba. It seems her step-mother done died.'

Remembering that Vicky Abdee had long-ago married a Cuban aristocrat, Naomi's voice hardened. She said, 'Tell me! Tell me everything that pervert said!'

'He didn't talk too much sense, Mistress Naomi. He was nervous. Twitchy. He was thinking, I guess, about what he's up there getting right now.'

Naomi sat upright in the chair behind her desk. The black lace veil hung in neat folds around her head and fell around her thin shoulders. She folded her white-gloved hands in front of her on the desk and began to give the waiter instructions to watch this Creole lawyer, Jerome Poliguet, who talked so unguardedly—so snobbishly—about upcountry planters. The Negress madam of the bordello, *Petit Jour*, had a special interest in the Abdee family, their plantation, Dragonard Hill.

Book Two

RIPENING

Chapter Nine

TREETOP HOUSE

A brief spate of early summer rain did not improve Claudia Goss's ill temper. A steady downpour pelted against the window pane of her small cabin in Grouse Hollow, drumming down onto the roof, creating a claustrophobic prison in which she had no other choice than to mull over the idea of being civil to a black person.

The more Claudia considered Jerome Poliguet's advice of visiting the colony of freed slaves called Treetop House and being polite to a black man, the more annoyed she became with the prospect. She remembered the advice which Poliguet had given her—not to 'antagonize' the free Negro, Lloy—and she brooded even more about the manner in which a white person was supposed to address a free black man.

Claudia had no one to turn to for advice on deportment. She briefly considered about acting her usual self, to forget about kowtowing to any person she called a 'coon'. But remembering the urgency in Poliguet's voice when he had instructed her not to vent any prejudices toward Negroes at this free farm called Treetop House, she ultimately convinced herself that she would not be paying court to some black person for his or her own worth but that she would be treating them as 'humans' only to strike a fatal blow upon the Abdee family living at Dragonard Hill. Claudia decided that, given a choice between the Abdees and black people, she would choose black people anyday—at least she could order 'coons' around when she finally won her cause! And, so, in such a frame of mind, she informed her farm slave, Jack, to hitch-up the mules to the wagon. She decided to seize the first break in the inclement weather to try her luck at Treetop House in making initial contact with Lloy.

The slave, Jack, stood alongside the wagon to which he had obediently hitched Claudia's mules. He had brought the wagon to the front porch of the cabin and helped his pudgy mistress step across the puddles left in the yard from the torrential three-day downpour.

Claudia held the hem of her linsey-woolsey dress above the mud and said to Jack, 'I won't be needing you to drive me today.'

Jack remembered the harangue which his mistress had delivered to him only a few weeks ago, that sharply delivered speech about white ladies never driving their own mules. He looked at Claudia in amazement, asking, 'You sure you can do it, Miss Goss, Mam? You being a fine lady and all?'

'You do it, don't you?' she snapped. 'Anything a coon can do, I can do, too! Here! Give me a push, boy,' she ordered, motioning for him to stand behind her and to help her climb up into the driver's seat.

Once settled on the wagon, Claudia held the buckskin reins in one hand and repositioned the straw bonnet on her head. She pulled a black shawl tighter around her shoulders; she sniffed and, rubbing her stubby nose with one raw knuckle, she said, 'The fact is, Jack, I'm driving over to that place called Treetop House. It's some crazy danged place where coons gallivant around like white folks. It would be bad, real bad for you to see such nonsense with your eyes. You might get crazy notions in your head. And on top of all that, Jack, I don't rightly know what them niggers over there would have to say about me arriving with a coon slave driving my mules. They might keep you over there once I got you inside the gates. They might keep you for a free nigger. Then what would I have? Nothing!'

She reached toward the brake and, grunting as she tugged and pushed on the rod, she then snapped buckskin reins. She shouted, 'Hey! Get going you lazy critters!' The wagon slowly bumped down the road pressed over the quack grass bedding the ground which belonged to Grouse Hollow.

*   *   *

The countryside was lush from the weekend rainfall, the sun glistening against the branches and boughs still beaded with raindrops from the deluge. The wheels of Claudia Goss's wagon slipped and churned in the mire of the dirt public road. She whipped her mules harder, though, and, by late morning, she reached the white-washed fences enclosing the farm for freed slaves called Treetop House.

The farm appeared no different than many small plantations dotted throughout the countryside, its buildings well-kept and the fields planted with crops. Treetop House also boasted a quantity of out-buildings like other plantations—barns, dairies, looming houses, chicken coops, even potteries and brick kilns. Treetop House was a self-sufficient community having all the similarities of a slave-run plantation with one noticeable exception—there was no main house at Treetop House, no pillared or galleried big house where the owners lived. The black residents of Treetop House lived in small communal houses and dormitories, the original building for which it had originally been named having long since been razed and its lumber put to more advantageous use.

Claudia stopped inside the gates of Treetop House, sitting on the wagon and looking in bewilderment around her as she wondered how she was going to find the person here she wanted to see.

A voice called behind her, 'Good morning, Mam? May I help you?'

Claudia turned in her seat and saw a black woman dressed in a blue-and-red checkered frock. The black woman wore a white apron over the frock and carefully held one end of the apron to cradle a collection of brown eggs. She smiled at Claudia, not a subservient smile which Claudia was used to seeing on black slaves, but a smile of equality—a neighbourly welcome.

'I'm looking for a . . . boy named Lloy,' Claudia announced gruffly.

'Lloy? Oh, you'll find Lloy over in the school house. Least that's where he's suppose to be.' She nodded to a shingle-roofed building setting across a field of corn.

'School house?' Claudia repeated. 'He still young enough to be going to school?'

The amiable black woman laughed. She answered, 'No, Lloy is not attending classes, Mam. He's teaching classes. Three days a week now.'

Claudia took a deep sigh. Coons! Coons teaching other coons! She quickly reminded herself, though, that she had

124

set out on this mission for revenge against other parties. That she must not let her personal convictions keep her from achieving the vengeance she desired more than anything else in the world. She lifted the reins to drive toward the school house.

The black woman called, 'I'm afraid you can't go to the school house now, Mam. Not in the morning. You see, you'd be disturbing school-teaching.'

Claudia's mouth dropped open. She could not believe that she was being told by a black woman what she could or could not do!

'You are welcome to come to the Refectory for a cup of coffee while you wait,' the black woman kindly offered. 'If we're lucky, we might even be in time for some of Mary Ellen's raisin cake. That goes mighty good with coffee. And by the time we finishes that—'

Suddenly stopping, the black woman held onto the apronful of eggs with one hand and raised the other hand to shade her eyes to look in the distance. 'I do declare. You are lucky today. I do think I see the little children coming out for their morning recess. Yes, I do. They're coming out now. Why don't you head over and try to see Lloy for a few minutes if you're in a real big hurry to talk to him. I'm sure he can spare you the recess time. Then if your news is important and takes long, you remember my invitation to coffee and raisin cake. Lloy will tell you how to find your way over to the Refectory. You can wait there and talk more with him over lunch-time. My name's Deline Ford. See you later, Mrs . . .?'

Claudia grunted again. She reached for the reins. She forgot about refectories and lunch-breaks. She saw no reason to thank the black woman for the invitation nor to introduce herself. What is she anyway? Claudia asked herself. Nothing more than just another coon. And I don't like the idea of her having a better dress than me. Deline Ford? Hmmmph! Snooty wench!

* * *

Lloy was a young man in his mid-twenties with skin the colour of coffee stirred lightly with milk, and gleaming black hair which curled in tight wool against his skull, forming

125

a neat line across his forehead. He had a strong chin. His shoulders squared inside his white home-woven shirt. His waist was neat and stomach flat.

Claudia immediately detected a faint similarity between this young man and the slave she had known as Monk, that both father and son had flared nostrils and dark, gleaming eyes. But the likeness stopped there. Monk had been a short, muscular man whereas Lloy was sinewy, his strength wiry rather than brawny.

Lloy's flashing black eyes showed immediate suspicion about this white woman coming to see him. His face quickly changed from the carefree expression he had worn when allowing the children to go out into the play-yard. It eclipsed into a sombre, almost cloudy expression. This again reminded Claudia of Monk.

'You ain't the spitting image of your pappy, boy,' Claudia said as she stood in the doorway of the small schoolhouse. She surveyed the wooden benches neatly lined facing a table at the front of the room, saying, 'But then your pappy couldn't read nor write. I guess education is bound to make some changes in a . . . man.'

'You obviously know who I am,' Lloy said in a deep-chested voice. He kept his eyes on Claudia's puffy red face as he asked, 'Have we met before?'

'Claudia Goss is my name. I live nearby at Grouse Hollow. I always meant to stop by this place for a gander around. But I've been feeling poorly. Never got around to it till now.'

'Goss . . .' Lloy repeated. 'I think I've heard of you. You sell slaves from the back of a wagon.' It was not a question.

Claudia had anticipated this knowledge. She answered with the lie which she had already fabricated. 'That was in the old days. Before I seen the . . . light.'

'You've been converted to religion?'

'Not exactly religion,' she answered, lowering her eyes to Lloy's body, imagining what a good time she and her first husband, Chad Tucker, would have had with a finely set-up black buck such as this one. She saw Lloy's hands hanging big and pawlike by the sides of his muscled thighs. She imagined him holding the perforated paddle called 'the hornet' in those hands, the wooden paddle which Monk used to smite Chad Tucker's naked buttocks with to induce

126

him to drive his penis deeper into Claudia's stretched vagina. The memory of those good times fluttered quickly through Claudia's brain, making her nostalgic for the old days at Dragonard Hill.

Intent to concentrate on the future, she said to Lloy, 'The fact is, I used to know your pappy. I knew your ma, too. When she was on Dragonard Hill.'

'My mother's dead now.' Lloy showed neither sentiment nor anger.

'I'm sorry to hear that,' Claudia quickly consoled. 'She must of died a young woman.' Shaking her head, she continued, 'But death ain't nothing none of us escape. As you see, I ain't no spring chicken anymore myself and I just wanted to "straighten-out-my-books" as they say before I'm called from this earth.'

'Are you suffering from any particular complaint, Mrs Goss?' Lloy's manner was courteous but not friendly; concerned but yet formal.

'My spells of ague get worse with the passing years. I want to be prepared for my final departure but—' She shook her head again, saying, 'There's so many people in this neck of the woods who ain't willing to bury old hatchets. We was talking about Dragonard Hill a second or two ago. Take them folks there for instance. The Abdees. I went over there a few days back to pay my condolences on the death of that Peter Abdee's late wife—'

Pausing, she eyed Lloy, saying, 'You ain't never seen Peter Abdee, I bet. Being a slave-owner and all, he's probably never made himself known to you over here.'

'Dragonard Hill sends us a parcel at Christmas.'

'Christmas? Probably guilt money!' Claudia said. 'You'd think a free-minded man like Peter Abdee sets himself up to be would come over here himself to see his nephew instead of just sending a gift box to . . .'

Lloy widened his eyes. 'Nephew?'

'Didn't you know? Your pappy and Peter Abdee come from the same pappy. They was brothers near enough. A Richard Abdee on some island down in the West Indies called St Kitts sired them both. Monk done told me and my first husband, Chad Tucker, all about it. Your black grand-mammy was a lady's maid to Peter Abdee's ma. Your grandmammy shot your pappy when he and Peter Abdee had them that big fight on Dragonard Hill. That's when your own ma was freed from Dragonard Hill and sent here and then—'

'Mrs Goss. I appreciate you taking the time to come here today. But I don't see any good in telling me all these facts. My mother left Dragonard Hill. She and my father are both dead. I live here. I didn't know that . . . Mister Abdee was my uncle. But . . .'

Don't go telling him I told you that fact!' Claudia quickly said. 'The words just slipped out of my mouth in conversation here with you. I was just standing here chewing the rag with you and the facts just slipped out!'

Although Lloy nodded his head in agreement, Claudia saw that she had caught his attention. But also guessing that he was a headstrong young man, she said, 'But you're right. There ain't no point of us labouring old facts. If some white folks ain't willing to face-up to the past why should we force them? That's what I told them Abdees when they danged near turned me off their land when I went to pay my respects.'

She moved away from Lloy, reaching to grip onto the door for support, saying, 'I won't be taking-up your time neither. You've probably got the little ones coming back in pretty soon. I got my own work to do, too.'

Lloy stood in the doorway of the school-house and watched Claudia waddle toward her rough-board wagon. He foresaw the difficulty she was going to have climbing up into the seat and he moved quickly to help her.

Claudia mumbled her thanks as she struggled up into the seat. She settled herself behind the mules and, gazing down at Lloy, she said, 'You sure a mighty fine-looking lad.'

'Thank you for coming to see me, Mrs Goss. I don't know exactly why you've done it but a person always likes to learn something about his past. Expecially a black person. Black people know so little about where they came from, who our fathers, mothers, grandparents were—'

He reached for her hand and, squeezing it, he said, 'Thank you.'

'Don't you mention it . . . son,' she said, reaching for the reins of her mules. 'I have a feeling that you and me see things the same way. Or, at least we could given the

128

chance.' The wagon rattled away from the schoolhouse.

*   *   *

Lloy watched Claudia Goss's hunched figure departing down the lane which led to the public road. He kept staring at her, oblivious to the shouting of the children behind him in the play-yard. He kept hearing the echo of her voice, the facts which she had told him about his family, the most nagging ones being that his own grandmother had killed his father to save Peter Abdee in a fight, and that Peter Abdee was his own flesh and blood.

Damn it, he thought. Damn it. Why wasn't I told these things before? My Mama was a good woman but slavery beat the poor brains right out of her head. She slinked away from Dragonard Hill when they told her to go, coming here with me in her belly as if that would extinguish forever all my ties to the past.

Lloy knew that he had to decide whether he was going to rekindle old flames—perhaps even avenge old wrongs done to his mother and father. He had not even known who his grandmother was up until today. But a stranger came here and told him that his grandmother had shown more loyalty to the son of her mistress than to her own flesh and blood. That his grandmother had shot her son to save the life of the white man who now was the master of Dragonard Hill.

Lloy broke the wooden pen he held in his hand. He tossed the pieces to the dirt.

Chapter Ten

THE PATROLLERS

The rains—which were over almost as quickly as they had begun—brought sickness to the neighbourhood. Young David Abdee caught a chill during the inclement weather and word reached Dragonard Hill that the boy was confined to his bed at Greenleaf. Barry Breslin sent a rider to Peter Abdee saying that David's condition was not serious but that Peter should consider extending the boy's stay at that plantation, that David should not be travelling back home this week as originally planned.

Peter consented. He dispatched the rider to Greenleaf with the instructions to call Doctor Witherspoon from Carterville if David's condition should worsen—and Vicky offered to go as an emissary from Dragonard Hill to see personally that the young boy's complaint was not serious.

The visitation to Greenleaf provided Vicky with the excuse she had been waiting for to take another temporary leave from Dragonard Hill, a brief escape without arousing her father's suspicions. She realized that if she announced she was making a second trip to Troy that she would have to explain every detail of her last visit there to him. As matters now stood between Vicky and her father, he had not mentioned the subject of signing notes for Barry, and Vicky had not pressed him for further explanation. Nor had any further mention been made about her source of information. She had decided to keep secret her private store of knowledge—including the fact that her grandfather,

Richard Abdee, was still alive in Havana. Vicky was trying not to think about her own life in Havana. She had not even decided how long she would stay at Dragonard Hill.

*   *   *

Neither Ralph Webster, the clerk at Troy's mercantile store, nor anyone else in town, knew exactly what form of address to use when speaking to Vicky. They knew that she was Peter Abdee's daughter, but they also had heard the rumours that she had married a titled personage in Cuba. The few patrollers sitting behind the window today and Webster discussed this dilemma when they saw Vicky alight from her carriage and come in the direction of the store.

Vicky entered the store more businesslike today than on her previous visit. She moved in a quick rustle of crinolines past the wooden kegs, moving directly to the narrow stairway which led up to Poliguet's office.

Webster called from behind the counter. 'He ain't up there today . . . mam. Mister Poliguet ain't arrived yet in town.'

Vicky stopped. She turned toward the counter and stared at the clerk. She did not understand. Today was Wednesday, the day on which Poliguet was always at his midweek practise in Troy.

Shuffling nervously, Webster said, 'He didn't arrive on the New Orleans coach . . . Miss Abdee. He didn't send no message. It's the first time this has happened and . . .'

'Thank you,' Vicky said in a brusque manner, turning toward the door.

'I'll tell him you called,' Webster offered.

Vicky stopped. The last thing she wanted Poliguet to know was that she was dropping in on him, to suspect that she was dependant on his attentions. She ordered, 'Do no such thing—' She softened her voice, adding with a smile, '. . . kind sir.'

Ralph Webster blushed. He mumbled, 'I won't say nothing.'

Vicky again moved toward the door, calling, 'It was only a bit of unimportant business I had to discuss with him anyway. Nothing that can't wait.'

131

She nodded to the men seated in front of the window, saying, 'Good day, gentlemen.' She opened the door; the bell tinkled, and she moved across the boardwalk to her carriage waiting on the street.

Lawyers! Sick children! Barry Breslin who can't even conduct his own business affairs! Vicky fumed over all these matters on her return to Dragonard Hill. Curlew asked her if she wanted to stop again at Greenleaf Plantation to see young David as she had originally told him she intended to do.

Remembering the lie, the excuse she had given Curlew for taking her to Troy, she quickly answered, 'No! Mister Webster didn't have the rosehip tonic I needed in the store. Forget it now. Just take me home.'

Vicky had seen this morning on her visit to Greenleaf that David was suffering from no more than a cold. She did not want to linger too long in a child's sickroom, anyway. A child only reminded her of her own son miles away from here in Havana. She could not start thinking about Juanito at this moment. She could not think of Juan Carlos. She knew that she was powerless when pitted against her husband. She realized she had to take a stand soon as mother and wife but, for the moment, she knew that she could only enjoy peace-of-mind if she put the thoughts of Havana out of her head. She told herself, forget, forget, forget.

Vicky was trying to eradicate the horrifying thought of Juan Carlos seeking an annulment from her in her absence when she realized that Curlew was slowing the horses. She remembered how she had climbed alongside him on the seat last time. She suspected he was slowing for her to join him again. She called, 'Don't get any ideas, Nigger! I'll tell you when I want you!'

Curlew called, 'I'm slowing for . . . patrollers, Miss Vicky.'

Sitting to the edge of the seat, Vicky saw three men on horseback blocking the public road. She said to Curlew, 'Let me speak to them.'

'We got nothing to fear, Miss Vicky, Mam. They know me and this carriage from Dragonard Hill. I'm just driving you . . .'

'I said, let *me* handle this!' Vicky impatiently ordered as she pulled at the shoulders of her dress. Damn it! she

132

thought. If I can't get Poliguet now when I need him I'll get somebody else! I don't have to throw myself at niggers. I can have white men, too! I can have anyone I want and Juan Carlos cannot do a damned thing about it!

'Good afternoon, gentlemen,' she called from the back of the carriage, noticing that one of the patrollers was younger than his two companions, a young swarthy farmer whom she could not remember having seen idling at the mercantile store. He was broad-shouldered and had black stubble on his lantern jaw. His ruggedness immediately tantalized her.

'Afternoon, mam,' one of the older patrollers called from his horse. 'We just conducting a check on all passing wheel traffic. There's been a runaway just south of here.'

'A runaway?' Vicky exclaimed in mock horror, her eyes quickly surveying the cottonwoods lining both sides of the road. She looked back to the patrollers, her eyes lingering on the swarthy young farmer as she asked, 'Should a lady be alarmed?'

'We'll take care of you,' the young farmer answered and grinned at her.

Vicky momentarily debated whether or not she should acknowledge the saucy innuendo of his words. Her frustrations, her anger at Poliguet for not being in his office today, her feeling of abandonment by her husband—all these things made her decide to forget about the decorum expected of a white lady.

She held the patroller's suggestive gaze and answered, 'I am most certain you could.'

The man danced his horse closer toward the carriage; his two companions pulled their hats forward; Curlew remained motionless in his seat. The moment was tense; the feeling of such bravado thrilled Vicky.

She pursued her brash intentions, tilting her head to one side, coyly saying, 'As a matter of fact, I thought that I *did* see some . . . activity in that cottonwood break just back yonder—' She pointed her parasol at the trees alongside the road.

Curlew spun around on his seat and glared at his young mistress. He reached for her arm as she moved to step from the carriage.

Vicky turned on him, ordering, 'Nigger! Mind yourself!

133

Do you know the punishment for someone who stops the cause of law and order? If there is a runaway nigger near here, every respectable, able-bodied person must try their best to locate him and return him to his rightful owner!'

Curlew shrunk back on his seat.

The darkly-featured patroller now trotted his horse alongside the carriage, saying, 'Them words be mighty dangerous for a fine lady like yourself to be saying. If you'd be so kindly disposed as to tell me exactly where you think . . . an able-bodied man should look for that runaway nigger . . .'

Staring him straight in the eye, Vicky announced, 'There are times when a female must forget she's a lady, sir. Times when she must be willing to meet . . . situations when they are presented to her.'

'I do believe I take your meaning.'

Holding up her hand to him, Vicky said, 'If you would be so kind as to help me from my carriage, sir, I will show you quite precisely what I do mean and then—if there proves to be no danger—we can both resume going our separate ways.'

'That's a manner of thinking a man like myself always respects.' His dark eyes twinkled.

'Then you are the man I shall show the place where I saw danger lurking.' Vicky now flounced down the road, the patroller quickly dismounting from his horse.

The underbrush alongside the road was thick. The husky patroller proceeded Vicky through the brambles, holding back the branches to prevent them from scratching her skin. They were barely out of view from the carriage and the other two patrollers when Vicky saw that he was of the same mind as herself. She saw that he was already working one hand on his crotch.

She continued with her make-believe game. She said, 'There seems to be no danger here—' She knew she should not talk any more. Her voice was beginning to quaver. She was shaking with excitement at the idea of being alongside the public road with a patroller who was so devastatingly alluring to her. She felt as if she might faint with excitement.

The patroller's voice deepened. He eyed Vicky's voluptuous bosom, saying, 'I think there still might be one or two surprises we'll find here.' He reached forward and grasped one of her hands. He smiled as he appraised the smooth whiteness of her breasts and then looked again at her widening eyes.

Vicky held the patroller's gaze long enough to know that he wanted her, too. She did not care about debasing herself. She could not let such a thrilling opportunity pass. Such a moment was worth all the scandal in the countryside.

The patroller now rested his hand on her thin shoulder. He pulled down one side of her bodice. Then, the other. He stared appreciatively at her breasts, his hand now working again on his crotch.

A voice inside Vicky told her that she had to match his aggressive move, to say one thing to give this assignation its final push toward what some people would call total degradation.

She lowered her eyes to his crotch, saying, 'You are a very . . . big man.'

Those words, that signal that she was thinking in purely physical terms and had no respect for her womanhood, eradicated the final barrier of decorum between them. The patroller lowered his trousers. His penis bounced strong and hard into view. Vicky first gasped at its size, the fullness of its crown, and then she pushed her naked breasts against the man's rough shirt and grabbed for his manly hardness. And whilst holding onto the phallus, she guided the patroller's hand under her skirts and frilled crinolines. She listened to the words he was now murmuring to her. She spoke in return to him. They talked about size, visual excitement, one another's appetite for various fulfilments.

The patroller soon lay upon Vicky; she held her legs akimbo in the air as he drove his manhood into her furry patch. She made him pull back onto his knees—and then stand in front of her—before he exploded inside her. She told him that she wanted to mouth his masculinity. He reached for her breasts as she knelt on the ground in front of him satisfying this lust.

At the moment of feeling her sucking him toward the ultimate excitement, the patroller roughly pushed Vicky back down onto the ground and resumed slicking himself into her vagina. He planted his arms on both sides of her, holding her gaze with his black-lashed eyes, contemptuously calling her 'bitch', 'whore' other abusive names he saw her enjoying being called.

Vicky crested in a thrill of giving herself to this rugged slave patroller at the country roadside, realizing that his two companions sat on horseback nearby and knew that the white 'lady' was giving herself to their friend, and that Curlew also was aware of her profligacy. And it was with those thoughts that Vicky contracted and squeezed her vagina to milk the last drops of seeds from the phallus of the patroller enjoying the insults he hurled at her.

* * *

The three patrollers galloped down the public road toward Troy, echoes of laughter trailing behind them with the dust of their horses. Curlew sat rigidly in the front of the carriage, trying not to look at Vicky as she pulled and patted at herself to repair the disorderliness of her clothing which the brief assignation alongside the road with the swarthy patroller had caused. The men's laughter made her fleetingly think about the crude tales they would inevitably tell at the mercantile store but, reassuring herself that she had no reason to go there again, she decided not to trouble herself over the possibility of village gossip.

The sight of a man alighting from a horse in front of the main house at Dragonard Hill reinforced Vicky's thoughts that she no longer had to visit the mercantile in Troy. As her carriage clattered up the driveway toward the house, she recognized the caller as Jerome Poliguet. He had come to see her!

'Monsieur Poliguet!' she called in newly found confidence, a self-composure advanced by her recent physical release with the patroller. 'What a surprise to see you at Dragonard Hill.' She felt in full control of herself.

'I arrived in Carterville this morning. Instead of taking the coach on to Troy, I rode on this mount I retain at the Carterville stables.'

Accepting his hand offered to help her from the carriage, Vicky said, 'I've just come from Greenleaf. My young stepbrother caught a chill in the rain over last weekend.'

'It is about Greenleaf I wish to speak to you, Condesa.'

'I'm afraid that your last news upset me so much—'

Vicky's mind was still on the patroller, the state of her clothes, the idea of perhaps even making love again but this time with Poliguet.

'This is good news about Greenleaf,' he assured her. 'I was hoping to speak about it with your father.'

'I do not think that that is advisable, Monsieur. Father is very techy on the subject of Greenleaf. You will appreciate that matter, remembering that the plantation was once the home of my late stepmother.'

Poliguet said, 'I do not mean to pursue the matter, Condesa, but I have a matter which might interest your father. Do not fear. I will not depress him. I appreciate his mourning.'

'You are very kind.' Although Vicky still found this Creole attractive, she now noticed something troubling about him. Something she could not quite understand. It had to do with his deportment, his almost . . . subservient manner.

'As I told you at our last meeting, this community is small. Word is hard to contain.' He eyed her and said, 'Do you not think it's strange that even I—an outsider—have heard about a boy called Lloy who lives at Treetop House? He is the son of a woman manumitted from here when you, I dare say, were probably only a mere infant, and sired by a slave called Monk who once lived here.'

Vicky was not interested in the past. She knew of Monk. She knew he had been killed in some gruesome manner. Such atrocities were the consequences of a slave system to her. She did not question them. She was more interested in deciding what had changed in her estimation of Jerome Poliguet since she had last seen him. Was it only because she had just enjoyed abandoned sex with the rugged patroller? Or was Poliguet not the man whom she had originally imagined him to be?

Mounting the white slate steps, Vicky swept past Poliguet saying, 'You most certainly must come inside, Monsieur. I do not know if my Father is even around the house. But after I brush the dust of the road from my hair and freshen up a bit, I shall be most glad to entertain you.'

Poliguet followed her into the house, paying more attention to the lavish appointments in the entry-hall than he did to his young hostess proceeding him across the highly polished floors.

137

                    *   *   *

Jerome Poliguet sat alone in a sitting-room lined with moire silk the colour of crushed raspberries. Vicky had gone upstairs to make repairs to her clothing and, when Poliguet heard the door open to the room, he rose from the divan expecting to see Vicky standing in the doubledoors. He instead faced a tall, thin man dressed in kneehigh black boots, nankeen trousers, and a shirt with sleeves rolled up to his elbows.

'Mister Poliguet, my daughter told me you were here. My name is Peter Abdee.'

'Ah, Mister Abdee! It is you I have come to see!'

Nodding to the divan where Poliguet had been sitting, Peter said, 'I have heard you were practising law in Troy. I wish you good luck.' He sat in a chair across from him.

'Thank you, sir. I am pleased that word of my small practise is spreading. I have the good fortune of seeing quite a few of the citizens. I am growing to love this country. The plantations. The farms. The towns. It is because of one local plantation that I am approaching you today, Mister Abdee, on a rather . . . delicate matter.'

Peter waited.

Lowering his eyes, Poliguet said, 'It is no secret that the plantation, Greenleaf . . .' He stopped, adding, 'I am very coarse, Mister Abdee. My Creole ancestors must be cringing in their graves with shame. Forgive me for not offering my condolences for your late wife. I have not met you before yet I rush straight to business matters. I have heard of your sad loss. Accept my condolences. And my apologies for bad manners.'

The mention of Greenleaf instantly cued Peter as to whom Vicky had gathered her information from in Troy. He remembered Curlew telling him about leaving her at the mercantile store. He knew about the upstairs offices.

He answered, 'Thank you, Mister Poliguet. I accept your condolences. That is most thoughtful of you. As to the subject of your manners and Greenleaf, you do not have to apologize. I do not wish to discuss that plantation in any way.'

'But I have a buyer for it!' Poliguet said setting to the edge of the divan.

'A buyer?' Peter wrinkled his brow. 'What makes you think Mister Breslin is interested in selling his plantation?'

'This might be his last chance.'

'Chance? Last chance?' Peter arose from his chair, saying, 'No, I do not wish to discuss this matter. It is not for me to discuss and if Mister Breslin were to sell Greenleaf, I am sure he would offer me first refusal.'

'*You* would buy Greenleaf?'

'It was my wife's home.' Peter answered blandly. Then moving toward the double white doors, he said, 'It is most kind of you to come by to introduce yourself and offer your condolences. I am sorry that we had to meet under such sad circumstances. But at least we have met. Good-day, Mister Poliguet.'

*   *   *

The fact that stories were already spreading in the countryside and towns about Barry Breslin's financial troubles made Peter realize that he must do something immediately to stop them. But Barry always refused to talk about money, saying at one moment that this year's crop would solve all problems, and moaning in the next moment that even a bumper crop would not save him.

Idle rumours often grew into serious, malicious scandals, Peter knew. He did not feel that Greenleaf was beyond salvation. But his westerly neighbours, the Witcherleys, had offered to sell him two of their fields and he desperately wanted to put his money there. The Witcherleys had lost a son and no longer pursued an ancient feud with this land. Peter was willing to forego buying the Witcherley property, though, to put money into Greenleaf to save it if for no other reason than he knew that Kate would have liked that.

Or would she have liked it? he asked himself tonight. His mind was now so confused since her sudden death that he could not decide if it had been wise to sign for Barry's loans. Or to pay more direct money. Would Kate have changed her mind, too? Would she decide that such an action would again be providing a bottomless purse for her feckless nephew?

Peter saw that he, first, had to clear his mind of Kate before he could see the best way in which to deal with this increasingly dangerous situation. Poliguet's visit told him that rumours were fastly spreading. Peter secretly feared rumours. He recognized them as being instruments of vengeance. But to tackle them he first had to have a lucid mind, to be in keen condition, not muddle his way and perhaps even lose Dragonard Hill. He realized that anything was possible once rumours started.

Kate! He again returned to his thoughts of sex as being an antidote to this cumbersome melancholia. He appreciated the indulgent—even frivolous—aspect of such thinking. But it could work. He had at last found someone to serve as a new sexual partner, embarking on a pursuit of passions.

One entire phase of his lifetime had passed, Peter realized, one complete adult phase since he had last sought to lose himself in sexual pursuits. Was it young manhood or middle-age which had eluded him? He did not know. He did not feel like an old man but yet he felt that he had seen enough of life to disqualify him from being young.

A domestic schedule no longer mattered to him. That change had only happened in the brief time since Kate had died. Even supper at night no longer provided enjoyment. He had anticipated the arrival of his daughters home, to have them all around one table but what had happened to that hope?

Tonight he had eaten alone in the dining-room with Vicky. She did not again mention the subject of Barry and money. She talked about the past in a detached, careless way. She even had mentioned a young black man named Lloy. Why would Vicky ever talk about Lloy, Peter wondered, a free Negro now living at Treetop House?

Peter was becoming suspicious, distrusting with the immediate people in his life. He did not recognize this feeling as being part of his nature and it troubled him.

Can a man change so quickly? he asked himself as he ambled alone tonight after supper to meet Belladonna at the place where they had prearranged for tonight's assignation. Can one death throw a man's entire pattern of living so much out of keel? He was strangely grateful for his concern over his attentions toward Belladonna. It diverted him from problems he could not immediately solve.

The original feeling that he was participating in an almost incestuous act by having sex with his daughter's lover had passed when he had seen Belladonna physically responding to him on their first night together. He had not questioned her why she had chosen to meet him. His masculine pride needed some bolstering. He was not a proud man but he was pleased to see a young woman enjoying herself with him.

Enjoyment was the key to his interpretation of Belladonna's interest in him. He surmised that she no longer enjoyed a sexual life with Imogen. He had never doubted that the two women practised a perverse love affair in the old house where they lived. His knowledge of such relationships was that they were not lasting.

The sight of Belladonna standing at the appointed spot alongside the path made him forget about all these doubts, ideas, observations, and opinions. He knew that she also had spotted him. She was backing into the thicket.

Peter did not speak to the tawny-skinned girl as he approached her. He squeezed the slim hand which she extended to him. He wrapped both arms around her and he felt her return the embrace.

Many things had changed since their first meeting. This was their third assignation but, already, Belladonna lifted her mouth to his without prompting. He did not like imposing himself on females. He felt excited that Belladonna welcomed him.

Holding the slim girl in his arms, Peter tasted her sweet mouth as their tongues met, their lips moistly slid against one another's, their kisses turning into a desperate exchange of tongues, saliva, even one another's breath.

Peter thought about this girl making love to his daughter. He wondered if she and Imogen kissed in this same manner. If Belladonna gave herself to Imogen . . .

The mounting passion of his own love-making soon cast these thoughts from his mind. His only wish now was to be closer to Belladonna, to feel her smooth skin against his naked body.

Belladonna momentarily refused to relinquish her grasp.

141

She also had quickly grown to enjoy this development of feelings between them, a beginning of what seemed to her to be a new life, a new awareness in herself.

The image of Imogen also passed through Belladonna's mind. She remembered Imogen pressing her for details about their first meeting, demanding to know how her father had responded to her body, if he was weakening for her.

Belladonna had anticipated such questions from Imogen. She knew Imogen's perversions, her thoughts of power, her curiosity about males' bodies. But the last time that Imogen had questioned Belladonna, the black girl was more hesitant to speak. She did not know whether she could share the stories of this love-making any longer with Imogen. These moments with Peter Abdee were becoming almost sacred to her.

Lying on the ground, Belladonna cradled Peter between her legs, reaching to hold his head between her hands as she kissed both his eyes, rubbed her face against his weathered skin.

Peter gently began nibbling her ear as he lay down upon her, easing the fullness of his masculinity into her, a phallus made of flesh and blood, an instrument of true passion instead of a blunt object hewn from wood and stretched-over with leather. Belladonna adored the reality of his manliness. She felt beautiful, needed, the most complete she had ever felt in her life. She wondered if Imogen realized what she had given to her by sending her to make love to her father. Belladonna doubted it. She even feared it. But nothing could stop this now.

* * *

Malou was pleased that her mistress was tired tonight, pleased because she saw that her mistress was finally fatigued from sexual satisfaction. She did not know where her mistress had met a man to satisfy her but she knew that it was not on her father's land and this pleased Malou. She had fears that her mistress would become the instrument for trouble here.

Despite that the black people lived in slavery here as in Cuba, Malou saw that the black people here did not suffer like so many blacks did on the island of Cuba. There the slave owners did not respect the family on their plantations, the farm lands they called *fincas*. The Cubans bought more men in the slave markets than women because men were stronger and the Cubans did not care if they died after four or five years of work because the price for a strong black man was low and profits from sugar were high.

Malou saw—and learned from her new black friends in Town—that no new slaves were purchased by their master and any seldom sold. The most suffering she saw amongst the slaves was caused by one another. She saw the child named Fat Boy wandering around the plantation. Malou was glad that the women in the house for children, The Shed, were giving him a home. She saw that the child suffered from the influence of the black man in the kitchen who dressed himself in women's clothing. But she also saw a deep strength in that black man. She saw a strength which others could not see in him.

Many black people concerned themselves with learning truths and facts about a life around them, and the spiritual life of future happiness. Malou knew this from her past. She also saw it here on Dragonard Hill. But the black people here were still frightened of punishment. That fear was instilled in them by the system which held them here as slaves.

Although Malou talked to more people in Town with each passing day, telling them about their African gods— the orishas—she saw that most men and women preferred to learn the answers from the religion of white people. They saw that as their truth. They had been gone too long from their homeland. Malou considered the black woman, Maybelle, to be a perfect example of a black woman in this new world who had a good heart, a strong soul, but held doubts about the words which Malou spoke of African gods. Malou was sorry that Maybelle had gone from the plantation with her mistress's sister. She would like to use Maybelle as a disciple, a woman to be an example to other black women in Town.

Malou's trust in Maybelle was based on the good woman's belief in families, children, future generations of black people. Maybelle had a son. She had given him to the white master but, instead of harbouring bitterness, she raised all the black children as her own.

Thinking about this matter tonight as her own mistress slept, Malou wondered if in fact she might learn something herself from Maybelle. She still had bitter hatred raging inside herself not only against white people but for the black people of the Dahomey tribe. She remembered that it was the Dahomey tribe who had raided her village when she was only a girl, had taken all the people of the Yoruba village and sold them to white slave traders on the Niger River.

Black people had sent Malou into the world as a slave. They had killed her mother, father, sold her brothers and sisters, destroyed the hut in which the ceremonial instruments were kept. Malou had been marked as a child to become a priestess in the Yoruba nation. She had been sent to learn the sacred tales from the *hougan*. She had been in his hut that night when the *hougan* had drunk too much palm wine, had not ordered the change of night guards on the village, had been sleeping drunkenly when the Dahomeys' arrows pierced the sacred hut, when the fires spread over the grass roofs of the village, the night on which Malou had been taught that she must trust no one—not even a sacred *hougan*—but to place her faith only in the gods . . . and herself.

Distrust also bred cunning. Malou had learned that it was as difficult to stay alive in the white man's world as it had been in the forests towering along the River Niger. That a person must be cunning as well as protective. Malou knew all these things but still did not see how she was meant to teach them here successfully on Dragonard Hill. She would try to show the black people the similarities between the two religions, that the sky was big enough for many gods and saints and all their ancestors, but that the world would not be inherited—as the Christians said—by the meek. The strong, the cunning would inherit this earth. Malou prepared all this in her mind tonight for the meeting tomorrow night in the chapel at the crossroads in Town.

Chapter Eleven

CORN WHISKY

Imogen lay awake on the corn husk mattress in the darkness of her bedroom upstairs in the old house. She did not move when she heard bare footsteps stealthily ascend the wooden staircase outside the room. The hinges creaked as the door slowly pushed open; the footsteps softly entered the room. Whilst lying awake here in the darkness waiting for Belladonna to return home, Imogen had resolved not to abuse her for coming back at such a late hour. She remained motionless on the bed, listening to Belladonna pull the dress over her head and surmised that her next movements—the soft rustling of clothes—came from Belladonna carefully arranging the dress over the back of a chair.

The pussy, Imogen cruelly thought. The pussy took off her frock and fixed it prettily over a chair so the ruffles won't get mussed! Just like a . . . pussy!

The corn husk mattress creaked as Belladonna slipped naked into bed. Imogen waited for her to snuggle alongside her, to wrap one arm around her and report that she had again obeyed her instructions tonight.

No arm advanced across the lumpy mattress. Belladonna made no move toward Imogen. She did not even tug at the flannel sheeting nor whisper in the darkness to Imogen.

The pussy's scared stiff of waking me, Imogen guessed as she lay with her back still positioned to Belladonna. Well, let her just lie there and worry. I'll be damned if I'll ask her any questions. Why make her think that I'm interested

145

in what *he's* been doing to her . . . pussy. I just want the wench to get him hooked on her. I'll soon be giving all the orders around here. The old man will soon have Kate out of his mind, will have forgotten about chasing other pussies, black or white. He'll be so head-over-heels crazy about *my* black-skinned pussy here but I'm the one who'll be giving the orders!

Pleased with what she believed to be the progress of her plan, Imogen closed her eyes in an attempt to go to sleep. She soon heard soft breathing coming from behind her back, a sound which told her that Belladonna already had fallen asleep.

Imogen remained wide awake. She had consumed more than one jug of whisky after Belladonna had gone to meet Peter tonight but even the strong alcohol did not make her feel drowsy.

Lying awake in the darkness of the bedroom, Imogen continued thinking about Belladonna, imagining how she had made love again tonight with her father, still contemplating the idea of awakening the girl and forcing her to tell her specifically what they had done tonight—if her father had screwed her more than once; if he had eaten her cunt; had Belladonna sucked his pecker; did she enjoy his cock better tonight than last time; did he keep it hard for her; did he maybe even stick it up her ass!

The whisky had given Imogen a craving to enjoy sex, at least vicariously. She wanted to hear a report from Belladonna's own mouth, to kiss Belladonna and taste the hint of her father's penis in her mouth.

Convincing herself that she was not really concerned with the matter at the moment, Imogen again rejected the idea of awakening Belladonna. She decided that she would benefit more from a good night's sleep. She still was unable to drift off to sleep, though, and the grey light of morning soon began to filter through the curtains on the window. Imogen finally felt her eyelids become heavy. She dozed briefly to an outside morning chorus of birds. But, then, at the sound of a rooster crowing in the distance, she knew that she must get out of bed and go to work, that she had virtually lost a full night's sleep.

A hard day lay ahead of Imogen. She had told the driver in Town that she would join him and a chopping crew after daybreak, that they would take axes, saws, mallets, and wedges to a back timber patch on the plantation where they would fell trees and cut the fence posts which were needed to make a markation line on the far boundaries of Dragonard Hill.

Throwing back the bed covers with the day's work in the forefront of her blurred thoughts, Imogen stepped from bed and reached for the clothing she had left strewn on and around a chair on her side of the bed. She finally sat upon the chair to pull on her boots. It was then, seeing Belladonna curled in a comfortable semi-circle in bed, that she clearly remembered how she had waited for her last night to come home from the love-meeting with her father.

Glancing down at the black girl luxuriating in sleep, Imogen shouted, 'Wake up, you bitch!'

Belladonna groaned, stretching like a cat.

Infuriated by her feminine movements, Imogen pulled open the bedroom door, slammed it behind her with a loud bang, and stamped down the wooden staircase. 'Bitch!' she repeated as she passed into the kitchen. 'Bitch whore!'

One tin plate, one bowl for porridge, one coffee mug, and cutlery set on the table where Belladonna had left them for Imogen last night before creeping upstairs to the bedroom. Imogen sent the collection of cutlery and tableware to the floor with one sweep of her hand and moved angrily toward the kitchen door.

* * *

The work in the back timberland on Dragonard Hill continued throughout the day as Imogen had predicted. She joined in the felling and limbing of trees, rolling the larger logs into piles which would be pulled by horses to the timber mill; they next began sawing the smaller trees into lengths which could be used to build zigzag fences for boundaries of this land. The steady, hearty work kept Imogen's mind off the subject of Belladonna and her father. She ate a frugal midday meal with the black workers who had brought food in cloth bundles from Town. Their work continued into the late afternoon. It was near sundown when Imogen returned to Town on foot with the gang of slave workmen; she proceeded from Town on horseback to the old house as dusk was shading the sky.

'Belladonna?' she called, entering through the back door into the kitchen. The aroma of freshly baked bread hit her nose and the smell of a stew simmering on the stove smelled undeniably delicious to her. She saw one place set on the table, though, the same tin plate, cup, and cutlery which she had sent flying to the floor this morning.

After calling again for Belladonna but still receiving no reply, Imogen went to the cupboard where she kept her supply of corn whisky, the alcohol distilled by white men in this district and which Imogen periodically purchased from the men who served as patrollers. She uncorked a brown earthen jug and, splashing a cup full of potent alcohol, she took a long drink. The whisky burned her throat but warmed her stomach. She suddenly felt ravenous. She remembered that she had eaten little more today than a piece of cold bread.

Imogen kept the whisky jug alongside her on the table as she greedily spooned, first, one plateful and, then, a second helping of the chicken-stew-and-dumplings which Belladonna had left for her on the stove. The tastiness of the dinner did not lighten her mood toward Belladonna, though. This was the first time that Belladonna had not been waiting in the kitchen for her when she had come home from work. Imogen poured generous cupsful of whisky and, washing down her supper with the alcohol, she grew more angry as she thought about Belladonna. She remembered how the black girl had sneaked into the bedroom late last night without saying a word. She remembered the precise instructions she had given the girl about how she must deal with her father. She thought how she had originally brought Belladonna to live here with her in the old house. These memories, reflections, instructions grew more turgid in Imogen's alcohol-fuelled mind and, by the time that darkness totally enshrouded the house, Imogen realized that she had to make a drastic change of plans. She herself had to intervene in the plan she had originally organized for Belladonna to pursue alone.

Damn that pussy bitch, she mumbled to herself as she shoved back her chair in drunken anger. That bitch is a nigger and what happens when a nigger disobeys? Gets whipped! That's what! Gets stripped of their clothes! Gets stretched out and . . . whipped!

Although Imogen could not remember the last time she had used a bullwhip on Dragonard Hill, she knew exactly where she kept one hidden here in the old house. She went to the wood pile alongside the stove and, throwing the chunks of wood to the floor, she opened a small door behind the wood-box where the forbidden instrument was concealed—the instrument which her father refused to be allowed on this plantation.

Jerking out the coil of black leather, Imogen gripped the whip's leather butt in one hand and unfurled it with a loud crack across the kitchen floor.

'Yeah!' she said, biting her lower lip with pleasure as she heard the sound of the whip fill the room. She snapped the whip a second time and repeated, 'Yeah!'

Anxious now to dominate, to punish someone with this whip as she had not been allowed to do in a long time, Imogen grabbed the whisky jug from the table and stomped toward the door.

'Yeah!' she called into the night, snapping the whip against the dirt yard behind the old house. 'I'll find my black pussy . . . Pussy? Where you hiding, pussy? Yeah!' She snapped the whip again.

Imogen was not too drunk to remember where Belladonna had been meeting her father on the path joining the main house with Town. She staggered in that direction, dragging the whip behind her across the yard as she took yet another burning drink from the whisky jug. She shouted into the night, 'Pussy, I'm coming to get you. And you, too, Pa, you old . . . tit-sucker!'

*   *   *

Imogen's fury increased at each turn and bend of the narrow path connecting the main house to Town. She had not found Belladonna and her father in the low brush where she had first seen them lying. She wondered if she had made a mistake, if she had miscalculated their usual meeting spot.

Stumbling along the fern-festooned paths, Imogen decided that they obviously alternated their places of rendezvous. She now refrained from shouting out into the

149

night for Belladonna, instead muttering to herself how she would surprise them. Her boots tripped over roots snaking across the path. The whip trailed behind her, its tip gathering leaves and dried grass and catching in the entanglement of underbrush.

Emerging at the far end of the path, Imogen stood facing the awkward skyline of Town, the tall-legged houses lining the two dirt streets and silhouetted against the starry darkness of night.

They've found themselves a new place here, Imogen told herself. The pair of them are tired of humping on the dirt like dogs and they've found themselves a new place.

Narrowing her eyes as she wondered where her father might take Belladonna for a night of abandoned lovemaking, Imogen's eyes settled on the small, steep-roofed cabin built at the crossroads.

The chapel! The old chapel! That's where they are, she told herself. She knew nobody used that old place-of-worship any longer. And finishing the whisky with one gulp, she tossed the brown jug into the bushes; it landed with a loud clatter as Imogen moved toward the wooden front door of the chapel.

Convinced now in her alcoholic stupor that her father and Belladonna were inside the chapel, Imogen first considered the idea of standing on the road and demanding in loud shouts that they come outside to receive their punishment in front of all the black slaves in Town. She was intent now to inflict the lash on both of them. She retained no sense of balance. She ruled this land now in her mind. She held the whip. She did not have to wait for anyone to bestow further power upon her. She possessed it all.

Deciding that she would rather catch them in the act, she stumbled up to the door and, kicking it open with one booted foot, she flailed the whip into the darkness. She screamed. 'Come out, you sons-of-bitches! Come out or I'll come in there and strip the hide off both your bare asses!'

A circle of black people sat around a small tallow candle in the middle of the chapel floor. They looked in astonishment at Imogen standing in the doorway. Malou crouched in the centre of the circle of black men and women.

Surprised as the black people, Imogen drunkenly demanded, 'What you doing here, you black . . . sons-of-bitches?'

The tallow candle was quickly snuffed. The people rolled back into the shadows. But one Negro, a man who had worked alongside Imogen today in the timberland, saw her inebriated condition. He moved toward her, generously offering, 'You looks like you needs some help, Miss Imogen, Mam.'

'I need no . . . help!' she slurred, pushing his arm away from her. She stumbled farther into the room, saying, 'This is a meeting. . . . You niggers are having a secret meeting!' She snapped her whip into the near darkness of the chapel, repeating, 'A secret meeting!'

The sound of toppling benches, quick gasps, and the flailing whip suddenly spread through the chapel. Imogen drunkenly pursued any figure whom she saw move in the shadows in an attempt to escape her. She snapped the whip against the floor. She occasionally landed a strike on a black man or woman; she raised back her arm to strike again with the bullwhip.

Her mind was now blurred with reality and her original intent; she ranted one moment at the Negroes for holding a meeting which was forbidden to them, and, in the next moment, she called abusive names to Belladonna and her father whom she had expected to find here. The black people who had come to the chapel to listen to Malou now had all managed to escape out the front door as Imogen stumbled around and around in the chapel, knocking over more benches, snapping her leather bullwhip in the darkness, profaning both Belladonna and her father.

'Imogen!'

The thunderous voice stopped her. She turned and squinted her eyes toward the door behind her. She saw the outline of a man standing in the doorway. She lowered the whip in one hand. She stared at the door, asking, 'Who you?'

'Imogen, you are drunk. You are disgusting.'

'Who you?' she asked in a louder voice.

'You know we don't whip people here!' Peter Abdee stepped forward and snatched the bullwhip from his daughter's hand.

Momentarily staring at him, Imogen then threw back her head and laughed. She said. 'We don't whip our . . . people! Hell no! We just . . . screw them!'

The flat of Peter's hand struck Imogen's cheek. She staggered back from the blow. She caught herself against a wooden post, muttering, 'You . . . bastard.'

'I'm not going to take any abuse from you. Not even when you're drunk.'

'You're not ordering me around like a wench. You're talking to . . . me! To . . . me!' she said, thumbing her chest. 'Who do you think runs this place? Me!'

'Not any more.'

The words took her by surprise. She asked in a meek, almost childlike voice, 'What you say?'

'Not any more,' he repeated. 'From this night onwards, Imogen Abdee, you are no longer the overseer of Dragonard Hill. You're just one more of my daughters. And a rather disgraceful one at that. Let me tell you this, too, Imogen. If you try to go against my word I will personally drive you out of your house and off this land. There is no excuse for conduct like I've seen tonight. None!'

He then turned and left her, walking away from the chapel as Imogen shouted after him, 'You son-of-a-bitch. You pussy-mouth! Who wants to do your filthy work anyway? Not me! Take it! Take all of it! Take all of it! I'll see you dead and her, too!'

*   *   *

Peter walked angrily back to the main house. He had left the house shortly after supper for a solitary stroll to reconsider the idea which had occurred earlier today. In thinking today about Belladonna, he had remembered that Posey was without Fat Boy to help him in the kitchen and he had thought that Belladonna might assume her long since given-up post as cook's helper. Belladonna had been in the kitchen all day today—and evening—with Posey except for the time she had taken a pot of stew down to the old house for Imogen. Peter had been strolling alone after supper, wondering about the wisdom of keeping Belladonna so close to his bedroom. He knew that such an arrangement would keep her away from Imogen and a sexual

152

arrangement she no longer enjoyed. But he wondered what this nearness to him would accomplish. Had that been an incorrect choice to make for both of them? But all these thoughts were now gone from his brain as he stormed back to the main house. He was determined that Imogen should not keep her post as overseer at Dragonard Hill. He remembered the days when the kind-hearted black man, Nero, had held that position here and it was then that he recalled the idle prattle which Vicky had recently told him—that the young man, Lloy, lived nearby in the farm for free Negroes called Treetop House.

Slowing on the path, Peter thought about giving the position of overseer again to a black man. A Negro had done the job before and performed his work well. Excited by this idea, Peter foresaw that—yes—instead of having a black slave act as overseer he would pay a wage to a free Negro. Why not? He thought about the objections which certain white people in the neighbourhood might raise about such an innovative idea. But he knew he could cope with narrow-minded critics. He not only would be paying a wage to a Negro—elevating at least one of them to a position of paid employment—but he also would be mending old ties with someone who was connected to him by blood.

The more that Peter thought about the idea the more excited he became about Lloy replacing Imogen as the overseer of Dragonard Hill.

*   *   *

Malou crept from house to house in Town in the late hours of that same night, shaking the pole ladders which led up to each of the tall-legged houses in which she knew she had followers. When a head appeared at the door in answer to her rattling signal, she whispered, 'Have no fear, brother. Our meetings continue. We'll find a new place of worship. The master is more worried about his own blood than us.' She made a sign-of-a-cross to them with one hand and proceeded to the next tall-legged house with her message of hope, to have faith in themselves, that whips were not to be feared, that not even fire could destroy their spirits. Fire had driven her out of the *hougan*'s sacred hut many years ago in Africa and she had learned only more truths about the gods, the spirits, the saints, the crucifix, all the black ancestors in the sky.

Chapter Twelve

A CLUB WITH NO NAME

No shortage of hospitality awaited Veronica in her spontaneous visitation to farms and villages lying to the north of Dragonard Hill. Having originally planned to go no farther than the Mississippi border in her excursions, she had found herself approaching the stateline of Tennessee by the end of her first week away from home. Arkansas had only been considered a state by the United States of America this year—1836—and, in the throes of the excitement of travel, Veronica even momentarily entertained the notion of travelling to the northwest in that direction. But the people whose names Royal had sent her from Boston to visit all politely dissuaded her from such an idea, urging her instead to pay only calls on farms or towns which lay toward the northeast.

The Duprees. The Breakwaters. The Lewises. The Sells. Veronica visited all the families listed in the letter which Royal had sent her, the letter which he had intimated that she destroy after reading. Veronica received names of new hosts at each household upon which she called, being promised a warm reception at her next stop if she again explained who had sent her and the two black companions with whom she was travelling.

Maybelle and Ham proved to be excellent companions for Veronica. They had both seemed shy, seldom speaking, on their first day away from Dragonard Hill. Veronica suggested to Ham to stop the wagon at the small town of

Keybury on their first afternoon; she had timidly knocked on the door of a small white cottage, knowing only that she would announce herself as 'Mrs Royal Selby from Boston' and that her husband had suggested that she visit them during her stay here in the South.

The name of that first family in Keybury was Westcott. Mister Westcott was a lanky man with bushy red sideburns. Mrs Westcott was equally tall and equally as insistent that Veronica, Maybelle, and Ham stay with them for the night. Veronica was as surprised as Maybelle and Ham when the Westcotts firmly insisted that they all—Ham and Maybelle included—sit at the same table in the kitchen to eat their supper. Mister Westcott said grace before the meal and, by the time that Mrs Westcott served a cherry cobbler for dessert, everyone—Maybelle and Ham included—were exchanging stories about planting, the new people coming to this region, settlers moving west to the Oregon Territory. The Westcotts ignored the fact that Maybelle and Ham were not familiar with the table manners followed in a white household; Mrs Westcott ate a chicken leg with her fingers, licking the grease from her thumb and making a joke about food often tasting so much better when you didn't have to use a fork.

Maybelle and Ham quickly learned the smattering of etiquette needed to live under the same roof as white people. Maybelle said to Veronica the next day in the wagon, 'You know, Miss Veronica, I never sleeps on white cotton sheets before.'

'Did you like it?' Veronica asked.

'I just don't want to get spoiled!' Maybelle laughed.

Veronica examined the straw hamper of food which Mrs Westcott had prepared for them and, seeing a plentiful amount of cold meats, pickles, freshly baked bread, she asked Ham to look for a spot where they could have a picnic by the side of the road.

Thus, Veronica, Ham, and Maybelle progressed from Keybury, to Haddleytown, to Rockdale, to the Pointers' farm near Hononga Falls, calling upon one family after another who welcomed them into their homes; they were all comfortably-living but not ostentatiously prosperous people who refrained from questioning Veronica about her personal life, nor did they question Maybelle's and Ham's relationship to Veronica's family, only extending hospitality like members of a club with no particular name once that Veronica announced she was the wife of Royal Selby of Boston, Massachusetts.

*   *   *

Ham was the first to mention the subject of Abolitionists. He held the team of chestnut mares at a neat trot on their travels this afternoon south from Horton on the second day of their return trip home to Dragonard Hill.

He said, 'If I didn't see no slaves at some of them places we visited, Miss Veronica, I would swear we've been calling on slave-runners. Them folks who white folks around here call that Underground Railway.'

Maybelle sat alongside Ham in the front seat of the wagon. She slapped him on the shoulder, saying, 'Shame on you, man. What you thinking Miss Veronica getting us mixed up in? Shame on you!'

Veronica rode in the seat behind Ham and Maybelle. She had been watching them enjoying the summer warmth, riding side-by-side like any ordinary man and wife.

She called, 'I know as little about Abolitionists as you do, Ham. It's no secret that I'm married to a man whose skin is darker than my own. We have three children. Maybe some people would call *me* an Abolitionist. Royal and I live in the North. Our children aren't slaves. But to put your mind at ease, not one of the kind people who we've visited mentioned even a . . . peep about slave-running or railways under or over the ground!'

'Don't mind him,' Maybelle said, leaning back to hand Veronica a lap robe. She warned, 'You watch yourself, Miss Veronica. The weather seems warm but I see a few clouds up ahead. We could be heading into a storm.'

Enjoying the fresh air herself, Veronica said, 'We can always take shelter under a tree. Mister Ruley said that we'd be passing through a thick forest before we come to Reverend Machim's home.'

Ham called, 'Do you knows anything about this Reverend Machim?'

'No. Nothing except that Mrs Ruley said that the Reverend would be pleased to have our company.'

157

Maybelle joked, 'This man here is just wondering if he's going to have fancy decorations on his bedsheets tonight. That's what. He's getting so spoiled with all this high living that I don't know what I'm going to do with him once I get him back home. The only high living there is our house built on . . . legs!' She laughed at her joke.

Although the prospect of returning to Dragonard Hill excited Veronica, she had been thinking about what returning to the plantation would do to Maybelle and Ham. She hoped to find another letter from Royal waiting for her, some news of her children, perhaps even the name of the mysterious man who was supposed to contact her about Royal's puzzling business. She wondered, though, how Ham and Maybelle would adjust to living in the plantation slavequarter again, sleeping on a straw pallet on a board floor. She somehow thought that bringing them on this trip with her had been wrong, that they had tasted a way of life which they would never again enjoy.

'Looks like we got visitors up ahead,' Ham said, slowing the horses.

Veronica sat forward in her seat and, reaching for her purse where she kept their documents, she said, 'We have no need to worry. Just keep driving, Ham. Just keep—'

She stopped. She looked alongside the wagon. She saw one horseman, then a second riding alongside them. She immediately recognized these riders—as well as the three men blocking their passage on the road—as belonging to a local element called 'red neck farmers', the men who also volunteered their services to be slave-patrollers on the public roads.

The first rider called from alongside the wagon, 'Where you headed, young lady?'

Veronica answered, 'My name is—' She hesitated. She had just been speaking that it was no secret that she had married a black man and moved North. Why chance mentioning her married name to these men who might have heard about Royal? She decided to use her father's name. She knew that he was well-known and respected. 'My name is Abdee. These are two of our people. I have been visiting friends.'

'Abdee? From Dragonard Hill?'

'Yes,' Vernoica said firmly to the patroller. 'That is where

158

we are headed now. We plan to stop the night in the next town.' She reached again for her purse, saying, 'If you care to examine our papers—'

The rider was not listening. He raised his head and called to a rider up ahead, a dark and swarthy young farmer who was sitting on his horse with two older men astride their horses on either side of him.

'Hey, Billy! Here's another Abdee woman for you. Do you think you can handle her like the last one?'

Maybelle turned quickly on the seat to glance at Veronica. But shaking her head, Veronica reached deeper into her purse. She gripped the small pistol which her father had given her as protection on this journey.

The darkly featured farmer now galloped toward the wagon and, smiling as he saw Veronica setting in the back seat, he asked, 'You have a sister living at Dragonard Hill?'

'I do not understand such a question. I told you who I am. I have papers to prove all our identities. If there are no further questions, please let us pass.'

'Oh, you're a feisty one! Well, I always say, if there's one bitch in a litter, dig around the ma's tits and you'll find another.' He leaned from his horse to grab Veronica's arm.

Quickly withdrawing the pistol from her purse, Veronica threatened, 'If you make one more move I'll...shoot you...'

'Ah, a real feisty one, you are! Well, you're messing with the wrong man, lady. Your sis showed me how hot you Dragonard ladies are under all your fine manners and high-faluting ideas. I ain't been able to think of nothing else but getting me more of the Abdee poontang ever since I sunk my pecker into your sis.' He shouted to his companions, calling, 'Come on, boys.' The other patrollers had already raised their long-guns.

Veronica saw that her weapon was outnumbered. She murmured to Ham and Maybelle, 'Don't do a thing. They'll kill us as soon as look at us. Don't...do...a...thing.'

The two other patrollers rode quickly from down the public road and, whilst one steadied the horse team, the other held his long-gun on Ham and Maybelle. The young patroller named Billy dismounted from his horse and, grabbing for Veronica's hand, he said, 'Your sis got me into the

159

bushes. But I still have nettles in my hair. I think I'm going to take you right here smack in the middle of the road.'

Veronica said in a quavering voice, 'You'll never get away with this.'

Pulling her toward him, he grinned at her and asked, 'What you like to hear, honey? You like dirty talk, too? You like to be called "bitch" and "whore" and "cunt"? Do you like to beg for pecker, too, just like your sis does?'

One of the patrollers called from his horse, 'Billy, it ain't fair you having all the fun again. What about us taking this nigger wench?'

'Leave her be,' answered Billy. 'You can always get black tail. But white poontang—fine, well-brought-up white meat. We're all going to get a taste of that now.'

He ripped at the pearl buttons on Veronica's dress, saying, 'Let's get a look at your titties, sister.'

A surge of anger suddenly replaced Veronica's fear. She did not know that she was capable of physically fighting for her honour in a situation as uncouth as this but she slapped at the patroller's hands, saying, 'Don't touch me . . . trash!'

He slapped back at her. She fell to the ground. He stood towering over her, saying in a deeper voice, 'I didn't plan on playing dirty, sister. But you've pushed me. You've pushed me too far.' He than began to unbutton the fly of his trousers, saying, 'Now I'm going to show you what your sis got. But I'm going to give you more. I'm going to wetten you up a bit first, Miss High-and-Mighty. I'm going to cool down that hot temper of yours. You can go home and tell *this* to your sister—'

He held his penis in his hand. It was not hard but, large in its softness, he rested it on the middle finger of one hand and a stream of urine suddenly gushed forth.

Veronica rolled to one side. She missed the degradation of his action. But another patroller jumped from his horse to grab her whilst Billy shouted, 'Hold the bitch! Hold her while I cool her down! I want to see her drinking my piss!'

The sudden volley of gun shots sounded in the distance in front of them. The patrollers quickly looked in the direction of the sound.

Bill muttered, 'Shit!' The second patroller moved toward his horse and shouted, 'We better get out of here. I don't know who that is but I ain't staying to find out.'

The third patroller had already lowered the grip on the horse team and was galloping down the road.

Ham jumped from the wagon in the dust left by the five patrollers' horses. He lifted Veronica in his arms and, handing her quaking body to Maybelle, he jumped onto the seat alongside her. He snapped the reins of the horses and the wagon leapt forward into the opposite direction from which the patrollers had fled.

A bend lay ahead of them in the road and, as Ham hurdled toward it, a small buggy turned the bend. He veered his team to miss the buggy but one wheel cracked against a granite boulder on the roadside.

A white-haired man sat in the buggy and, doffing his black flat-brimmed hat, he announced, 'Reverend Machim.'

'Reverend Machim!' Veronica gasped, lifting herself from Maybelle's protective grasp. 'We were on our way to see you . . . We were just stopped by patrollers . . . It was awful . . . Horrible . . . I didn't think . . .'

The apple-cheeked man looked at the rents on Veronica's dress and, then glancing down the road into the direction in which the patrollers had ridden, he said, 'There are more than one set of patrollers who cover this area. One is very much in evidence. As you yourself saw. But the others . . .'

Reverend Machim smiled, suggesting, 'Let us just call the second group of patrollers who keep to the trees, let us just call them "the hand of the lord" and leave the matter at that. Come now. Ride with me. We'll send someone back to mend your wheel.'

Ham looked in surprise at Maybelle who, in turn, glanced at Veronica. They were all remembering Ham's earlier question. But nobody dared mention a thing about what now more than ever seemed to be a well-organized, far-reaching organization, a club which still had no name.

Chapter Thirteen

THE WHITE SLAVE'S STORY

The young black man, Lloy, reported to the main house at Dragonard Hill on the morning following the day on which Peter Abdee sent a message to Treetop House stating that he had a proposal to put to him. Peter was impressed with Lloy's physical presence but, detecting a defiance in the young man's attitude, he decided to tell him what facts he knew about his background before they pursued any discussion in detail about him being the overseer here. He waited until they had left the main house and were cantering toward the front fields where green cotton first grew on this plantation until he began speaking to Lloy about his parentage.

Peter said, 'I trust you know that your mother had been a slave on this land. That she was freed and sent to live at Treetop House before you were born.'

Lloy also had premeditated tactics. He had foreseen the advantages of not being too forthcoming with the small scraps of knowledge he possessed about Dragonard Hill, the Abdee family, and himself. Also, he still was confused as to why an invitation to Dragonard Hill should arrive so soon after Claudia Goss's visit to Treetop House.

He answered, 'I was still young when my mother died. She told me very little. But, yes, sir, I know that she was a slave here.' He forced himself to keep his words as polite as possible.

'Your mother did not tell you why she was freed?'

'No, sir, she did not.'

'Your mother was pregnant with you at the time—' Peter paused. He had rehearsed this speech the night before but, in the company of Lloy, words failed him.

The horses now barely moved at a trot. Peter looked at the field slaves divided into groups working the dips and rises of brown earth. He said, 'Many people would say that I am doing a dangerous thing by inviting you here. I do not even know if you will consider being the overseer for me—'

Lloy interrupted, 'As I told you in the house, sir, I might not be qualified for such a position. I have done field work like any other man at Treetop House. We rotate responsibilities there. Everyone man and woman is given an opportunity to understand authority but also to toil under supervision. But to oversee a plantation as large as—' He extended his hand toward the fields, the hills, the forests of Dragonard Hill.

'Please let me continue,' Peter politely but firmly insisted. 'You will learn in time why I have asked you to come here. If you stay here, you will learn about the black man, Nero, who was once overseer here. You will also undoubtedly hear stories about my daughter, Imogen, who held the position up to now.'

Pushing the wide-brimmed straw hat back on his head, Peter said, 'But these details are all secondary to the fact why you are a free man and not enslaved yourself on this land. Yes, that was a very likely possibility. You could be living in the slave quarter here called Town. You could be one of those workers there tending the cotton plants. A drastic series of events changed those possibilities, though, Lloy, and I would like to make them known to you as quickly as possible. I would like to prevent the likelihood of any bad blood existing between us in the future. We have had enough in the past.'

Lloy did not question Peter for details. He knew that they would now all be forthcoming.

Peter began, 'I won't delve too intricately into the details about how I came to Louisiana myself. I wasn't born here. My father was English. He fled England for personal reasons I do not know and he settled on the island of St Kitts.

My mother left my father as your mother left here—with a child inside her body. I was born when my mother, a Frenchwoman, was fleeing from a husband who had mistreated and cheated her, returning to her homeland to try to start a new life for her and her unborn child. That was in the days of the French Revolution. The convoy in which she was travelling anchored on the Florida peninsula before even taking to the open sea. Also, I should add that my mother was not travelling alone. She was with a black servant, a devoted woman called Ta-Ta, and a young half-caste child whom my . . . father had sired with Ta-Ta. The child was a boy.

'A sequence of events, which I can tell you later if you are interested, led up to the sad fact that my mother died shortly after my birth in the Florida swamps. Ta-Ta guarded me as closely—even closer—than her own son. She was alone in the wilds of Florida and, after being physically abused by a band of white brigands, Ta-Ta, her son, and myself were sold in a slavehouse in New Orleans to an upcountry planter called Albert Selby.

'I came to this land as a piccaninny slave, Lloy. This land was then called The Star. Albert Selby had a wife named Rachel, a devoutly religious woman who had sent her husband to New Orleans to buy a tutor for her small daughter, Melissa. Instead, he brought home a Negress and two . . . piccaninny boys. To her horror, Rachel Selby discovered that one of the piccaninnies was white. Albert Selby insisted that I be kept in their home—the place we now call the 'old house'—and that Ta-Ta be allowed to live there, too, and serve as my nurse. Her own son was sent to be a fetch-and-carry boy for the white man who then acted as overseer on The Star, a man named Chad Tucker.

'In retrospect, Lloy, I suspect that that action proved to be the most fatal for Monk . . . that was what Ta-Ta's son came to be known—Monk. But that also could be seen as the reason which ultimately lay the path for your mother's and your own manumission. Chad Tucker is now dead. I won't malign the dead. But he and his wife, a woman who still lives in the neighbourhood under a new name, were— in my opinion, a very bad influence on Monk.'

Peter paused, then asked, 'Bad? That's how the Selbys saw it. And badness was certainly the Tuckers' intention

164

in my opinion, too. But the facts they filled Monk's head with—that he had the same rights as myself—whether *they* are bad, I cannot truly say. I keep slaves because that was the world I was born into. That was the work force which toiled the land I inherited from Albert Selby after I married Melissa his daughter. Monk thought that he should at least be overseer here. That he should have as much say in running this land as myself. He presented his case in a violent way, burnings and destructions, all ideas planted in his head by the Tuckers. His ultimate recourse was to challenge me to a duel. The weapons were whips. I will not lie, Lloy. Your father was a strong man. Much stronger than myself and quicker with a whip. He would be alive today and myself dead if it had not been for Ta-Ta shooting her . . . own son . . . to save . . . me.'

Lowering his head, Peter said, 'A black girl named Lilly was pregnant at that time with Monk's child. Monk's body was buried by an old slave woman here called Mama Gomorrah. Lilly was sent away from this land. You are her son. Her and Monk's son.'

Resting his hands on the saddle horn, Peter now sat silently on his motionless horse. He looked across a valley as he said, 'If our world was not turned upside down, Lloy, by the colour of people's skin, you and I would be nephew and uncle.'

Lloy stared soberly ahead of him. He realized that the story which Peter Abdee had just told him coincided with the story he had only recently heard from Claudia Goss. He also realized that it would not be prudent to tell Peter Abdee about Claudia's recent visit to Treetop House. He wanted time to think. He had other ambitions than being an overseer.

He asked, 'But why have you sent for me to come to Dragonard Hill now?'

Peter replied, 'One reason, Lloy, is that I need a man who is not directly involved with the plantation to serve as my overseer. For another reason—'

Turning to look at Lloy, he said, 'The only way I can really answer that, Lloy, is to say that we have to find out the answer together.'

'That seems fair enough.'

165

'A man learns that he must at least try to be fair in his dealings with people regardless of their colour.'

'You consider black people to be human then.'

Peter answered, 'Many people would argue with me on that matter but, yes, of course I do.'

Lloy said, 'But still you keep slaves.'

'I inherited this land as I said. I also inherited this work force. Slaves are the muscle of this land. Of the entire South. Do you expect one man to fight an entire system?'

'Then, sir, you are a slave to your inheritance.'

'Many white men might strike you for what you've just said to me. But you are right. Very astute. I came to this land as a slave. My skin is white. But, yes, Lloy, I am still a slave in many respects. A white slave.'

'Why, sir, did you change the name of the land from The Star to Dragonard Hill?'

'That was Albert Selby's suggestion. He felt I needed some link to my past. He saw that black people are cut-off from their heritage. He feared the same thing might happen to me. One of the few facts known about the background from which I was taken was that my father had once been a public whipmaster on the island of St Kitts. The English called such a man the "Dragonard". My father eventually used it for the name of his sugar plantation there. When Albert Selby heired me this land he suggested I call it Dragonard Hill. Perhaps it was a wrong choice, considering its cruel connotations but—' Peter laughed an empty laugh '—it certainly evokes the background from which I came into this world.'

'Now you are offering me a place in this... Dragonard world,' Lloy said soberly. He turned to Peter, continuing, 'I will accept the position as overseer but only on a temporary basis. We can see if I'm qualified for one thing.'

'Good. I accept your condition.' He extended his hand toward Lloy.

The offer of a handshake momentarily stunned Lloy. A white man had never offered him his hand to shake before. He had never heard of it happening in the South. But slowly reaching forward, he gripped Peter Abdee's hand and began to shake what he immediately felt as a firm, honest grip.

The two men rode down the grassy slope whilst Peter called, 'There's a lot to show you, Lloy. Let's go to Town first. I want you to see where the workers live. Then I'll show you a small house behind the main house where I thought you might be comfortable.'

'I'd rather live alongside the workers.'

'As you wish, Lloy. As you wish.'

*   *   *

Jerome Poliguet's first rule for success was to look for a man's secret longing, to try to fathom a man's hidden ambition. He sat in the parlour at Greenleaf Plantation on the afternoon following his visit to Dragonard Hill and intuitively recognized that Barry Breslin had no interest in running a plantation, that he was miserable here and probably wished that he could be living far away from this Louisiana backwoods. Poliguet also believed that it was often prudent to say exactly the opposite to what he believed.

He praised, 'You have a comfortable home here at Greenleaf, Mister Breslin. Very comfortable indeed.'

'It's exactly as my aunt left it.'

'Before she moved to Dragonard Hill?'

Barry slowly nodded, one long leg dangling over the arm of a chair. He added, 'Aunt Kate liked coming back to check on things.'

'You must miss her. I offer my condolences. But you are lucky to have such an interested guardian as Mister Abdee.'

'Guardian? He ain't my guardian!'

'A bad choice of words. A bad choice. Should I have said . . . protector?'

'He ain't that neither.'

'He certainly has your best interests at heart. I know that for a fact.'

'Mister Poliguet, when you came here today you said that you could help me out. Now I know it ain't no secret that I'm in a little money trouble. Hell, even if my crop is bumper this year I'll still be in debt. So I guess that it is because of money that you came here today about my best interests.'

'While we're being perfectly honest with one another, Mister Breslin, let me first tell you that I have already been to see your uncle.'

'For what?'

'You spoke about public knowledge of your precarious position. That is true. I have not been practising in Troy for a year yet and even I know of it. I also was approached by a party . . . someone who showed great interest in buying your place, buying the bank notes. Putting more money in their place.'

'Who'd do that?'

'At this point I am not at liberty to disclose the interested party's identity. But knowing your uncle's concern—through marriage—in Greenleaf, I first approached him.'

'I don't like you going to him but I guess you did right. He endorsed those loans with Aunt Katie.'

Poliguet nodded. He had planned to acknowledge the fact to Barry Breslin that he knew about Abdee's endorsement of money loaned to Greenleaf. He was pleased, though, that Breslin had admitted it.

'So what did Peter Abdee say to you?' Barry asked.

'He totally disapproved of you selling this land to any outsider. He said that he would buy Greenleaf himself before he'd allow it to go outside the family.'

'It ain't his business to say that.'

'True. Perhaps. But . . .' Poliguet did not like to appear the antagonist. He wanted to keep appearances that he was defending Peter Abdee's integrity.

Again studying the floral-papered room, Poliguet said, 'Yes, you have a very nice home here. Tell me this. Have you ever—in your wildest dreams—thought about leaving it?'

'Plenty of times lately.'

'Where would you go? Mexico?'

'Why Mexico?'

'Oh, no reason in particular. I just said Mexico because I was talking to a friend of mine in New Orleans who'd moved there. A totally different situation from yours. This fellow came back to New Orleans with his wife on a short visit. They moved to Mexico—what?—three years ago. Now he brings her home. They move in the best circles. No problems at all.'

'What did Mexico solve? What problems did he have before.'

'As I said, it is a totally different situation from your own but this friend of mine—his wife is a lady of . . . colour.'

Barry's eyes opened. He blurted. 'White men can marry black women in Mexico? And lead normal lives?'

'Most of the women there have tawny skin! Intermarriage is quite the accepted thing.'

'I never knew that.'

'But that's beside the point, Mister Breslin. I was just complimenting you on your home. I must say I don't disagree with your opinion to stay here. To fight for what you believe in. You're happy in Louisiana. This is your home so why should you give up all this happiness?' He held his hands out to a room which he knew was no more than a shrine to a woman now dead, a female who in no way could provide Barry Breslin with the needs he now required. He asked, 'Why give up all this?'

On leaving, Poliguet said, 'I visit Troy two days in every week. But here is a card for my offices in New Orleans. If you're ever down in the city you must drop in.' Jerome Poliguet departed from Greenleaf, knowing that he had enjoyed more success there than at Dragonard Hill, and more impressed than ever with Claudia Goss's network of backwoods gossip. She had told him that Barry Breslin was partial to black girls. And, again, she had been right. Poliguet had seen that for himself.

* * *

Barry Breslin rested the brown girl's naked leg on his bare shoulder, tongueing the soft skin on the inside of her calf, first kissing then licking a path along her skin toward the dimpled knee as he rubbed the heel of her other foot on the semi-hardness of his penis. The girl's name was Gigi, a quadroon slave girl who had been Barry Breslin's mistress at Greenleaf for more than two years now. Because of young David Abdee's sickness which still made his presence necessary in the main house at Greenleaf, Barry made love this afternoon to Gigi in a haybarn.

His darting tongue moving like a cat's tongue on Gigi's creamy-brown skin, Barry's mind wandered back to the meeting he had had earlier this afternoon with Jerome Poliguet. As he reflected on the thought of leaving Greenleaf and perhaps moving to Mexico, he licked his way back up

Gigi's leg and began kissing her toes. He soon moved her foot toward his mouth, his lips enveloping all of her toes.

These must be the most beautiful little feet of any gal I've seen, Barry thought as he tightened his wet lips around the clutch of small toes. He next lifted her dainty foot above his head and pressed it against his face, rubbing its sali-vamoist warmth against his cheek. He reached to his phallus to work it with his hand as he pursued this obsession of kissing and rubbing his face against Gigi's feet.

'You sure loves me to be kissing my feet,' Gigi whispered as she studied Barry's smooth-skinned body kneeling be-tween her spread legs.

Barry murmured his consent. He reached for her other foot. He held them together—sole to sole—and stretched his mouth to encircle all of her toes with his lips.

Gigi squealed pleasurably; the warmth of Barry's mouth was both satisfying and ticklish to her; she squirmed on her makeshift bed of straw.

Barry lowered her feet to his chest, pressing them against his heart, below the V on his skin tanned by sun along the line of a shirt. He held Gigi's feet to his heart and lowered his head.

Gigi asked, 'Barry honey? What's the matter? Why you suddenly stop? You feel sad about something?'

Shaking his head, Barry said, 'I just thinking. Just think-ing about . . .' He stopped. He did not want to tell Gigi about Mexico. How a white man could marry a quadroon girl and live there happily as man-and-wife. He decided that he definitely would talk again to that Creole lawyer, Jerome Poliguet.

The prospect of Mexico was suddenly driven from Barry's mind when he felt Gigi playfully jerk her feet away from his grip. She turned around on the straw and, ex-tending her naked legs out in front of Barry on the barn floor, she lay her head between his legs and lifted her mouth to chew the sac hanging between his legs. She reached with one hand, too, to hold his penis as she sucked the one testicle inside his scrotum.

It was Gigi's acceptance that he only possessed one tes-ticle which had made Barry first become seriously attracted to her. She did not treat him as if he were improperly developed. Now, as she devotedly worked to give pleasure

170

to his masculinity, Barry fell forward over her outstretched legs and began to tongue the patch between her thighs. He stretched his mouth so wide, trying to work his tongue so deeply, to stir the farthest reaches he could with the tip of his tongue that his jaws began to ache. The only perfection would be if this act could be performed in their own house—not here at Greenleaf but in some place where they could live happily together as husband-and-wife.

*   *   *

'So then what do you like to do in bed?'

Claudia Goss's direct question made Jerome Poliguet sit upright in the chair across the table from her. He had ridden to Grouse Hollow from Greenleaf before he caught the coach in Carterville to New Orleans. He had come to report on the progress of his work and did not expect her to inquire about his private life.

He answered, 'I was merely telling you the talk among the patrollers in Troy. How they say that the Abdee girl, Victoria, found pleasure with one of them alongside the public road.'

'Victoria? She's the one you found attractive.'

Poliguet could not deny to himself that he had once found Vicky to be very attractive, but that had been when he interpreted her authoritative social presence as being a hint as to how she would conduct herself in love-making. Now knowing that she liked to be subjugated, even abused by her lovers, Poliguet knew that they would never enjoy a sexual encounter. They both looked for domination. Poliguet saw no reason, though, to inform the slatternly woman, Claudia Goss, of his sexual preferences. They were allied in matters of business. He preferred to keep their relationship within those boundaries.

Claudia remained sitting by the table long after Poliguet had departed from Grouse Hollow to catch the coach in Carterville. She thought about his report of Abdee's coldness to him, about Barry Breslin's response to the mention of Mexico, about Lloy being called to Dragonard Hill to become overseer—facts all gleaned by Poliguet from Dragonard Hill or today at Greenleaf.

That was one development which even she and Poliguet

171

had not foreseen. That Peter Abdee would contact Lloy. They had planned to utilize Lloy themselves if—when— they acquired Greenleaf from Barry Breslin. The fact that Peter Abdee had offered Lloy a position on Dragonard Hill even gave them cause to consider a new overseer for Green- leaf once Claudia bought the outstanding notes from the bank.

It was not these matters which intrigued Claudia, though, as she sat alone in her cabin in Grouse Hollow. She was still obsessed with the thought—*What does that Creole dandy like to do in bed*? She considered this matter to be important not only as sheer curiosity. She believed that a knowledge of someone's sexual preferences could prove to be highly advantageous in dealing with them in business. She foresaw herself and Poliguet working closely together in the near future as they closed in around Dra- gonard Hill. Greenleaf was only the beginning.

'Damnit! What does he like doing in bed?'

Claudia had long-ago replaced her own sexual appetite with a hunger for gold. And it was in that greed for increased riches that she now puzzled over Poliguet's well-guarded sexual pastimes. She had known him for four years and his private life was still a mystery to her.

Chapter Fourteen

'MEDITERRANEAN OF THE AMERICAS'

The Gulf of Mexico bordered the southern coast and delta of Louisiana and the land which was, in 1836, called the Territory of Florida. Beyond the Gulf of Mexico, south from the boot of Florida, lay the Caribbean, the warm bay which early Spanish settlers had called the 'Mediterranean of the Americas'.

At the beginning of the nineteenth Century, Mexico was dependant upon Cuba for military protection. Havana was strong but Spain did not worry about internal struggles amongst the white population of Cuba because there was such a vast majority of black slaves to free whites: Cuba still looked to her mother country for protection.

It was the whites' fear of the large black populace in Cuba which also kept America from making encroachments on the riches of that island. Thus, it was only in matters of commerce which allied Cuba with the North American states, territories, and colonies.

Despite the black majority in Cuba, the slave dealers constantly increased the number of slaves which they imported in shackles from Africa, continuing the trade long after the North American people imposed laws that no new black slaves be brought to their colonies, states, or territories.

Competition between Cuban slave dealers was keen; they seldom spoke to one another and often employed privateers to seize the competitor's cargoes of slaves in the Trans-Atlantic Passage. But there were other times, such as controlling prices, when the slave merchants saw it to their advantage to meet. They also chose to communicate for personal reasons, and it was for a personal reason that Conde Juan Carlos Veradaga, a slave dealer as well as sugar planter, sent a messenger to Richard Abdee on the *Calle de Esclavos,* an invitation to meet the Englishman in private, on a common ground for a meeting involving both their personal lives. Veradaga suggested a curtained public carriage encircling the *Plaza des Armas* for their meeting.

* * *

Richard Abdee suspected that the reason for Veradaga's invitation for a meeting involved the infant, Juanito, whom Abdee had bribed the black woman, Malou, to bring to his slave house on the *Calle de Esclavos.* Abdee was in fact surprised that Veradaga had not contacted him before now regarding that matter, even sending him a challenge to a duel. Although having never met Veradaga, Abdee knew not only that he was crippled but also that Veradaga was a proud aristocrat and an infirmity would not prevent such a man from defending his *honra*—a Spanish pride which included vengeance against having his son kidnapped, if only for a few hours from the family home. Veradaga could well appoint a man to represent him in a duel against ageing Abdee. Age nor infirmities mattered when *honra* was involved.

Veradaga's calm composure surprised Abdee. The crippled aristocrat sat crouched in one corner of the heavily curtained carriage with a vicuña blanket covering his withered legs. He nodded for Abdee to sit across from him, saying, 'We should have met before now, Senor Abdee. I knew your former partner in business, Don Ignatio Soto.'

Abdee did not wish to discuss Ignatio Soto, not even after the twelve years since his death. Soto had rescued him from a slave station in the Leeward Islands—*Castelo Novo Mundo*—and brought him here to Havana as his partner in his slave house. But Soto's terms of partnership had been so mean, so exacting, that it had taken Abdee many years to achieve, first, an equal footing as a partner and, hen, complete control of Soto's business. Abdee ignored he rumours in the city that he had cast his own lot with Moroccan pirates, blacks, and a whore from Tangier to achieve not only control of Soto's business but cause his death as well.

He answered over the sound of the coach rumbling around Havana's main square, 'I had feared that my blood ties to your wife would have brought us together before this.'

'No. I knew if you wanted to make yourself known to my wife that you would have. But you English are cold and do not respect families like the Spanish. I did not wish to force you in that matter. You turned your back on your wife, then your son now living in Louisiana. Why should I expect you to open your arms to a mere . . . granddaughter?' Veradaga smiled, his head bobbing against his ruffled shirt as the coach kept its rhythm.

'You know much about me,' Abdee said.

'I know that many men in Havana say that you have no principles.'

'And I know men who say that you have too damned many!' Abdee answered, looking at the nobleman sitting across from him but seeing little more than his pointed goatee and darkened skin circling his eyes.

Veradaga smiled. He nodded his head, asking, '*Verdad*? Too honourable? I wish that were true! Perhaps it is. That is not far from the reason why I have asked for this meeting. I do not intend to bring you close to a family which holds no interest for you. But, at the same, my wife is of your line and I am asking you to help me solve the problem of her first husband.'

'She was married before you?'

'To what Americans call a "Yankee", a Northerner, and a man whom the English call a "bounder"—a man with loose ways, a man who lives on his wit, charm, appeal to the ladies. An adventurer who abandoned your granddaughter in New Orleans shortly before I met her. She spoke little about him. His name is Duncan Webb. The last time I heard of him he had contracted a venereal disease but—despite that affliction—he found a male admirer by the name of Hiram Heyward who took him to the colony of Australia.'

Abdee shook his head. He had lived in Havana long enough to know the slang for many words. One was for perverts and he said, '*Maricon*! Who'd think a granddaughter of mine would make such a mistake?'

'I do not find it advantageous to worry about mistakes. I think only about the future. This Duncan Webb has come to Havana. He is making threats to contest the annulment I received for Victoria's marriage to him. It was a mere civil ceremony not recognized by the Holy Catholic Church. I would ignore his threats but for the scandal they might cause for my young son. The slightest gossip now could prevent a good match for Juanito in the future when he is a fine young man.'

'You plan well in the future, Veradaga.'

'Again I am not asking you to understand Spanish ways. I am only asking you to—'

'Eliminate Duncan Webb.'

Veradaga nodded.

'Why do you think I could do it? I am not a young man.'

'I do not ask you to do it personally. I know you have men in your pay. I have counted many business losses to know that fact.'

'You want no part of this murder. You want to keep your son unsullied for marriage.'

Again, Veradaga nodded. He said, 'I thought that because you dislike families so much you might also . . . enjoy doing away with at least one of your sons-in-law.'

'You say this *maricon* is a rascal.' Abdee rubbed his jaw which was still strong, still well-formed in his late years. He said, "I have always liked bounders and rascals. Even the perverts of the lot.'

'On a grand level, *si*! But not a petty blackmailer. A man who wants no more than a handful of *pesos* to buy a few suits of clothing or a small *volanta* to drive around the square!'

'He asks for so little?'

'Yes. I would pay it. But you see he would quickly become a nuisance. He would talk. He would brag. I think—'

Abdee interrupted, saying, 'I think I'm beginning to understand Spanish honour, Veradaga. Worry about sons making a good match in the eyes of the Church and society but ask someone else to do your murdering in the back streets.'

'Ah, Senor Abdee. But a murder of which you'll approve. He's only a petty thief. A troublesome little rat. I have learned much from the English, too. To steal is honourable as long as you do it well. You talk to me about the Church. There are Spaniards who steal from the Church. But not the English! The English never steal *from* the Church. They steal the *whole* church!' His eyes twinkling, Veradaga leaned forward and said, 'Your king Henry the Eighth, *verdad?*'

'I'll do it,' Abdee said, smiling. 'But you must do me a favour in return.'

Veradaga showed no concern. He peered out the edge of the carriage curtain, saying, 'You tell me.'

Abdee said, 'Do not let your wife come back to Havana. She will seek me out for my curiosity to see my great-grandson. I do not want to meet the woman.'

Veradaga raised his hand. 'That matter. Do not mention that you wanted to see at least *one* of your heirs. It is the single flaw that showed me you are human—the one reason I knew I might trust you. And as for my wife returning to Cuba—' Veradaga shook his head, saying, '*Nunca* . . . never. She gave birth to my son but she is not a decent mother. The child will fare better in the world without a mother like that influencing him. Given the choice of having Victoria returning to Cuba or Juanito growing into a respectable man, I chose a brilliant future for my son. Senor Abdee, I have already decided that your grand-daughter will never return to Havana. You do not have to fear that.'

*   *   *

The *cantina* was crowded. The man in the honey-coloured suit stood by the bar, holding one arm around a Cuban girl whose black hair fell in ringlets to her shoulders. But whilst cuddling the girl, he eyed an older man sitting alone at a table. The Cuban girl tempted the young American in the honey-coloured suit but he saw the man at the table moving his hands inside the pockets of an expensively tailored suit of clothing. The old man was smiling at him, too. Duncan Webb knew it for certain now.

Dropping his arm from the girl's bare shoulder, Duncan reached toward his breeches, fondling himself to show the old man that he was built equally strong. He saw the old man at the table smile again, then push back his chair. Instead of walking toward Duncan Webb, though, the old man moved toward the door of the *cantina* and disappeared out into the street.

Duncan Webb planned to rise early tomorrow morning and try again at *Palacio Veradaga* to see Vicky's husband. He would put the pinch again on old Veradaga for some money. But he thought how nice it would be to have a little extra money tonight. He did not even know if Veradaga would pay. And he could tell by the old man's clothing and gold watch chain that he was a rich Cuban, that he would pay for whatever he wanted Duncan to do to him.

The night was warm. The street full of people. Duncan stood outside the *cantina* and looked up and down the cobbled street for the old man in the white suit. He finally saw him standing in the door to a courtyard. He saw his hand again digging on his groin.

If he thinks I'm going to suck him, he'll have a surprise, Duncan thought as he moved slowly toward the doorway. Let the old pervert suck me. And I'll make him pay first, by God!

The old man spoke, 'Good evening.'

'You are American?'

'English. Why don't you step back a little bit out of the street. I am well known here.'

Duncan smiled. How many times before had he heard that story! I am well known here! And how many times he had given thrills to rich old perverts who haunted waterfront bars but did not want to be seen groping peckers in the back street!

He obediently moved further into the dark courtyard, saying, 'I have just arrived in Havana. I would not normally say this but my baggage has been lost. And I must—'

'I understand,' said the old Englishman with twinkling blue eyes. 'I will reward you.'

Duncan proceeded, 'You are a gentleman like myself. And whilst we are speaking as gentlemen let me say that although I see what you . . . exhibit so interestingly inside

178

your pants I have something so much better that—' Duncan pushed his groin forward.

The old man did not lower his eyes, only saying, 'I also understand what you'd like to do with . . . that.'

Duncan shrugged. 'That is why you smiled at me, isn't it? You knew what you would be getting.'

'I knew. I knew when I looked at you—'

'I tell you, you will not be disappointed,' Duncan bragged, reaching again for his crotch.

'Nor will you be disappointed . . . Mister Webb.'

Duncan stared at him. 'How do you know my name?'

The old Englishman did not reply. He moved further back into the dark courtyard as two men emerged from the shadows behind Duncan Webb; one man reached to grab Duncan's hands, the other pointed a long, thin blade toward his throat.

Richard Abdee warned, 'Do not struggle, Mister Webb. You are coming to my house. It is near here in the district called Regla.'

A carriage rumbled in front of the door to the courtyard. Abdee nodded to the two men to move Duncan Webb toward the carriage.

*   *   *

Pitch torches smouldered in the damp room deep below Richard Abdee's slave house in Regla. Duncan Webb had been stripped of his clothing, his mouth had been gagged, and his arms spread over his head, the wrist of each hand tied to iron rings embedded deep into the stone walls. Abdee stood a short distance behind him, holding the butt of an oily black whip in one hand, studying the nakedness of Webb's tapering back. He said, 'You will excuse the cloth around your mouth, Mister Webb, but I have learned that fine gentlemen such as yourself often lose all self-respect during punishment.'

Duncan Webb's hands twisted in the iron rings; the muscles in his back contorted as he squirmed.

Letting the splayed tip of the leather whip fall to the floor, Abdee said, 'If you are wise, Mister Webb, you will not move. The chest and stomach are tender areas. Your movement will allow my whip only to wrap around you when I strike.'

Abdee wore boots, trousers, and a shirt with the sleeves rolled up to his elbows. He positioned his feet on the floor a short distance behind Webb, his face fixed with a half smile. He appeared to be enjoying himself for the first time in many years.

A loud crack of the whip echoed in the stone room. Abdee lowered his arm and saw Webb's body lock with tension.

'Don't be such a coward . . . *maricon*. I didn't even touch you. I was just trying my whip. It's been a long time since I've used this one. But it's no ordinary whip I'm using on you. This whip has a forked tongue. Like a dragon. You are special so you get the—'

The whip snapped in the room again, the splayed tip catching against Webb's back. Abdee's strike was perfect; he had caught Webb directly between the shoulder blades. He lashed a second time, striping Webb a short distance beneath his first target. He repositioned his feet, saying, 'I hear that you enjoy debasing people, *maricon*. I might as well have a little enjoyment with you. I shall start by making a ladder of red stripes down your back, like this . . .' He struck again, and then quickly again, proceeding to lower each hit down Webb's back.

Abdee's blue eyes soon dulled as he lost himself in the act of inflicting punishment on Duncan Webb. He no longer noticed that Webb was refraining from struggling, that all the stamina had disappeared from the young man's body. Nor did Abdee count the number of his lashes; the long, tapering black whip struck out again and again in the torchlit room; Richard Abdee stood steadfast in his position; he twisted with the agility of a much younger man as he performed his part of the bargain which he had made with Conde Juan Carlos Veradaga. But not thinking of this as fulfilling an agreement, Abdee even had forgotten that Duncan Webb possessed a name, or had once been married to his grand-daughter. Abdee increased the force of his whipping as he remembered back to the days of being the 'Dragonard' on St Kitts. He had never thought of a person's name—nor the colour of their skin—in those days. Nor did he now. He enjoyed the power which a whip gave him over

180

another human life. This excitement was increased by the fact that he could whip this particular man until he was dead. Abdee continued to keep his strokes neat, though, maintaining a uniform pattern of striping the flesh on Duncan Webb's back, of moving up and down the ladder of bleeding welts until Webb was no more than a dehumanized, lifeless hunk of flesh hanging from two iron rings embedded deep into the stone walls. And Richard Abdee was once again the Dragonard.

Book Three

THE REAPERS

Chapter Fifteen

A NEW BUCK

Croney laughingly informed Lloy how she had never received so many offers from the young girls in Town to help her in the chicken coop since he had come to live in her tall-legged house. She assured him and the other four black people sitting tonight around the firegrate in the middle of the floor, 'And I ain't going to tell none of them eager gals that this young buck here ain't mine to be setting-up with a wife! No, you bet not! You think I'm crazy? Let them young things keep helping me with my work. Let them think I'm going to put in a good word for them with this Lloy here.' Croney threw back her head and laughed, patting Lloy on the knee.

Lloy had learned much about black people in the week he had been at Dragonard Hill. He had seen the natural warmth and friendship amongst the people at Treetop House. But he also saw a similar conviviality here in the slave quarter at Dragonard Hill. Regardless of how hard the slaves worked during the day, despite the few comforts they had in their lives, Lloy found that black people understood one thing—they enjoyed friendship. They relied on companionship. He saw as much charity and hospitality here in Croney's meagre board hut in Town as he did around the table in the Refectory at Treetop House where the black people were all free and working for themselves.

The job of overseer was a challenge to Lloy. He caught glimpses of resentment in the eyes of male blacks who had

185

lived here all their lives—older men, men his same age, young boys. They all resented an outsider coming onto the plantation and giving orders to them.

Recognizing this jealousy as part of any human's nature, Lloy forced himself to show every consideration to the workers but yet maintain the authority with which Peter Abdee had entrusted him. He knew he was the link between the black people in Town and the white owner in the main house.

Lloy had seen little of the life in the main house. He knew that Peter Abdee had recently lost his wife, and that two of his daughters had come back to the plantation to visit him. One of the daughters was named Victoria—'Miss Vicky' to the slaves. The other daughter was 'Miss Veronica'. Lloy had not seen either of those two girls. But he had heard the stories about Veronica being married to a black man. Croney had told Lloy how Peter Abdee had freed Royal and, after securing him a job in a Boston bank, he allowed his daughter to marry him. This fact intrigued Lloy more than the gossip circulating in Town about Vicky, rumours speaking that she was a slut and the bane of her family. Lloy preferred to hear about Veronica. He wanted to learn as much about her and Royal as he possibly could. Lloy also had his plans.

The third Abdee daughter, Imogen, still remained an enigma to Lloy. The black slaves never spoke about their former overseer to him. Lloy gleaned a few details about Imogen—her rough manners, the fact that she lived in the old house—but he could not understand yet why Peter Abdee had relieved her of the position of overseer. The slaves did not talk to him about the matter. Lloy had ridden by the old house but had seen no sign of life, no smoke even curling from the chimney, not even sight of the black girl who supposedly lived with her. He was preparing himself for a meeting with Imogen.

The basic structure of obedience on a large plantation increasingly fascinated Lloy. He had never before realized how the house slaves felt themselves to be—and often treated as if they were—superior to the field slaves. True, he heard the black people in Town giggling about the head cook, Posey, but Lloy had seen them nod politely when Posey made an appearance in a shed or the vegetable garden. They *did* respect Posey. They *did* envy the house-servants. Lloy wished he could at least alter this feeling of inadequacy in the field slaves, to show them that their work was not ignoble, that to till land was in the age-old tradition of African people.

Although the black woman, Malou, served in the main house, Lloy saw that she not only spent much free time in Town but that the black people here shared a definite camaraderie with her. This puzzled him. He knew that Malou had only been here for a short time from Cuba with her mistress but, yet, he saw her being accepted in Town as a friend.

* * *

Croney's throaty voice cut into Lloy's thoughts as she said, 'You've got a gal back home where you come from?' She patted his forearm.

Lloy shook his head.

'Don't be bashful, boy. You hardly talk about yourself. You done nothing but work, eat, sleep since you got here.'

Lloy thought better than to tell Croney and her house-mates that he was a free black. He had suggested this to Peter Abdee himself, saying that the fact he was from Tree-top House should emerge at the correct time. It was not unknown in the South for one white planter to lease a slave to another. Peter agreed to allow Lloy to appear as if he were working here until a permanent man was found for the job, to imply that Lloy's presence here might only be temporary.

The time still had not come for him to make his real identity known. Perhaps it never would. He now answered Croney, 'What of us black people know much about ourselves anyway to tell?'

'That's what Malou says,' Curlew called from across the coals blinking on the iron grate. 'Malou claims that—'

Croney glanced at Curlew and shook her head for him to desist from talking about Malou. Curlew raised his head toward the smoke hole in the middle of the roof and, pointing to the dark sky outside, he said, 'Look there! A falling star!'

The awkward attempt at diversion did not work. Lloy

187

had seen Croney's signal of disapproval about Curlew mentioning Malou's name to a stranger. He knew that there was an undercurrent of excitement in Town. He sensed it in the peoples' talk and actions. He had heard that many things had been happening lately on Dragonard Hill, true, but he knew this excitement involved more than workers having a new overseer and a death in the main house.

Lloy remembered Claudia Goss's visit to Treetop House. He was reverting to his original opinion about Claudia Goss, that she was a trouble-maker, but he still felt that she, too, had been a harbinger of changes soon to happen here.

During his first week at Dragonard Hill, though, Lloy decided to keep all these opinions to himself. He still had much to learn about his father who had lived—and had been killed—on this land as well as gleaning what facts he could about his grandmother who had shot her own son to save Peter Abdee.

The first fact which Lloy had learned about his grandmother was from Croney. She had told him how the old black woman, Ta-Ta, had fallen to her death from a window in the old house. Ta-Ta had lived in an attic room there. The black people still held that Ta-Ta had been a witch. And although few field slaves had ever been inside the old house, they told how Ta-Ta had drawn on the ceilings and walls in her attic room, covering every possible space with cryptic pictures and words which told the history of her— and Peter Abdee's—past. Lloy suspected that such pictures must also reveal details about his own father and, thus, decided that the attic room in the old house was the one place he wanted to visit on Dragonard Hill regardless of how long he stayed here.

*   *   *

Belladonna slopping for Posey . . . a new nigger taking the job of overseer . . . the field niggers having secret meetings in Town at night to plot some sneaky up-rising . . . But nobody doing a damned thing about nothing . . . These were Imogen's repetitive thoughts as she spent the passing days alone in the old house. She had quickly depleted her supply of corn whisky and, sobering long enough to realize that she had not eaten in three days, she made a foray for food in the cupboards and pantry. She was nearing the end of the few scraps she had found to eat in the old house when she suddenly began discovering food trays left for her on the back steps of the kitchen.

Damn them! she cursed to herself. Damn them all to hell! They're treating me just like a prisoner. A prisoner here on . . . my own land!

Still undecided about what revenge she was going to seek against her father for replacing her with a black man, Imogen concentrated on what she considered to be a more pressing matter, the task of replenishing her whisky supply. She had always gone to Troy in the past to buy the corn whisky from the patrollers who met at the mercantile store. They distilled it themselves at home.

Ashamed, though, to show her face in Troy for fear of talk having reached it about a black man replacing her as overseer, Imogen decided instead to visit the house of one of the men who served as a patroller, the farmer named Claude Fonk who distilled the whisky on his land.

Imogen saddled her horse in the stable of the old house early the next morning, riding down the weed covered road which had once served as the main entrance to this land. She unlatched—and relatched—the gate hanging from the posts from which had hung a wooden star from its cross beams, and she galloped in the direction of Carterville.

Claude Fonk was a sallow-faced man who wore his greasy brimmed hat turned-up at the front. He sent his wife from the cabin when Imogen arrived at the door. He guessed that she had come here to buy whisky but he also had news which he wished to discuss with her, facts which Fonk believed were not fitting for his wife to hear. He considered Imogen to be more of a man than a woman.

Nodding for Imogen to sit upon a wooden bench alongside the plank table, Fonk shoved a jug of his latest brew across the table for her to sample whilst he asked, 'You talked to your sister?'

'Don't mention that bunch to me!' Imogen lifted the jug to her lips. She had forgotten the relief which good liquor gave her. She already felt better.

Fonk nodded for her to take another swig, saying, 'Then you don't know about the trouble?'

Imogen's stomach warmed from the liquor. She enjoyed the rush of heat then asked, 'What trouble?'

'It started with Billy Sandell. Stories have it that your sister—the fancy-dressing one from down Cuba—that she done coaxed young Billy to join her in the bushes alongside the road down back.' Fonk knew he could speak to Imogen about such matters.

Wiping her mouth on the sleeve of her nankeen shirt, Imogen muttered, 'You must mean Vicky ... the slut.'

'Billy Sandell, he ain't no angel. But then when he and some other boys were doing a spell of patrolling up north towards Horton, why they run into your other sis!'

Imogen began to show interest. She knew that Veronica had gone north to visit friends from schooldays. She asked, 'Veronica?'

Fonk shrugged. 'Don't know her name but she was travelling with two coons, a buck and a wench—'

Imogen remembered the story more clearly now. Her father had insisted that Veronica take somebody with her for protection. She said, 'That's Veronica all right. She went visiting old friends or something.'

'Don't know about the reason she was trailing around the country. But Billy being the horny devil he is, he decided to repeat the fun he had with your fancy-ass sister, that Vicky one, but—'

Imogen laughed. 'Billy Sandell! That dirty-peckered polecat! He tried to pester old iron drawers?'

'He tried!' Fonk said, also laughing now, shaking his head. 'That danged Billy tried. But it didn't quite work out that way. They got interrupted or something.'

'Just as well,' Imogen said, studying the whisky jug. 'Veronica, she prefers black pecker.'

'You don't say?' Fonk nodded for Imogen to help herself to the jug.

'She married that coon who my Pa freed. She has three kids by him. They live up in the North.'

'You got a sis married to a ... coon?'

'Lots of strange things happen over at Dragonard Hill, Claude. Lots of strange things. That's why I ain't the overseer there no more.'

'You ain't the—' This announcement stunned Claude Fonk.

The corn whisky gave Imogen confidence. She enjoyed talking to someone again. She was ready to start venting her hatred. She took another drink from the jug, wiped her mouth again on the sleeve of her shirt and shoved the jug back across the table toward Fonk. She said, 'Fact is I might be leaving these parts. Pulling up roots.'

'You don't say?' Fonk took his first drink from the jug.

'Fact is, Claude, I think you and the men should keep an eye on the place. A close eye, if you know what I mean. The niggers are having secret meetings at night. And what's more, my Pa's allowing it to happen. That's why him and me ain't seeing eye-to-eye.'

'Meetings? Niggers holding meetings? But that's against the law!'

'That's why I think you and the rest of the patrollers should keep an eye on the place. Secret meetings and a black taking over my place.' She paused, deciding that she might as well break the news as anyone else. She lowered her head, saying, 'You see, Pa's got a coon now for overseer. I don't know where he got him. He ain't one of ours. But he's a coon.'

Shaking his head, Claude Fonk said, 'Your Pa always was a queer fellow. I know he's your Pa and all but—'

'You don't have to make apologies to me for your opinions, Claude. Just do like I suggest. Have the boys keep an eye on the place because once Pa goes broke—'

'Your Pa's going broke?'

'Who do you think has been plowing money into Greenleaf like it was bullshit? Barry Breslin don't know a crop from a tit. Pa's been backing him. Has been throwing good money after bad. He ain't as much as told me this in so many words but I know he's in trouble. Money troubles. Bad money troubles. So, if he loses Dragonard Hill on account of notes he signed for Greenleaf, and the niggers at home are holding secret meetings . . . well, nobody has to be too smart to see that that adds up to trouble.'

Claude Fonk shook his head again. He understood the volatile situation she described without listening to any elaborations. He said, 'That could mean trouble for the whole countryside. Niggers get tetchy when they know they might be sold off a place. Like living right next to a keg of dynamite.'

'Worse, Claude. Worse! Like living right next to a keg of dynamite but with a nigger holding the candle!'

'It's that bad?'

'Worse,' Imogen assured him, fuelled again by whisky. 'So pass the word around to the other patrollers. Keep your eye on Dragonard Hill.'

* * *

Posey was suspicious of Belladonna coming to work again in the kitchen; she had not been a kitchen helper since the Abdees had moved from the old house. As Lulu could not cope with the many chores Posey needed done, though, he reluctantly agreed to have the black girl assist him as a helper. He made the fact clear, though, that she was not to sleep in the kitchen. That was his territory at night. If Belladonna were to work with him, and be attached once again to the main house, she must spend her nights in the loft built over the kitchen annex.

Peter Abdee gladly granted Posey his condition. The proposal for Belladonna to sleep in the kitchen loft temporarily solved his quandary about her moving into the main house as his concubine, perhaps even prevent widening the rift between himself and Imogen.

Peter was suffering many misgivings about his relationship with Belladonna. She finally had confessed that it had been Imogen's plan for her to seduce him. The idea repulsed Peter as well as appearing to him to being a rather crude, even infantile gesture.

Preferring not to concentrate on the dilemma which Imogen presented to him, Peter chose to concentrate on clarifying his situation with Belladonna. He saw that the girl would soon become increasingly involved with him. He had wanted and still wanted a physical diversion from his loneliness. Belladonna had provided this. But he now recognized that he had a responsibility to protect her from a hurt which might mar any future she could hope to have for an enduring relationship with someone who could give her a home, a family, or both.

Belladonna noticed Peter's distracted mood as they met to make love tonight on a mossy knoll in the woodlands. She lay curled against his naked body, content to lie on this warm night snuggled against him. She gently brushed her lips against the side of his naked chest as he lay with both hands locked behind his head.

She whispered, 'You thinking about somebody?'

Peter did not want to tell her that he was thinking about Kate. He answered. 'Uh-huh.'

'About me?'

'What would you like me to be thinking about you?'

She traced the tip of her forefinger up his arm, through the coarse hair growing in the pit of his arm, smiling as she saw him flinch with the touch. She answered, 'I don't know exactly just what—'

'I'm thinking that I'd like you to be happy.'

'I *am* happy,' she said enthusiastically, jumping to straddle his groin with her naked legs.

'This is . . . physical happiness. I mean truly happy. Like you marrying . . . someone who could make you truly happy.'

She hung her head. She was not pouting. She looked reflective, pensive.

He asked in a quiet voice, 'Have you ever thought about having children?'

Belladonna began, 'Imogen says—' She stopped. She had promised herself never again to discuss Imogen. To try to block her completely out of her mind. She answered his question with a shrug of her bare brown shoulders.

Peter reached forward and, rubbing the back of his fingers against her forearm, he said, 'Girl, I never want to hurt someone as sweet as you. Never. And there are so many ways I could.'

'You could never hurt—' Belladonna stopped. She threw back her head and, looking at the stars twinkling in the sky, she took a deep sigh. She closed her eyes and, as if the night air were a spray from a waterfall, she gyrated herself in its imaginary pinpoints of mist. Then, quickly scooting back on Peter's naked legs, she lowered her head to his groin. She buried her face in his crotch and, holding his penis to her mouth with both hands, she began to suck him for hardness.

Peter remained motionless with his hands clasped behind his neck. He felt the warmth of Belladonna's mouth awakening excitement in him. He felt how she had finally

193

learned to satisfy him without allowing her teeth to cut against his phallus, to take long and deep pulls, swallowing him deep into her throat and then pulling up her head to his crown whilst slicking one hand with her saliva to keep the movement constant, perpetual, one long cycle of satisfaction for him. But Peter suspected that he must soon forego this satisfaction. He believed that no physical satisfaction was worth an eternal wound in somebody else's soul. He must not allow Belladonna to become his mere concubine. She had helped him accept his loneliness after Kate's death but he must not transfer his suffering to her. He did not believe that love was a sequence of passing pain from one person to another like a child's game involving a handkerchief, a ring, an apricot pit.

* * *

Maybelle and Ham kept close to their long-legged house after they returned to Dragonard Hill with Veronica. They worried about Veronica recovering from the shock of the patroller attacking her; they were satisfied at last that her condition would not be serious.

They also were pleased that they had not been here on the night when Imogen Abdee had barged unexpectedly into Malou's meeting in the Chapel. They were certain that they would have been amongst the black people attending that meeting.

Although speaking little when they were alone about Malou—her teachings that black people should include African gods and frenzied devotional habits in their religion—Ham and Maybelle knew that one another was thinking of the Cuban slave's preaching. Ham and Maybelle also knew that they were both remembering the physical comforts they had enjoyed in the white people's homes with Veronica.

Maybelle's only vague reference toward that joyful time spent with Miss Veronica in the outside world were the words, 'We've got something to pray for. We've seen how people's supposed to live and we've got something to pray for.' She did not expand beyond that.

The first intimation that Ham was thinking about their future life came when he asked Maybelle about their young son when she returned from the Shed. He called the boy by the name they had given him. He asked Maybelle, 'How's Tim? He growing well?'

Maybelle had made a practise not to think of Tim as their son. That was the only way she could accept the land's law that she must not claim a child born from her womb. She tried to think of all of the black children at The Shed as her children, tried to show them all an equal amount of love. She answered Ham that the boy would be strong.

Ham and Maybelle's one moment of luxury in these first days following their return to Dragonard Hill was their few hours spent alone in the long-legged house. They lay curled together tonight; Maybelle's naked legs were wrapped around Ham's buttocks. His love-making was particularly tender tonight. Hers was hungry, showing a need for his attentions. He knelt between her legs, holding her up on the incline of his muscled thighs, pumping his hips toward her, feeling the sensation grow more tingling inside his penis. He did not want to stop. He could not stop. They had long-ago decided that they did not want to have any more children, to give no more slaves to this land. But as they clung desperately to one another, as Ham's hard penis drove deeper, quicker into Maybelle's moistness, he whispered, 'Let's make a baby, Honey. Let's make a baby in you.' Maybelle clung onto his neck, digging her fingernails into the mahogany-brown skin stretched over his back, whispering, 'Make a baby in me. Make your baby in me for good.' She testified her words with a kiss, taking Ham's long tongue into her mouth as he thrust his groin in strong, final movements against her stretched thighs. The seed exploded deep inside Maybelle like a long-held secret as they clutched one another in this unexpected moment of joy and fear.

Chapter Sixteen

TWO SISTERS

The figure of the darkly featured patroller still haunted Veronica's dreams, the rapist appearing to her in a variety of disturbing spectres ranging from a man towering over her with threatening talons which she had to keep from rending her naked breasts into bloody shreds, another image being of a shiny black horse rearing over her recumbent body, a stallion that whinnied as urine gushed forth from a greasy shaft between its hind legs. Veronica tried to conquer the fears in her awakening hours by prayer, thankfulness for having been spared the basest of degradations.

Having had ample opportunity to reassemble the words which the patroller had threatened her with by the time she finally returned to Dragonard Hill, Veronica now clearly remembered him taunting her with stories about Vicky, lurid tales how Vicky had accompanied him into the bushes alongside the public road.

Veronica saw that her father's troubles had increased in her absence; she heard that Imogen had been replaced in her position as overseer by a black man; that Belladonna now worked for Posey in the kitchen annex. Veronica did not want to add to her father's burden by reporting to him about narrowly escaping being raped on a country roadside; she pleaded with Maybelle and Ham also to remain silent about the incident. But there was no reason not to confront Vicky and demand an explanation for her scandalous activities.

A month had almost passed since Vicky's arrival from Cuba and she still showed no signs of going home. Veronica knew her own reason for lingering at Dragonard Hill but she could not understand why Vicky remained here, especially when she obviously hated the place and all her family.

Veronica received the opportunity to speak to Vicky on the second morning back at Dragonard Hill about the matter of her conduct with the patroller. Vicky was bored with rural life and had been going to bed early. She often came down to the breakfast alcove when Peter and Veronica were finishing their coffee. This morning Vicky arrived after Peter had already departed from the main house.

Veronica began her accusation slowly, confidently, commencing with the words 'I am surprised at you, Vicky', reaching a pitch in this opening attack with 'You should at least have more respect for your family!'

Vicky stared at Veronica sitting across the rosewood table from her, first, in shock at the sudden accusation for behaving indecently with a white farmer alongside the public road. Next, her expression turned to anger and she flared, 'How dare you believe the gossip of white trash farmers!'

'Then you do not deny it!'

'I will not dignify your shabby accusation by even answering you.' Vicky pulled the ruffled edge of her *robe de chambre* tightly around her throat.

'Victoria Abdee!' Veronica screamed. 'Or Condesa Veradaga as you so grandly call yourself these days. You and I both know that you have no control over your wicked tastes. Father has overlooked it all his life. Everyone always said, "Poor Vicky! Oh, Poor Vicky! She suffered that nasty incident as a girl with that pedlar man!" Well, Vicky, let me tell you this! I do not believe that story about a pedlar man raping you. I never did. If anyone was raped I believe that you were the aggressor! Even as a child. I know you too well. So do not try to play holier-than-thou with me. Do not forget, we were at school together in Boston. Do not forget that I saw how you conducted yourself with . . . Duncan Webb!'

Vicky's voice was low, brimming with hate. She warned, 'Do not mention his name to me or—'

'Oh, yes, that is just the reaction I expect! "Do not mention his name!" You followed Duncan Webb to New Orleans, didn't you? You married him! You let him make a fool out of you here at home. In front of all your family. You foisted him and his insolent ways on everyone. You let him beat the house-slaves—one of whom turned out to be my husband! But you still say "Oh, do not mention his name".'

Holding her head at a pert angle, Vicky said, 'Veronica, I would not be so sanctimonious if I were you. Everyone knows why white females chase after . . . black men.'

'Why, Vicky?' Veronica demanded, her fingers curling in anger as she sat to the edge of her chair. 'Tell me why!'

'You tell me, my dear. Or isn't your . . . Royal built quite so big as other bucks?'

Veronica forced herself from flying across the table and striking Vicky on the face. She fought to keep a balance to her voice as she said, 'There is more to life—and love—Vicky, than the . . . size of a man's genitals. But that is one thing you obviously have never discovered. That is why you are having such a miserable life.'

'My life is *not* miserable!' Vicky quickly retorted.

'You are very wretched!' Veronica argued. 'Do not try to play games with me. You do not write letters home to your husband. None arrive for you. You rarely talk about your child. I would not even be surprised if you do not return to Cuba!'

'And why wouldn't I?'

'Possibly because your good husband might not want you coming back home. It could very possibly be that you conduct yourself in Havana in the same shocking way as you conduct yourself here. Sneaking into the bushes with every stranger like a . . . harlot!'

Vicky had received enough abuse from Veronica. She airily announced, 'The fact that I might have gone into the cottonwoods with a patroller is no reason for someone in your position to cast aspersions on my family life!'

'There! You admit it! You did . . . rut with that patroller!'

Realizing that Veronica had tricked her into confessing to a profligacy, Vicky stared in amazement at her sister. She said, 'Veronica, you are more artful than I ever gave you credit for.'

'Stop trying to flatter me. I am a ninny and I am the first to admit it. Who but a ninny would have protected you all these years?'

'The trouble with you, Veronica, is not that you're a ninny but that you are dreary and boring!'

'Fine. Neither do I deny that. But at least my "dreary" and "boring" ways do not place other people in danger. And I am not talking about your actions merely affecting me. I mean Maybelle. Ham. Two innocent people.'

'You worry too much about niggers.'

'And why not?'

'We are talking in circles, I think, Veronica. I think you are a nigger-lover and you think I'm a slut. Let's leave it at that.'

'Oh, no! Let's not leave it at that. Let's start there! I fell in love with a man who happened to be black. Brown. Whatever colour you care to call him. I married him. I believe that no people—regardless of their skin colouring—should have to be placed in subjugation, bondage, slavery to another person.'

'Then I suggest that you go back to the North where other people share your sentiments. Because you are quite in the minority here! In the South!'

'I will. I intend to go home soon. But I also love my father very much. I came home to him when he needed me. And I also looked forward to seeing you and Imogen after all these years.'

'I suppose you'll have a talk with her next.'

'Imogen? Why? About what?'

'About her trying to arrange for Papa to sleep with Belladonna.'

'Stop being so disgusting, Vicky,' Veronica said, pushing a coffee cup to one side on the table. 'You always reduce everything to . . . sex!'

'Disgusting am I?' Vicky laughed at her sister. 'It's the truth! Imogen did plan such a thing. And it worked! But it worked too damned well! Why do you think Belladonna's in the kitchen? To be close at hand for Papa, that's why!'

'Vicky, you are despicable.'

'I am despicable only if I stay here listening to you speak from your pulpit in the sky, a place where a view of the

199

world is so dim you don't even know what's happening around you!'

Standing now next to the table, Vicky continued, 'I am also in the wrong if I stay here and watch Imogen throw her cast-off lovers to my . . . father. If I stand around watching that, then, no, I do have no pride.'

'What are you implying,' Veronica asked, still seated in her chair in the breakfast alcove.

'I imply nothing,' Vicky said moving toward the double white doors leading to the hallway. 'I am *saying* that if I embarrass you, cause you trouble, I will leave. There is no reason to stay on Dragonard Hill—at least not whilst you and Imogen are here. And maybe you're right about my life in Havana. Perhaps it is not a picture of marital joy. But, by God, Veronica, the world is a big place. There's someplace in it for me. And I also intend to help my Papa. And I am certain I can help him better than all of you! I will go to New Orleans and prove that I can!'

'What good will you do in New Orleans?'

'I know more about this family than you do, Veronica . . . Selby! You concentrate on kindness and goodness in the future. I will build on the wickedness and torture we came from in the past. I know the scum, the addictions, the passions we've picked-up along the way. You concern yourself with good will and charity, Mrs Selby. I will tend the darker side.'

Vicky opened one of the double white doors and, stepping out into the hallway, she called, 'Malou! Malou, you bitch! Pack my clothes! We're going to New Orleans, you voodoo bitch!' She slammed the door.

* * *

The brothel, *Petit Jour,* was the one place in New Orleans where Vicky knew she could find a likely accomplice for her plan. She regretted that Jerome Poliguet was not on the Carterville-New Orleans coach to make the tedious trip south speed more quickly but, having only sober-faced Malou, and two chubby-faced farm women for travelling companions inside the bumpy public coach, Vicky employed the time brooding upon the sudden turn in Veronica's temperament.

The thought that word about her assignation with the patroller already spread in the countryside made Vicky feel relieved that at least she was escaping this backwoods community. She looked blankly at the water oaks suspending curtains of moss as the coach travelled farther south; she hoped that she would never have to go upcountry again. Home had always been misery for her.

Vicky had no idea what the future held in store for her. Considering the prospect of returning to Havana, she remembered Veronica's accusation about her not caring for her husband, of talking so little of her son.

Perhaps I am not meant to be a mother, Vicky told herself as she saw the first storage sheds on the northern skirts of New Orleans. The prospect of being once again in a vibrant city began to revitalize her. She had always believed that a city held some secret strength for her; New Orleans was especially an elixir with its mysterious architecture, the cries of the black people, a night-long cacophony of 'hot coffee!', 'sweet pies', even *biere du pays*—pineapple beer!

Unlike Vicky, Malou sat soberly as the coach now travelled over cobbled streets through rows of tall houses crowding one another. Malou had left many friends on Dragonard Hill. She also had left work undone there. She felt that she was abandoning the black people in Town at the moment when they might be needing her the most. She thought about the black overseer, Lloy. Something troubled her about Lloy. He was not telling everything he knew. Malou had no choice at the moment but to obey her mistress's commands and accompany her to New Orleans. Where they would go to from here was a mystery. Malou had often prayed for the gift of foretelling the future but the gods had always denied her the gift. She only knew the next point of her destiny when she heard Vicky call to the black driver of an open public carriage which they hailed at the coach-house. Vicky ordered the black-driver wearing a feather cockade on the band of his tattered old hat, 'Hotel LaSalle!'

*   *   *

'You once ordered me to leave this establishment,

Madam,' Vicky said as she sat across the desk from Naomi, the veiled woman who owned the bordello, *Petit Jour,* on Rampart Street. Vicky had come here from the Hotel LaSalle after she had bathed and changed into a crackling emerald gown—the first dress she had worn that wasn't black since she had left Havana. She held her hands pointed on the crystal knob of a green ruffled parasol and proceeded, 'You once suggested that life's answer for me was to go home and live with my father on Dragonard Hill. I did not follow your advice. I married a Cuban. I live in Havana.'

Naomi looked at the card which Vicky had sent in with the bodyguard to Naomi's office. She said, 'Yes, I see. The Condesa Veradaga.'

'My family name was Abdee.'

'I remember you well,' Naomi assured her in a raspy voice. 'The passage of years have not taken a toll on your attractive appearance, Miss Abdee.'

'I am called "Condesa".'

'None of your pretences, girl!' the veiled Negress named Naomi said, throwing down the card to her desk. 'Come to the point! I remember that you did not speak with a guarded tongue in the past. What do you want from me now?'

'Fine,' Vicky said, sitting primly in the chair across from Naomi. 'I'll tell you exactly what I want. A girl. One of the most beautiful young girls you can find here in New Orleans.'

Naomi lifted her cane and, pointing its ebony tip at Malou standing soberly alongside the door, she said, 'I see you have an attendant. You do not come here for a body slave. Usually women approach me for a handsome young man. A buck. I have the occasional request from a female for another . . . woman but—'

'I do not wish the girl for myself. I want her for my father.'

'What is the matter? Has Dragonard Hill depleted its supply of wenches?'

'My father is an honourable man, madam. He respects his slaves. He does not forcibly bed them. I recently returned home because of the death of my step-mother. She and my father were happily married. But—'

'Yes,' Naomi said. 'I heard of her death.'

'That surprises me,' Vicky sniffed.

'Don't be so surprised. A whore has ears as well as a cunt!' Naomi laughed as she saw Vicky pale at her crudeness. She said, 'Ah! the pretences of a fine titled lady. I remember you coming here swearing like a roustabout on the wharf. Let us not play games, condesa. So, your father has lost his wife. He does not want to bed a wench on the plantation because he's too humane, too considerate. And you thought I might have a little filly who . . .'

'Not a . . . whore, madam!'

'Oh, of course not. Not a whore. Not for such a fine gentleman as your father.' Tilting her veiled head, Naomi said, 'It is too bad you did not come here six months ago. The annual Octoroon Ball is held in New Orleans then. That is where most white gentlemen find the mistresses they keep in very nice little houses. These girls are illegitimate. They have impeccable pedigrees on their father's side—usually married Creoles—and their mothers are ravishing beauties. The girls are educated to be perfect ladies. The ultimate of femininity. The best a man could wish for in a mistress. Such a girl would suit your purposes.'

The idea of an octoroon girl immediately appealed to Vicky. She knew that her father would respond to a well educated young companion. She said, 'But surely you must know one who is not taken.'

Naomi smiled behind her veil. She recognized the Abdee eagerness in this young woman, a willingness to buy or sell anyone at anytime. Speaking about a girl as if she were a horse for a carriage. She is just like her grandfather, Naomi thought.

Rising from the chair behind her desk, Naomi said, 'Come back this evening. I'll see what I can do for you by then. At least I'll be able to give you a lead I should think.'

'I am most appreciative,' Vicky began.

'Spare me the rubbish. Show your appreciation with gold if I find you something.'

Naomi did not escort Vicky and Malou to the carved door of her office but, remaining standing behind her desk, she waited until her black bodyguard returned from seeing the visitors to the courtyard.

Naomi informed the burly black man, 'I want to make some changes in tonight's theatrics. The young lady you saw is returning this evening. I will allow her to sit in one of the curtained boxes upstairs in the theatre. I want her to see that she has more than one acquaintance in New Orleans.'

For the rest of the day, Naomi remained in her office, making plans and sending messages, waiting to see what customers reserved a place for tonight's theatrics. Finally, by early evening, she heard that Jerome Poliguet had sent word to *Petit Jour* that he was coming later this evening as was previously arranged. Naomi then went upstairs herself. She hurried to ascend the red-carpeted stairs before the hour that Vicky was to arrive back in her office. She ordered the bodyguard to inform Vicky that she was indisposed and, whilst waiting for her, Vicky was to be escorted to a small room upstairs in the theatre herself.

* * *

Vicky stared at the white man's naked body trussed with black leather thongs by two voluptuous black women. She sat in the niche protected from the stage area by thin gauze curtains, a protection which covered her presence from the eyes of the men lounging on chaise longues encircling the stage but a curtaining which was sheer enough for her to see that the white man was Jerome Poliguet. Vicky watched with growing fascination as Poliguet gasped, moaned, struggled against his leather bindings as the Negresses pulled him toward a black woman sitting upon bales of cotton. Poliguet was trussed to be only one more bale of cotton being loaded for the North by African workers. Vicky complimented herself for having guessed that Poliguet's lean body was firm and well-proportioned, that his manhood was of a size which would have pleased her. She could see all those physical attributes from where she sat. But she also was most pleased that she had foreseen that Poliguet would have been disappointing in love-making. Vicky guessed that—regardless of his theatrical moanings and protests—he enjoyed being dragged from his chaise longue, stripped of his clothes, and tied into a bundle by domineering women. Yes, she was certain that Poliguet thoroughly enjoyed his role. And watching him now being forced to lie facedown on the floor in front of a Negress and

204

kiss the toes of her thigh-high leather boots, Vicky decided that she had yet one more favour to ask of Naomi. The bodyguard had told her that Naomi would see her after tonight's theatric. Vicky now planned how she would ask Naomi—even pay her— to allow her to participate in a future theatric. Perhaps even a later performance tonight. Yes, and she would ask Naomi to keep Poliguet in bondage until that time. Vicky decided that if she was going to have a bad reputation in certain parts of Louisiana, she might as well debase herself in New Orleans as well.

Chapter Seventeen

THE BOSTON-NEW BRUNSWICK

Mister Reginald Snelling, Mister Cartwright Burney-Jones, Mister James Fitzpatrick, and Mister Joseph Llewelyn represented a token committee of the Board of Trustees for the Boston-New Brunswick Bank at a meeting held this grey morning in the Adams-style boardroom in the bank's main office on Beacon Street, Boston. The four sombre-suited gentlemen had assembled to give their chief clerk, Royal Selby, instructions on how to proceed—or not to proceed—with the loan of money being considered to the charitable group, The Deliverance of Neglected People to Safety.

Royal understood the four gentlemen's hesitation to speak in specific terms about the society they were to discuss at this meeting, a charity which he knew them all to be members of, but, nonetheless, a group unchartered by the State of Massachussetts and considered to be financially as well as politically risky for any bank to have dealings.

The state of Massachussetts was known for its cotton mills in Lowell, Hutton, other industrial towns; the mills' chief source of cotton came from the South; the South's work force was slave labour; Royal knew the commercial dangers for a bank as esteemed as the Boston-New Brunswick to be connected in any way to a charity such as The Deliverance of Neglected People to Safety—a title thinly disguising the fact that the society assisted black slaves escape to freedom in the North.

Since the days when Peter Abdee had first written to the Boston-New Brunswick Bank and found employment for his future son-in-law as a teller there, Royal had enjoyed considerate, pleasant treatment from everyone on every level within the bank. He had expected to be greeted by a stony wall of emotionless civility but, instead, had been warmly welcomed as a member of a small community of businessmen and their wives.

Royal's dedication to his job, and his long hours of study at night to improve his knowledge of accounting and commercial banking, had helped his progress at the bank. He and Veronica had both decided to keep themselves away from social affairs as much as possible, not to flaunt their marriage to eyes in Boston which were supposedly easily shocked by appearances.

The first hint that there was a faction within the bank—indeed in the entire city of Boston—which was violently opposed to slave-owners had been made to Royal when the bank vice-president, Mister Reginald Snelling, asked him if he would care to contribute in a modest way to a charity.

That had been four years ago. The charity had been The Deliverance of Neglected People to Safety. And in the meantime, Royal had learned more about the South from the four members of the bank's board than he had learned about the South in the entire time he had lived there.

Snelling, Burney-Jones, Fitzpatrick, and Llewelyn kept a growing list of names in the South—farmers, ministers of the church, businessmen—who not only contributed to the same charity but wrote covert letters in which they offered accommodations for 'Victims' to be enjoyed at a time when the society saw it financially able to bring its first 'testimonial' north.

The costs of bringing slaves from the South were surprisingly high; steamboat and railway passages were needed, bribes were necessary on many occasions; even military uniform. But most important were funds to create new jobs for the victims here in the North. The society had a small fund to date but, as each of the members had to be careful as to how much he or she could personally donate, the society hoped to establish a loan from the Boston-New Brunswick Bank to cover major expenses. The ostensible reason of the loan was to build a meeting house in Boston. The truth was—at long last—the society was going to bring the first slaves north. Royal had seized the opportunity of Veronica returning to Dragonard Hill as a ploy to alert their members in Louisiana, Mississipi, Tennessee that the plan was at long last going to be put into effect. He did not want to involve Veronica personally in the venture, though, not to ensnare her with information and details which might make her a criminal suspect, perhaps even to face execution.

* * *

Today, this bleak morning in Boston, Royal Selby listened soberly to the bad news. Messrs Snelling, Burney-Jones, Fitzpatrick, and Llewelyn told him in guarded terms that they had been over-ruled by the board's majority, that the Boston-New Brunswick Bank would not be forth-coming with a loan to the society for running slaves from the South.

Royal had learned a long time ago to protect his pride. He had learned not to beg, that begging achieved nothing but deterioration of dignity. He stood tall, sedately at the end of the polished mahogany board table. A stiff white collar hugged his cocoa-brown neck. He kept his head low; his chin was strong and firmly set as he received the bad news. He slowly drummed four fingers of each hand against the edge of the table.

Listening to each of the gentlemen express their deep regrets, Royal knew that they were as helpless as he was in this matter. At all times the prospect of a loan had been considered a gamble. But the disappointing fact to Royal was that each gentleman had assured him—separately—in the last months that they knew that the Board was going to vote unanimously to help the charitable cause, that he should begin laying the ground-work.

Mister Llewelyn now said, 'I suggest you call your wife immediately home, Mister Selby. To write to her immediately and urge her to return North.'

Royal shook his head. 'I am afraid it is not that easy. I have already written to the man we know at Treetop House. I have written him to go to Dragonard Hill and contact . . . Mrs Selby. He should have received the letter by now that they are to bring the first slaves.'

The four board members looked at one-another. They knew about the man from Treetop House, the farm for free slaves, the black man who was their integral peg in this entire works. If Royal Selby had already contacted the free negro, Lloy, they knew that it might be too late. That the society would be delivering the first victims—with the assistance of the black man, Lloy, and Mrs Selby—to the North at any moment.

*   *   *

Amongst the slaves to be taken North by Royal Selby's society were the two black people living at Grouse Hollow, Jack and Mary.

Jack was still waiting to hear from Treetop House for the appointed day—or night—that he and his wife would make a run from their mistress's farm.

No message had yet arrived. Mary pressed Jack for details but he confessed that, although the white-haired old chandler at Treetop House had told him about the plan, the designated date was not set—anyway not made known to the small handful of black people who would escape their owners' tyranny. The old chandler could not even divulge to Jack which of the people at Treetop House was the key man here in the South for the Abolitionist movement.

Mary sobbed against her husband's chest tonight; they lay hungry and cold on the floor alongside the cookstove in the lean-to which served as a kitchen at Grouse Hollow. Claudia Goss's snores drifted through the tattered curtain hanging in the partition.

Jack patted his wife's quaking shoulder with a reassuring hand, whispering, 'Don't you cry, honey. I loves you. That's all that matters for us. I loves you. And we're going to get out of here. We're going to get out of here one way or another even if I finally has to . . . kill her with my own two hands. Yes, honey, you and I are getting to safety.'

They had discussed many times about strangling Claudia Goss in her sleep, or sneaking up behind her with a board, hitting her over the head, and scattering her brains around the cabin. But they had agreed up to now that murder was not the price they wanted to pay from freedom and self respect, that when they left Grouse Hollow they would run away from a crime no larger than running for their right as free people. Jack no longer knew if he could remain true to that conviction. He had to do something soon. Claudia now let them eat no more than one potato between them a day. She chastised Mary when she did not clean the shack and derided her for the place being so dirty. Jack knew that Claudia would soon sell Mary. He had to hear soon from Treetop House if the black Abolitionist man there was going to help him and Mary escape. If not, they would run away from Grouse Hollow with no place to go.

Chapter Eighteen

JEZEBEL'S GRIP

Posey stood with his hands planted on his hips as he faced Lloy in the colonnade which connected the kitchen annex to the main house. He said, 'Boy, there's something quality about you! You done work in the main house of the plantation you come from?'

'I did work wherever there was work to do,' Lloy answered, not lying but still withholding the fact from everyone on Dragonard Hill that he came from Treetop House.

'How long Master Peter plan to keep you here then?'

'I can't answer that, Miss Posey, because I don't think even he rightly knows yet. I don't think anybody does.'

Posey lifted his head proudly, pleased that this handsome new black overseer addressed him by his preferred title, and had done so without any prompting. He decided to take the new boy into his confidence, leaning forward to impart, 'Certain talk ain't meant for niggers to speak but being you's overseer here and me's the head cook, I can say to you in secret-like that you're going to be a heap better at the job than that Miss Imogen was. I don't know beans about field work and tree-chopping but I can already see you'll be better than her. The job is meant for a man to do, anyway.'

Shaking his head, Posey continued, 'Miss Imogen, I don't know what's going to happen to her. Her world's done changed and it changed fast. I think she might lose her brains.'

Lloy had work to do this morning reorganizing the fodder system for the livestock but he did not want to cut short this conversation with Posey too quickly, too abruptly. He realized the value of having such a well-informed person on his side. Also, he preferred not to discuss his predecessor. He answered non-committally, 'Maybe time heals old wounds, Miss Posey.'

'Wounds? Miss Imogen suffering from worse than some wounds. She ain't got her job! She drunk all the time now on corn whisky. That Belladonna sleeps here up in the kitchen loft—' Posey reached for his apron and, wringing one corner of it in his hands, he said, 'I hope the White Lord God forgives me for my wicked ways. I done a few bad things. One be to Belladonna. I completely misjudged that Belladonna wench, I did. There's a good gal now. But the spirit seems to have gone plumb out of her in the last few days. She was bright and sparkly like sunshine when she came to work for me a few days back. But suddenly she goes all sober. I knows it ain't over missing that Miss Imogen. No, I knows it ain't because of that because no more than just five, ten minutes ago we seen Miss Imogen staggering to the hills. Belladonna done worried Miss Imogen's going to come to the kitchen to get her and drag her back to the old house. Belladonna runs hide and—' Posey continued to wring the white apron in his slender hands.

Alerted by Posey's announcement that Imogen had gone past the kitchen toward the wooded back hills, Lloy asked, 'You say you saw Miss Imogen walking away from the old house?'

'Old house? She was miles away from that tumbled down shack!'

Lloy had been waiting for an opportunity to go to the old house, to inspect the attic room where his grandmother had lived. He asked for safety's sake, 'You're certain Miss Imogen won't be meeting her father? That they won't be riding back to the old house together?'

'Meet her papa? Never! They still ain't speaking! Besides, Master Peter, he's gone to Greenleaf this morning to bring young Master David back home. I know that for certain because Master Peter tells me before he left what he wants me to fix young Master David for his first supper home tonight. Miss Vicky, she's taken off to New Orleans with that voodoo nigger. And Miss Veronica, I don't know where she be around here this moment. But Miss Imogen, no. I knows she's drunk cause I've seen her.'

Thanking Posey for his time, Lloy made an attempt to leave but Posey was hesitant to lose such an attentive visitor. When Lloy finally managed to move from the flagging under the colonnade, Posey excitedly called, 'I almost done forgot the reason I shouted for you . . . Master Lloy.'

The formal address of 'Master Lloy'—especially coming from Posey who recognized no peers amongst black people—surprised him.

Posey reached into the skirt pocket of his long white dress and, producing an envelope, he held it toward Lloy, saying, 'I can't read writing but I know from the tired-looking nigger man who delivers this letter to the back door, I know from the messenger the identity of the party who sends this to you.' Posey narrowed his eyes, asking, 'That Claudia Tucker woman, she ain't your rightly owner, is she, boy?'

The name 'Tucker' first confused Lloy. Then remembering that Tucker had been Claudia Goss's married name when her first husband had been the overseer here, he said, 'No, Miss Posey. That woman's not my owner. I don't even know why she would be writing to me. How she even knows that I'm here.'

Taking the letter, Lloy quickly opened it with one finger whilst Posey lingered alongside him, saying, 'I'm surprised she reads and writes herself, her being nothing but trash.'

Lloy read: 'CONGRATULATIONS ON YER NEW JOB. MEAT ME TONITE AT X-RODES NEAR TREETOP HOUS AT SUNSIT. RESPECTIFLY. C. GOSS'

Folding the letter, Lloy frowned. He had been expecting another letter. A message from Treetop House to contact a white lady here.

'What's the matter?' Posey pressed. 'She causing trouble for you, too.'

'She wants to meet me, Miss Posey,' he said, wondering what happened to the other letter. He hoped there was no trouble in Boston.

'Meet you? That trash woman? You watch out. You ain't

213

a half-bad looking buck. Fact is, you're down right hand some looking. And that ugly old trash woman's got a taste for handsome bucks. You be too good for her, Master Lloy Far too good for a trash woman like her!'

Turning to Posey, Lloy said, 'Do you know somebody here who would do me a favour, Miss Posey? I don't wan to meet Claudia Goss as she asks. But also I don't think it's wise if she comes here. Not at the moment. And she just might do that if I don't turn up at the meeting place she mentions.'

'Claudia Tucker come back to this place?' Posey said. 'Not at no time!'

'Miss Posey, do you know anybody who could go to the crossroads near Treetop House?'

'Treetop House? I know where that be. Master Peter sends Christmas packages there. I rode over last winter myself.'

'Do you remember the crossroads?' Lloy asked eagerly.

'Fact I do,' Posey answered. 'I remembered remarking about which road leads where.'

'Could you find some one with a pass to travel at night and have them go to the crossroads to tell Mrs Goss that I'll not be able to meet her at sunset but that I'll be in touch with her? Mister Abdee might not be home before sundown so he can't give a travel pass.' Lloy was thinking out loud now. He added, 'I hate sending someone to her place. I've heard awful stories about Grouse Hollow. How she treats her—' He shook his head.

'You leave everything to me, Master Lloy,' Posey said, snatching back the letter from his hand. 'You leave everything all to Miss Posey.'

Lloy profusely thanked Posey and, promising to come visiting him soon in the kitchen, he hurried off toward the old house, anxious to get a look at the attic room there before Imogen returned. The time then was shortly before noon.

*   *   *

Bill Sandell and the other patrollers collected in the chairs around the front window of Troy's mercantile store listening avidly to Claude Fonk's second-hand information bout troubles mounting on Dragonard Hill. Fonk repeated n detail the stories which Imogen Abdee had told him, mbellishing on the facts about black slaves having secret neetings in the slave quarter on Dragonard Hill and to mogen's claim that her father had replaced her with a Negro as overseer. Fonk likewise elaborated on the hearsay of Dragonard Hill's financial position, claiming that the bank had already foreclosed on Greenleaf and was now preparing to seize Dragonard Hill.

Leaning forward in his chair, he said, 'That be the big-log banks down in New Orleans. That's where the real money sits!'

'What do city bankers know about life up our way?' asked Warren Bell, a patroller and small farmer.

'Correct!' Fonk said. 'What in hell do city bankers know about planters going bust and the niggers heading on a rampage worse than the Indians who used to live around these parts? Savages are savages in my eyes and we're still civilized pioneers! And white Christians!'

'Lots of pioneers were slaughtered in the olden days,' muttered Emil Groggin.

Fonk added, 'And there still be slaughtering. But by *blackskins* this time! That's why old Imogen Abdee, she tells me to keep a watch on her pa's place. To protect all us innocent parties who really count around here.'

Billy Sandell stood behind Fonk's chair. He said now, 'We ain't seen hide nor hair of that Miss Vicky gal in town lately.'

'Nor the other one,' added Groggin who had been one of the patrollers riding with Billy Sandell when they had stopped Veronica's wagon on the road south of Horton.

'Something fishy's happening there, all right. She'd normally complain, a proud feisty woman like that sister. But we ain't heard one complaint yet. Not a peep. They're hiding something. They're trying to keep the top on a hornet's nest out there.'

Warren Bell suggested, 'I think we should ride over to see.'

'Don't expect to get nothing more from Miss Imogen,' Fonk warned, leaning back on his chair. 'She ain't the overseer no more.'

'Never did trust her much anyway,' Billy said. 'Any

woman who don't truck with no man ain't to be trusted neither.'

'She's a good liquor customer of mine,' Fonk reminded them.

'A little too good. No, I think we have to watch that Imogen gal, too.'

The men leaned their heads closer together, discussing who should go in what patrols, the amount of ammunition needed for such an outing, and the hour to start riding out to Dragonard Hill. They decided that the welfare of the community rested in their hands. Warren Bell said that he would bring his bullwhip as well as a squirrel gun. The time then was shortly past noon.

* * *

By mid-afternoon, Claudia Goss knew that she should start thinking about going to meet Lloy at the spot designated in the note which Jack had taken to Dragonard Hill. She decided to wait at Grouse Hollow at least another hour longer, though, to see if Jerome Poliguet would arrive from New Orleans. It was his day to return to Troy. She wanted him to press Barry Breslin into selling Greenleaf immediately. She also had another plot. She was going to offer a bribe to Lloy to start an uprising amongst the slaves at Dragonard Hill. She believed that every man had a price, even a freed black man—*especially freed coons*, she thought. But by late afternoon, Jerome Poliguet still had not arrived at Grouse Hollow and Claudia decided that she could not wait any longer. The hour was approaching to meet Lloy at early evening. She decided to leave. She also decided to travel alone, not to have Jack drive her to the rendezvous. She did not want him snooping.

* * *

Naomi was still impressed by Vicky's expertise last night in the theatrics upstairs in *Petit Jour*; she was pleased that she had granted the young white woman her request to keep Poliguet trussed in his leather bondage until last night's final show.

Vicky had met Naomi in the bordello's office after the

performance which she had viewed from the curtained box and had seen Poliguet for the first time here. She had anxiously said to Naomi, 'We can talk later about an octor-roon girl for my father. I saw a man upstairs I know. I want you to do me a favour. Please. There is no reason, I know, for you to grant it, but this is what I would like.'

Although Naomi had wanted Vicky to see the man who had been talking about her lately at *Petit Jour*, she was surprised when she listened to Vicky's request, and even more surprised when she watched her a few hours later put it into action.

Honouring Vicky's request to keep Poliguet in his bondage, Naomi ordered the theatre's Negresses to repeat the same performance at the last show but with one major alteration—Poliguet would be carried, trussed as a cotton bale, not to a black woman but to Vicky standing in the centre of the candlelit stage.

Vicky showed a natural talent for performing; she was not ill-at-ease in front of an audience; instead, she enjoyed standing in a domineering position over Poliguet's body with people watching her.

Gasping when he saw who it was wearing nothing but thigh-high black leather boots, Poliguet pulled back in surprise, in horror. His actions now were not make-believe.

But the Negresses held him. Vicky pulled his head toward her naked midsection. She pressed his mouth toward her furry patch, muttering, 'If you bite me, I'll have you stripped of your skin. Now eat! Eat this . . . pie!'

Poliguet buried his face deep into Vicky's thrusting groin. The spectators rose from their chaise longues to watch more closely, gathering around Vicky as she pressed Poliguet's head even tighter against her mound, ordering, 'Tongue deeper . . . deeper . . . get your lips in there if you can, you Creole bastard . . .'

She remembered the fantasies, the hopes she had had about him making love to her; she felt that he had betrayed her by being so passive; she now was seeking a proud woman's revenge. The sensation she felt from his probing tongue did not match her feeling of power and victory.

She looked down past her naked breasts and saw Poliguet obediently burying his mouth into her spread vaginal lips. He ate, tongued, delved deeper like a desperate man.

217

Smiling as she watched his eagerness now to please her, she reached toward his nose. She held two fingers forward. She pinched his nostrils shut with the tips of her fingers and—with her other hand—she firmed the grip on the back of his head which pressed his mouth even more tightly against her, locking his tongue deep into her vagina, creating almost a suction hold between his mouth, his lips, his tongue with her vagina. It was then that Vicky began to contract her vaginal muscles, tissue around his only access to air. He struggled. But she held his nose with her fingers and his head to her midsection with her hand. The Negresses held his arms, shoulders, legs into position. He choked. Gasped. Puffed. But his oral attempts were muffled by Vicky's clutching midsection as she continued to pinch his nostrils pressed tightly shut, maintaining the hold of her female orifice around his mouth. She watched as his face slowly turned blue. The blueness then darkened but she still did not release her control over him. She smiled as she looked down at him losing breath. He was physically weakening. There was no way he could escape from Vicky and the Negresses. The resistance finally vanished from his struggling arms. He grew limp. He fainted. He had been temporarily suffocated by Vicky's female expertise—and as she stood over his motionless body, she raised her arms to the audience of applauding men who cheered not only for Vicky's 'Jezebel's Grip' but for her—the first white female ever to appear in a dominating role in a theatric on the top floor of the bordello, *Petit Jour*.

*　*　*

This next day when Vicky sat in the office of the bordello on Rampart Street, she saw that Naomi was impressed with her. She was still thankful for the chance to appear in last night's theatric. She had come back to *Petit Jour* today without Malou; she arrived to hear finally what news Naomi had to say about the octoroon girl whom she had found for her father.

First, Naomi began to explain that Poliguet eventually had revived, dressed himself, and fled from the bordello at dawn, not even asking for details of what had happened to him. Naomi laughingly told Vicky that he obviously knew who she was. That she had sufficiently 'gagged' him so that none of them would hear from him again—or that he might come back and never leave the place!

Naomi waved her white-gloved hand, saying, 'Enough talk about that man. Let me tell you what I found. A young girl by the name of Chloe St Cloud. She was the mistress of a rich young dandy who was killed in a duel behind Saint Louis Cathedral. His family refuses to support the girl so her *tante*—all good octoroon girls have an 'aunt' who supervises their education and welfare—is at her wit's end over what to do with the young girl's future. I told the old woman that there was a position of governess which might possibly appeal to her.'

'Governess?' Vicky asked.

'With these young ladies every bit of propriety must be observed. They are not sluts. If you want a fine girl, then you must act accordingly. I want you to place a notice in the French edition of the *New Orleans Bee*. The paper called "*L'abeille de la Nouvelle Orleans*". I want you to place a discreet notice announcing that "Condesa Veradaga of Havana requests the services..." make up something about needing a qualified young lady of character and good breeding.'

Vicky shrugged, 'If you wish.'

'It is not for me. It is Mademoiselle St Cloud's aunt who wishes this formality.' Naomi stood alongside Vicky's chair and said, 'Now that was the good news. Are you ready to hear the bad?'

'Bad? But what else is there? You gave me a chance to take part in your theatric. You found me a very pretty girl. At least you say she's pretty and the Lord knows you've seen enough... young ladies. Even if this does not work out, I do have to admit that you've acted better than I might have in your position.'

Ignoring the surprise compliment, Naomi said, 'This arrived.' She held a parchment envelope toward Vicky.

'For me? A letter arrived here... for me?'

'I did not say it came for you. But it came. See. From Havana. And with the same coat-of-arms as your calling card.'

'My husband wrote to you?'

'I have never met your husband but he obviously has a

considerable knowledge of both you and New Orleans, young lady. He sent a letter to me here, stating that you were to be informed that an "Impediment of Entry" has been placed against your return to Havana. He calls it in Spanish an *"impedimento a contra entrada"*. He explained that the Cuban authorities will not allow you to disembark from any ship there, that you must not even try to return home or you'll be arrested and placed in prison.'

'He can't do that!' She could not believe that a feeling of victory could be so brief.

'Sail to Havana and see if he can!'

'But I *will* go back home. I'll go back and I'll—' Vicky's mind swirled with possibilities. She sputtered, 'I'll contact my grandfather! That's what I'll do. He's a slavedealer. He is powerful in Havana, too. He'll know how to deal with that . . . swine!'

'Your grandfather?'

'Yes,' Vicky said, too concerned now with her own problems to notice Naomi falling back against her desk, gripping onto the leather-top for support. 'My grandfather lives in the district of Regla. He's a despicable old tyrant. He even kidnapped my child. I don't have Malou with me today but you can ask her. My grandfather bribed that bitch, Malou, to bring Juanito to his slave house in Regla. I wanted to confront him but Juan Carlos would not allow it. He even insisted I did not punish Malou. He packed us both off here to Louisiana. And now—now I am beginning to understand why—'

'Richard Abdee is alive?'

Naomi's question took Vicky by surprise. She turned in her chair, asking, 'You've met him? My grandfather?'

'How do you think I know about your father? Why do you think I've bothered all these years about Dragonard Hill? Wasted my time with you? Oh, I've grown to like you in a strange way. Like one vixen respects another. I rant at you one moment. Help you the next. But my first concern always has been for your grandfather. Richard Abdee. I knew him on St Kitts. When he was only a—' She laughed '—the public . . . whipmaster! He left my bed to marry Honoré Jubiot. Her plantation was called *"Petit Jour"*. He changed it to Dragonard when he married her. That is where I got the name for my place here on Rampart

Street . . .' She paused and, grabbing Vicky by both shoulders, she demanded, 'Richard Abdee is still alive? You are sure of it?'

'He was,' Vicky said, staring at the face under the black lace veil, skin which she now saw was scarred and stretched into a grotesque shape. She pulled back in repulsion, murmuring, 'He was alive when I left Havana.'

Freeing Vicky from her grasp, Naomi stood over her chair saying, 'Tell me this now. Do you want to return to Havana? Truly?'

Vicky fleetingly considered the question. She shook her head, saying, 'I cannot answer that. Not so soon.'

'I will not press you. But I know this. *I* am going to Havana! And as long as your husband's threat is being held in effect by the harbour officials there, young lady, you cannot go near the place. So, I have a proposition to make to you, fellow vixen gal!'

Throwing back her head and laughing, Naomi said, 'The old bastard. I knew he was alive! I knew that we'd meet again!'

Stopping, spinning around in her office, Naomi faced an ivory-framed mirror hanging behind her. She slowly approached the mirror, looking at the veiled reflection of her face. She said as if she had forgotten that Vicky was sitting in the room behind her, 'I wonder how he came out . . . How he survived . . . Does he look as—bad as I do? . . . What happened to—him?'

*   *   *

Naomi had been young then. Her lover was the young Englishman, Richard Abdee, whose blond hair swept back from his forehead, the only white man whom Naomi had ever known to be built like a Negro. They were well matched as lovers. He enjoyed her independence. But, finally, that night he told her to leave him.

Another windmill had been set afire that night, its straw flaps slowly revolving—burning—against the streaked Caribbean sunset. And, again, Richard Abdee tried to persuade Naomi to leave the plantation while there was still time for her life to be saved. The drums told that the troubles were close.

But Naomi would not desert him. She said that she could not leave him—a white man—alone with the black people.

Richard Abdee was not frightened of the blacks. He treated them well and he did not think they would hurt him nor allow him to be hurt. But he repeated to Naomi how the Dragonard slaves hated her, were jealous of her position both as a rich free Negress and his mistress.

Naomi laughed at him, but her laughter was low, almost a growl, unlike its usual high pitch; it was nervous, showing that she was at last frightened. Her long black hair was brushed back from her prune-coloured face, her eyes painted with blue cosmetics, her fingernails freshly lacquered red. She told Richard Abdee that she knew black people better than he did. They would see her coming in her fine red dress and they would bow to kiss the feathers on her hem. She tried to laugh again, hoping to convince him of her bravery.

Naomi had come to the north end of the island to Dragonard Plantation after Abdee's wife had abandoned him, had sailed off to France with Ta-Ta, a slave boy, and Abdee's baby in her belly. Naomi had given up her bordello on Barracks Lane in the capital town of Basseterre to live with Abdee.

The last that Naomi had seen of Dragonard Plantation was the fire, the flames which climbed the fabric hanging from the walls in a garden room. She had heard Abdee lashing his whip at slaves rushing the house. She had known that Abdee was only a short distance behind her. She had heard a scream, then, a shout, and then she heard a ripping above her head and the last thing that she remembered was that the tented room was falling in around her, the flames enveloping Naomi as if she were being rushed into hell.

Chapter Nineteen

VENGEANCE

The stone gate posts flanking the entrance to Dragonard Hill stood golden in the sunset, the iron arc announcing the plantation's name silhouetted by the fading light of evening. No traffic had passed under the sign after Peter Abdee had ridden his horse down the hills this morning, going to Greenleaf to bring his young son, David, back home. The only other person to have left the plantation late this afternoon had been Posey. He had told Curlew that he finally wanted to take advantage of his offer of a wagon and a road pass but warned him not to tell anyone that he was going for a brief recess from the kitchen. Posey had already prepared the specially ordered supper for young Master David; he had instructed Belladonna how to arrange the food on the trays. Posey did not know how long he would be gone from Dragonard Hill, the duration of time it would take to travel to the crossroads near Treetop House and home again. The only person who would come to the kitchen annex in his absence would be Veronica. But Posey trusted her to hold the secret that he was not there. Belladonna had asked Posey what she should do if Imogen came to the kitchen. Posey had answered that Belladonna should keep Imogen away from her with his meat cleaver. But having second thoughts about that advice, Posey suggested that Belladonna should protect herself with a kitchen knife or to run to the main house for help. Then, Posey prepared the necessary equipment he needed for his brief journey into the outside world, and he departed from the kitchen to the stable, and, next, down the back road in a wagon hitched to a dappled mare. Posey thought that he saw a light in the attic room of the old house whilst he drove the horse toward the weed-covered road which led to the log gates. Telling himself that he was imagining things, Posey snapped the whip over the horse's head and quickly disappeared between the yellowing cypress trees which lined the old drive way. The sun was quickly sinking behind the hills behind him.

*　　*　　*

The thunder began at dusk, a rumble of horse hooves pounding down the public road from the direction of Troy, a cloud of dust rising in the growing darkness as a group of riders galloped toward the white-picket-fenced cemetery reining their horses in front of the stone pillars announcing 'Dragonard Hill'.

The main house set high, white, commanding on its lush grassy knoll in the distance. Lights blinked inside the front windows. Smoke curled from the tall white chimney in the kitchen annex. There was little to be seen of the main house except for the blinking window lights, the curling smoke, the white pillars standing tall and strong like proud sentinels against the public road below.

'Makes me sick just looking up there. They think they're God Almighty, they do,' muttered Emil Groggin. He took a drink from a brown earthen jug and passed it to Billy Sandell.

Claude Fonk had explained the details to the rider who had joined them along the road between here and Troy. He now said, 'A normal man would swear respectable, clean-living white folks live there. But that ain't the truth. The whole pack of them is nigger lovers.'

Billy called, 'That fact you told me, Claude? It's true? That other Abdee gal we almost gang-banged up near Horton, she's married to a coon?'

'Married? Hell, she's got three brats by him.'

'Makes a man want to puke,' muttered Billy.

Fonk said, 'That Imogen, she ain't much better. She living with that black girl. How's that for something? Not

224

only going to bed with your own kind but a nigger wench to boot! Two pussies rubbing against one another. What do you say to that?'

Bell grumbled, 'Scum like them should be wiped off the face of this earth.'

'Any wiping done, it'll be them niggers up there when they go on the rampage as soon as it's announced that their place is being sold at auction. You know how niggers hate to be sold. Think they're as good as people, they do. But once this place is sold, by God, the niggers will have to go, too. And then there's trouble.' Turning in his saddle, Fonk repeated the story about Dragonard Hill's financial crisis to the newcomers, magnifying the fact even larger now as he retold it to the newly-joined patrollers. There were seventeen men clustered on horseback at the foot of the hill.

'Look!' Warren Bell called, suddenly pointing up the hill toward the main house. 'There's something moving on that front porch. By them pillars. You see it.'

Standing in his stirrups, Billy Sandell said, 'Yes I can. It could be Abdee himself. Or it could be . . . it could be that Imogen.'

'She dresses like a man but what she needs is a good man. You think you could take care of her, Billy boy?'

'I ain't never seen a pussy yet too tight for me. I guess if she's been with women all her life then she must still be a cherry.'

'Feel in a mood for a cherry tonight, Billy boy?' Fonk teased.

Taking another swig from the brown earthen jug, Billy Sandell said, 'The woman asked us to keep an eye on the place, didn't she? So let's the hell do it!' He squeezed his legs against his horse's belly and called, 'Come on, men. Follow me up this little hill.'

*   *   *

Imogen leaned against one of the white pillars flanking the front gallery of the main house. She had been drinking liquor all day. She now was wondering who she should use her whip on first, the new black overseer who had taken her place or on Belladonna who had deserted her.

The sound of galloping horses attracted her attention

225

She saw through her whisky blurred gaze a group of men riding up the sloping driveway. She first recognized Claude Fonk as one of the lead riders. She raised her brown jug in a salutation of welcome and lowered the butt of the whip alongside her tall black leather boot.

'Where's your black gal friend?' Billy Sandell called as the horses surrounded the front of the house.

Imogen had expected friendly faces, not a group of leering men. Glad at least to see people she knew, though, she answered, 'The bitch is in the kitchen.' She nodded to the white annex attached to the mainhouse. She hiccupped and demanded, 'Who's asking?'

It was at that moment that Bell pointed to a ground floor window in the main house, saying, 'Hey, Billy! There's that feisty one peeking out through the curtains at you, boy. Too bad you ain't black, Billy. She'd probably invited you inside and spread open her legs for you.'

Imogen stepped forward, weaving in her drunkenness, and sank back to one of the pillars. She slurred, 'What is this? I asked you to keep an eye on this place . . . Not to ride in here like a pack of . . . fools.' She was beginning to move the butt of her bullwhip with one hand.

'Fools is we?' Claude Fonk asked.

Imogen looked from Fonk to the jug of whisky she had bought from him and now held in her hand. She hurled it to the ground and, as it crashed against the flagstones, she shouted, 'Yeah, fools! The whole damned bunch of you!' She was in a mood for a fight.

Two riders jumped from their horses; they grabbed Imogen's arms whilst another group of men moved toward the kitchen annex. Billy Sandell was running toward the doors of the main house. He threw open one door, and called inside, 'Nigger lover? Want me to give you a white baby to go with your little black ones, Miss Nigger Lover?' He disappeared into the house laughing, calling, 'Somebody in here looking for juice to make white babies?' The sound of Veronica's screams rose from beyond the open front door.

Claude Fonk produced the ropes. Warren Bell brought his bullwhip from his saddle horn. Another man seized Imogen's whip. Four patrollers were now leading Belladonna from the kitchen, dragging her by the arms as one man shouted, 'There was a piccaninny but she got away from us. She was too little, though. Just a nigger kid.'

Shoving Belladonna toward Imogen, Emil Groggin asked, 'This your lover, girl?'

Imogen looked from one whiskered face to another. She was sobering enough to realize how much she hated males. The whisky gave her courage to speak this hatred, and she began, 'You trash . . . you rotten, no good . . .'

'Trash now are we?' Fonk said. 'We're all right when you're needing our whisky. Or protection. But we're just . . . trash when we finally see through you.' He nodded at the men holding Imogen, saying, 'Why don't you start on her first.'

Billy Sandell called from behind them, 'Look who've I caught!' He moved forward, pushing Veronica in front of him, holding her hands gripped behind her back.

Fonk ordered, 'Tie her to—' He looked around him, his eyes lingering on the white pillars. He said, '—tie her and the coon gal up to them posts. Let's keep some order to this. The little lady here just says we're trash. We'll show her how orderly us trash can be when we has to. We'll start with . . . her.'

Imogen struggled against the male dominance. But she was no match for the strong grips of the men holding her. By the time that Veronica and Belladonna were tied with ropes to the Doric pillars, four patrollers pinned Imogen's legs and arms to the ground. Billy Sandell stood in front of her spread-eagled on the ground. He unbuttoned his pants, saying, 'We'll see, if she's a cherry or not.'

'I got an idea, Billy,' Fonk said. 'I always wondered what these kind of women use for peckers when they make love. What do *you* think?'

'They use fingers!' shouted one farmer.

'No,' called another. 'I think they use sticks!'

Warren Bell bellowed, 'No, I think they use one of these.' He raised his squirrel gun.

Laughter surrounded Imogen as she began to toss her head frantically from side to side, listening to the men debating what object they should stick into her vagina. One man had ripped at her shirt. More hands pulled at her belt, using the blade of a bowie knife to cut her breeches away from her groin. She felt a hand on one breast. She felt pressure against her other breast. She began to scream when she realized that the slim end of a whip had been tied around the base of each breast. She then felt the coldness of steel between her legs. She next heard a patroller urging, 'Prime her first. Prime her with some grease.' Another voice asked, 'Is it loaded?' Imogen's breasts were now being pulled in opposite directions by two different whips. The men holding each whip tossed them and the tips made her breasts shake, and feel as if they were about to be torn from her body. Her thighs felt as if they were going to be spread until her bones cracked. She felt the cold bluntness sink deeper into her vagina. She gasped; she screamed for mercy as the hammer of a squirrel gun cocked between her spread thighs and its barrel pushed deeper into her vagina.

*　　*　　*

A childlike drawing of a woman. A baby between her legs with the name 'Pierre' scrawled in crude lettering beneath it. Another crude drawing of a child with a tail attached to it. A drawing of a long-gun placed across this second child. And many whips, whips of all sizes but the tip of each whip splayed like a snake or a mythical dragon's tongue.

Lloy studied all these drawings in the attic room of the old house as well as the outlines of maps and pictures of houses drawn in a primitive manner on the walls and ceilings of the room. Must and old age discoloured many of the drawings done with a child's crayons but Lloy saw that they all were the work of a disturbed mind, by a woman—his grandmother—who had adored her blonde-haired mistress, and the son sired by the 'Dragonard' of St Kitts.

Trying to piece together a chronological sequence of places, names, and maps, Lloy had decided to make copies of as many of the drawings as he could. He knew he might never be able to come back to this attic room. He would take the copies with him, using them in the future to construct some sense of his own background. He found dusty boxes of crayons and wax pencils still in the room which he used to start making copies of the crude work.

It was whilst Lloy was still working in the attic room by

the light of a tallow candle that he had first heard the horse hooves moving up the drive. He immediately remembered Claudia Goss, of asking Posey to send somebody to the crossroads near Treetop House. He also thought of someone finally arriving from Treetop House to tell him that a letter had finally come from Boston to start the first slaves on their long journey north.

Quickly snuffing out the candle in the attic room, Lloy carefully found his way down the rickety wooden stairs as he stopped occasionally and listened for the sound of Imogen. But the house was empty, silent, creaking only with its own noise of time.

He reached the back door and, running quickly to the chinaberry trees where he had left his horse obscured from sight, he then heard the distant sound of screaming. He knew that the screams came from women—from women near the main house. He remembered the sound of horses galloping up the front driveway. No black people rode horses. Not in that number. He then remembered the white patrollers who roamed the countryside.

Realizing that he was no match alone for a group of white patrollers—men who were often drunk and fierce haters of black people—Lloy thought of the one way to stop whatever trouble might be happening in the main house. He could not go to neighbours for help. They might be amongst the patrollers. He had no choice but to go to Town. Only the black people might help the Abdee Family.

Lloy kept his horse to the woodland far behind the main house, taking the longer path to Town, but staying as far away from the main house as possible for the moment.

*　　*　　*

Wrapped in the dark grey horse blanket he had taken from the stable to keep his white clothing from shining in the darkness, Posey waited in the copse of cottonwood trees near the crossroads until he heard the clatter of a wagon coming down the road. He stepped further back from view, waiting to see if the driver was Claudia Goss and, seeing that it was, he slowly withdrew the meat cleaver from the folds of the horse blanket and muttered, 'Now we'll see who's a pansy boy . . .'

229

Claudia's mules came to a halt in front of the cottonwood copse. She lowered the reins and whispered, 'Lloy?' She sat on the wagon, repeating into the night, 'Lloy? Lloy, you here, boy?'

Posey considered answering that Lloy was here. But deciding that Claudia might want him to show himself for proof, Posey remained silent, hidden, prepared.

Claudia did not move from the wagon and, the longer that Posey stood in the trees, the more vitriolic his thoughts became as he remembered how Claudia's first husband, Chad Tucker, had ripped off his pants as a child and had laughed at his minutely sized penis, had fingered the area behind it where there should have been testicles, had repeated the story to his wife and the two of them had derided him constantly for being a freak in the world.

'*Lloy*?' Claudia whispered again.

She's no fool, Posey told himself. She's no fool. She might be trash through-and-through but that trash woman is crafty. She ain't going to go wandering in the bushes looking for Lloy. She's going to sit right there on that wagon and wait, and when she don't see Lloy, then she's going to leave.

Deciding to take a chance, Posey moved stealthily from the trees, stepping carefully not to crack even a twig. He kept his skirt held tightly around him as he moved—step by step—in the darkness behind the back of Claudia's board wagon. It was when he was a short distance behind the wagon that he threw a stone across the dirt road.

Claudia jumped at the sound. Posey rushed forward and, grabbing her by the arm, he jerked her to the ground. He pressed her to the dirt with one hand as his other hand raised the meat cleaver over her head. He hissed, 'You scream once, trash woman, and you . . . *die*!'

'Posey!' she gasped.

'*Miss* Posey!' he corrected her and brought the cleaver down sharply onto the dirt, only a few inches away from the side of her head.

Seeing that he was intent on murder, Claudia now began to tremble. She whispered, 'Sure, Miss Posey. . . . That's what we always called you . . .'

'Who always calls me?'

'Why . . . everybody. Why everybody knows you're "Miss" Posey.'

'They do, don't they, trash woman? And they know you nothing but . . . *shit*!'

'Listen here . . . Miss Posey. I've got gold. It's in the wagon there. If you let me get it—'

'I don't want your gold you got from selling sick niggers.'

'I don't sell niggers no more. I don't sell niggers, Posey.'

'What you call me?' he demanded, raising the cleaver above his shoulder again. But as he lifted his arm, Claudia gave a shove upwards with her stomach, using all her strength to dislodge him. She knocked Posey sideways, muttering, 'Damned nigger pervert!'

The sound of a loud thud echoed in the still night. A gasp followed. Then came a second thud. Next, a slice, the sound of a sharp blade cutting across flesh. The gasping soon became moans, then pleadings for mercy, but the meat cleaver moved up and down in the darkness, its steely edge catching the moon's glint as Posey now knelt over Claudia's body. He soon sat astride her, hacking away at her neck, her arms, her chest; he yanked off the bloody strips of her clothing and continued cutting and hacking at raw flesh; he rose to his feet and, jerking at her skirts, he tore the cloth with one hand and cut at her stomach, her fleshy thighs, her knees with his kitchen cleaver. He had stopped muttering to himself now, only silently stripping the cloth from her body and hacking away at her lifeless trunk and limbs, following no plan of butchering, only executing an ancient hatred on someone who had long ago ruined his most treasured world, a world decorated with the wild field flowers which he had loved to pick as a boy, the wild flowers from which he had got his name, Posey, the name which had no sexual connotations—neither boy or girl, male or female—until this white woman and her husband had told him that he was a deviate, a pervert, a freak of nature in the world rather than representing something beautiful in nature like a . . . posey.

*   *   *

Peter Abdee rode solemnly up the driveway to the main

house, holding young David's face to his chest, trying to protect the boy from seeing what he himself saw—he first saw the black people from Town standing with axes and pitchforks in a silent circle around the group of patrollers in front of the white house. He saw Veronica tied to one of the pillars. She was hysterically sobbing. He saw Belladonna tied to another pillar. As he continued riding toward the pillars, the white men backed toward their horses. It was then that Peter saw the object, the body which he did not immediately recognize. He at first thought that she was an animal, a slaughtered farm animal; he only recognized that it was a woman—his own daughter—when he saw one of Imogen's boots still snuggly gripping a leg which had once been attached to her body. Peter sat silently—dazed—on his horse, pressing David's face even more tightly against his chest as Lloy stepped from the circle of slave men and women who were holding the white patrollers at bay with hammers, axes, scythes, pitchforks. Lloy called to the white men, 'I think you should all go to your homes now. All of you. Just ride down the same way you came up that hill. These black folks behind me are peaceful. More peaceful than you've been here tonight. There ain't no uprising here. But there might be if any more . . . misery is caused here. Go. Just go now.' Lloy stood facing the white men, staring at them until—one by one—they began to mount their horses. The sound of the animals soon passed down the hills; Peter remained seated on his horse, holding his head forward, pressing his young son toward him, beginning to take deep gulps of tears, shaking his head as he began to cry. Maybelle moved from the crowd of slaves to lift young David from Peter's arms. Croney and Ham moved with Lloy to untie Veronica and Belladonna from the pillars. A group of black men came to cover the remains of Imogen's body with a blanket before they moved her from the front of the main house.

Chapter Twenty

THE TRAVELLERS

The two lovers had been carefully chosen, great care gone into scouring the city of Havana to find a Negress with the correct hint of blueness to her black skin—making the colour almost prune-like—and a search conducted for a sinewy young white man with flaxen hair which swept back from his forehead and with eyes that shone blue like cornflowers. The two lovers—the young white man and the lithe Negress—had been coached separately, not even allowed to meet one another before their encounter. The young man was American but his nationality did not matter; the accent of his speech, unimportant; he would not be speaking at his meeting with the Negress. And although the young Negress was a slave girl, she had been coached in the ways of how to conduct herself as if she were free, rich, an independent spirit willing to be dominated by no one, a female who would submit to her dominating lover only if he, in turn, allowed himself to be subject to her femininity. When the correct attitudes, confidences, desires, all the necessary traits were instilled into the two chosen people, they finally would be introduced to one another, an introduction following weeks of sexual abstinence, a meeting planned to be a culmination of passions between this sinewy young white man and the fiery young Negress with skin the colour of a prune. They had been separately coached by their tutors—their models—to go to their meeting feeling lust for—as well as suspicion of—their partner. The actors contributed only their ingenuity . . . and youth. The long-awaited encounter finally arrived. The stage was in a windowless room—a heavily carved bed on which was slung a feather mattress covered with a white linen sheet. The room was lit by a black iron chandelier suspended from the ceiling by chains with its three tiers of squat candles casting shadows onto the bed. There was no other furniture in the large room except for two wooden chairs and an iron table, both chairs comfortably padded, and the table set with chilled wine and two stemmed crystal goblets. Naomi came to sit in one of the chairs. She entered the room wearing her long black dress and black veil covering her face. She wore white gloves as she held her wine glass. Richard Abdee entered the room after Naomi's arrival, glancing toward the bed where the two naked lovers lay as if asleep. Abdee looked at them rather than at Naomi. Although this was the first time that he had seen her since she had come to Havana, he did not greet her nor did he make any inquiries about her journey from New Orleans. Her first letter to him from New Orleans had explained how she had learned of his whereabouts from his granddaughter. Their exchange of letters following her arrival in Havana, the correspondence to arrange the careful plans for this evening had been their only subsequent contact . . . until now. He sank into the other chair alongside the iron table and, pausing before he poured himself a glass of wine, he asked Naomi if he could refill her glass. Naomi shook her head, raising the glass toward her mouth, lifting the veil from her scarred face to sip the sparkling white wine. She kept her eyes trained on the bed: The naked lovers were beginning to move. Naomi quietly set her glass down on the table and watched with interest as the female meant to be portraying her now rolled away from the handsome young white man. He—the facsimile of young Richard Abdee—pulled her back toward him. They struggled. He reached to slap her. She grabbed his hand and, locked together in a momentary test of power, they glared at one another like animals but, unexpectedly, they lunged into a lustful grasp. They knelt kissing. The kisses turned into a gasping embrace; his white arms encircled her black body; her dark arms hugged his slim waist; their naked midsections pressed tightly together; the black girl then bent backwards into an arc as

234

the white man held her by the hips and looked proudly down at his penis driving in and out of her mound. He maintained the rhythm of his pumping motions as he rose to his feet, his knees bent, squatting now as he pulled away from and pushed harder against her thighs. The black girl herself then moved, pulling herself upright from the arc, springing to her feet, standing in front of the squatting man, putting the sole of one bare foot on his shoulder and holding her vagina toward his mouth. She no longer wanted him to dominate her. She wanted him to serve her femininity with his tongue like a slave. It was at that moment that Naomi felt Richard Abdee press the top of her white gloved hand resting on the arm of her chair. He patted her hand and, reaching toward her with his other hand, he removed the white glove and lifted the blotched skin—long ago marred by fire during the slave uprising on St Kitts—and he gently, slowly kissed each finger. He lay her hand back on the arm of the chair and, looking at the white man and the prune-black Negress now wrapped into a double-coloured ball of deep fornication, he asked, 'Is that how it was, Naomi?' She answered in her raspy voice, the first words she had spoken to him in over thirty years, 'You bet your white ass it was! And we were both *bad* enough to survive this long!' She turned her head to look at him. He studied the veil. The sound of ecstatic moans rising across the room from the bed were now obliterated by their laughter at this reunion, a long-awaited meeting in a windowless room deep in the slave house on the *Calle de Eclavos* in the district of Regla in Havana.

* * *

Vicky felt no remorse about not returning to Havana. She realized that her son would grow into a fine young gentleman, that his father would guide him into a world which would exclude her. She asked herself, Why suffer that pain later? Why give Juan Carlos more victories in embargoes he placed against me. I will live for myself. Vicky Abdee! To hell with Condesa Veradaga! And, thus, the one and only remaining detail in Vicky's life as the Condesa Veradaga was Malou but she decided to get rid of her, too. Instead of selling Malou in a New Orleans slave house, though, putting her on the block as she had often threatened, Vicky suddenly felt generous in her new life, freeing Malou and settling a small sum of money on her to begin her own new life. She had heard that Malou bought a small shop on Canal Street where she sold herbs and spices from the Sea Islands. Knowing Malou's propensity toward a religious life, and that similarly prone black people gathered here in New Orleans, Vicky surmised that Malou's stock included more amulets and potions for her voodoo religion than it did condiments for a kitchen. But, then, Vicky no longer cared about Malou. She was too concerned with her own progress. She slept days and stayed awake nights for her work at *Petit Jour* on Rampart Street. She devised new theatrics for the upstairs theatre. She railed orders at the black men who worked as waiters. She constantly inspected the girls for cleanliness, attractiveness, and disease. She found that juice from a lemon squeezed into a vagina was one way to check a prostitute for the pox. It was during such inspections that she enquired—and discovered to her surprise—that few girls knew about 'Jezebel's Grip'. Vicky gave them hints for this practise which increased sexual satisfaction for a male. As well as pursuing such a busy schedule, she also closely surveyed all the male guests, eliminating the drunk, the pugilistic, and the poor. She had placed Jerome Poliguet's name on a list of people to be barred from the bordello. She decided that exclusion from *Petit Jour* would be his supreme punishment. With all this work and dedication, Vicky hoped to make *Petit Jour* more profitable in Naomi's absence than it had been under the old Negress's surveillance. Vicky often thought, though, that Naomi might never return from Havana. She told herself, Let Naomi keep the secret to herself that Richard Abdee is alive. Vicky had severed all ties with her family since sending the octoroon girl, Chloe St Cloud, north on a coach to Dragonard Hill. Vicky was too involved with her new role in life—a bordello's mistress—even to think about her own physical pleasure. She sat behind the desk in the office at *Petit Jour*, sipping coffee in the early hours of the morning after a prosperous night of business and, looking at money heaped in front of her, she asked herself, 'Why have I never discovered money before now? The power of money? Its magic? I work at night but—

look—I have all this gold for my sunshine!' The only thought which troubled Vicky was that she might be similar to her grandfather in too many ways.

*   *   *

'Miss Posey?' the kitchen-girl, Lulu, asked as she sat on a stool next to the work table in the kitchen annex on Dragonard Hill. 'When we going to get us a new helper here, Miss Posey?'

'What you call me?'

The girl stared at Posey. She did not know what she had said wrong. 'I calls you—'

'Mademois*elle* Posey!' the lanky Negro cook said, throwing up his nose. 'Mademoiselle St Cloud, she's a fine educated young lady and she's teaching me French-talk. That is when she comes visiting here from Greenleaf where she and young Master David lives now that Mister Barry Breslin done left with a coloured gal for Mexico.'

Posey suddenly took a deep sigh. He also sat down on a stool next to the table, shaking his head with bewilderment over all the changes that had happened here. Master Peter had freed Belladonna. She had gone North to Boston with Miss Veronica. Master Lloy had gone North for a visit with them. But before he had left Dragonard Hill he had suggested to Master Peter that Ham be made overseer here. Master Peter, though, Posey learned, had his own plans for Ham. He was giving him Greenleaf Plantation to run now that he had bought it from Mister Breslin. Ham and Maybelle were living there, along with Mademoiselle St Cloud from New Orleans tending young Master David. The changes, the movements, the alterations were all too much for Posey's mind.

'What's the matter . . . Mam'selle Posey,' Lulu asked.

'This travelling. Everybody's going or gone some place all of a sudden.'

Lulu said, 'Like Miss Imogen? Her going to Heaven? Do you think Miss Imogen went to Heaven . . . Mam'selle Posey?'

Posey shot the skinny girl a nasty glance. The death of Imogen Abdee, the slaughter conducted by the patrollers, was not mentioned on Dragonard Hill. Imogen's remains lay in the cemetery at the foot of the driveway and the matter was closed. Peter Abdee did not press for charge of murder. He saw that no amount of vindictive courtbattling could repair the damage done, perhaps done a long time before the patrollers rode up the hill that night.

Lulu now pressed Posey, 'You ever done travelling?'

'I . . . I . . . I . . . have never stepped foot off this place. Not since I come here.'

'You went to Treetop House last Christmas when Master Peter sent over presents.'

'That? Well . . . I was with Master Peter then, wasn't I? I was not alone. I never gone travelling alone from this place. Never!'

Posey had feared reprisals when Claudia's body had been found near the crossroads. The blame was put on highwaymen, thieves, or runaway slaves, though, and because the patrollers had not been doing their dutiful job that night on the public roads, they did not pursue a possible suspect who might have murdered—butchered—Claudia Goss. Posey also was relieved that his dreams were not haunted by a bloody spectre as he had feared they might be. Claudia Goss was not coming back to spook him. She had done her evilness in life. He eventually saw his deed as the will of the Lord when he learned that Claudia Goss's two slaves, Jack and Mary, had gone to live at Treetop House until a relative could claim them as hereditary property. Everyone said that no relative would ever step forward, though, that Grouse Hollow would probably grow completely over with weeds, that Jack and Mary would live peacefully at Treetop House.

The only thing which confused Posey was that the new overseer, Master Lloy, had not stayed here at Dragonard Hill. Posey understood why Veronica would want to go home, and suspected that she might never come South again after her horrible experience that night with the drunken patrollers. Posey joined in thanksgiving that the patrollers had not had time that night to molest Veronica and Belladonna. Likewise, everyone agreed that Master Peter was kind to grant Belladonna her freedom and give her money to start a new life in Boston.

'I wonder if she'll stay there? Master Lloy, he escorted her and Veronica up North. He said he himself had business o settle there. Now, I know the world is changing, that a nigger... might, just might *possibly* have business to end to in the North. But do you think Master Lloy might get sweet on that Belladonna gal?' Posey turned his head and looked at Lulu. Focusing on the young girl, though, and realizing to whom he was directing such a deep question, he sat bolt upright on his stool and said, 'Why I'm asking you for? You nothing but a piccaninny.'

'Piccaninnies grow up... Mam'selle Posey!'

Standing up from the stool, Posey said, 'Well, don't you be in too much of a hurry to grow-up, black girl, because once you grows up you gots lots of decisions to make. Like me.'

'What decisions you have to make, Mam'selle Posey?'

Posey was not listening. He was standing by a window, looking down the colonnade toward the main house. He said, 'Shame... It's a shame. That fine house got less people in it then that old... boneyard down at the bottom of the hill. Shame. Nobody's in the big house no more. Just poor, poor Master Peter. Shame of it.'

* * *

Peter Abdee was pleased that Chloe St Cloud was happily settled at Greenleaf. He still did not understand why Vicky had sent her from New Orleans but, when the octoroon girl had presented the clipping from the 'New Orleans Bee', and said that she had been hired by the Condesa Veradaga to be a tutor to young David Abdee, Peter could not send her away.

After the troubles at Dragonard Hill, Peter saw the wisdom of David returning to Greenleaf. He also saw the advantages of having a tutor for him until he was strong enough to go away to military school. But, still, Peter thought that it was more like Veronica than Vicky to send a tutor.

Deciding that, in her way, Vicky might be trying to cover-up for some troubles she had caused, Peter accepted the girl's presence, and took advantage of Barry's growing dissatisfaction with Greenleaf. He bought the land and the house from Barry, giving him cash to go to Mexico with the quadroon girl, Gigi, and letters of introductions to banks

239

on which he could draw future payments. Peter also gave
Barry a firm promise that, whenever he wanted to return
to Louisiana, he would always have a home at Greenleaf.

Lloy's offer to escort Veronica to Boston still baffled
Peter. He saw that Veronica and Lloy became close friends
on the days following the disaster at Dragonard Hill. He
knew their new relationship was more than friendship. It
was as if Veronica had been waiting to meet him. They
spoke at length about Royal, even discussing names of banks
and institutions in Boston which Peter did not even know
Lloy was aware of, and they rejoiced that a certain letter
had not been delivered here from Treetop House. Their
rapport became so enthusiastic, so secretive, that Peter was
tempted to ask them if they were involved with something
covert ... like Abolitionism. But for some reason he checked
his question. He even put the thought out of his head. He
concentrated instead on filling out manumission papers for
Belladonna, wishing her to leave Louisiana with Veronica
and Lloy.

Although Lloy had suggested that the black man, Ham,
replace him as overseer, Peter rejected the idea. He already
had a plan for him—but, more specifically, a plan for Ham's
wife, Maybelle. If David and Chloe St Cloud were to live
at Greenleaf, then they would need someone from Dragonard Hill to look after them. Maybelle had been a part-
time nurse to David as an infant. The boy loved her. Peter
wanted Maybelle to be the housekeeper and main cook at
Greenleaf whilst Ham performed the job there as overseer.
They would live in the main house at Greenleaf; their son,
Tim, would live there, too, and be a playmate for David.
The boys were the same age.

The idea thrilled Veronica and, as she hugged her father,
profusely thanking him for such generosity, he said, 'Do
not act as if I'm ... freeing them!' He laughed.

'No, Papa, but—' Veronica took a deep sigh, saying,
'Maybelle will have a table! Forks and knives! Clean linen
sheets ...'

Peter interpreted Veronica's excitement over cutlery and
sheets as a womanly concern. He proceeded with his plan,
though, and on this warm summer Sunday night as he
cantered along the road leading to Dragonard Hill, he
thought that, indeed, everyone did seem very happy at

Greenleaf. Young David no longer asked about his dead mother, nor why those men on horseback had been there that night when they came home and found Aunt Veronica tied to the pillar. Maybelle asked Peter that afternoon if he had heard from Vicky and, when he said that he hadn't, she said, 'When you do, Master Peter, Sir, tell her to give a little message please to that Malou woman of hers. Tell her to tell that Malou woman that us black people here are going to make it just fine. We thank her for her kind words when she was here but we're finding our own ways.'

Still impressed that the black people from Town had come to his family's rescue as soon as they could on that nightmarish night, Peter thanked Maybelle and thought better than to press her for an exact explanation of her message to Malou.

As he rode home tonight, though, he lifted his head at the violet-tinted sky and thought about Maybelle's message. The horse's hooves rose and fell softly on the public road as Peter realized that, indeed, it was the black people who had stopped the white patrollers. With no one helping them but Lloy. And if any black person in the world had reason to hate the Abdees, to see them all destroyed, it would be Monk's son . . .

Peter wondered if his belief in black people—the convictions which other white people called criminal and ungentlemanly—was not so wrong after all.

True, he was working hard these days, performing the task of overseer himself at Dragonard Hill. But the work drained his body—and mind—of all energy. He fell onto bed at night, often going to sleep before he had removed his boots. He was close to the land again. Closer to his people than he had been for a long time. His only respite from work came on Sunday, the time he rode to Greenleaf to visit David.

David. Peter saw that his son and heir would be a sensitive, perhaps even a retiring person. But it was too soon really to be certain how David Abdee would mature. Peter hoped that the vivacious Mademoiselle St Cloud would instill some of her liveliness into him.

Stopping his horse on the public road, Peter looked to his right at the white picket fence surrounding the family cemetery. He saw the two white granite angels, each guarding one of his deceased wives, the mothers of his children. The mound of earth covering Imogen's grave was only just beginning to sprout tender grass.

Peter turned in his saddle and looked across the road at the gate announcing the name of his land. He took off his hat and, leaning forward onto his saddle horn with crossed arms, he thought about the past.

Settling his hat quickly back onto his head, he decided to forget about the dead, the murdered, the disappeared. He would think only about the living, yet try to learn a lesson from those recent days quickly becoming more history of this land . . . *The Siege of Dragonard Hill*.

THE END

DRAGONARD
by Rupert Gilchrist

Feared by some . . . despised by others . . . hated by all! Richard Abdee was the Dragonard.

For the first time on the Caribbean island of St. Kitts, an Englishman had accepted the position of professional whip-master to the African slaves . . . the hated Dragonard. But for Richard Abdee it was the beginning of a new life . . . a life of power, of violence, of lust—a life in which he intended to rule everything and everyone around him . . . both black and white . . . in a society where a thin layer of respectability barely covered the seething currents of sadistic passion and over-powering greed underneath. . . .

Dragonard is the first in a fast-paced, deeply-moving and, unavoidably shocking series by Rupert Gilchrist.

0   552   10149   4   £1.25

THE MASTER OF DRAGONARD HILL
by Rupert Gilchrist

Greed, jealousy and blood-lust were loosed on the Star Plantation in Louisiana when the owner discovered that the boy he had bought as a slave was the outcast son of Richard Abdee, the dreaded whip-master of St. Kitts and the ruler of the Dragonard plantation . . . a man held in fear and loathing by black and white alike . . .

Peter Abdee, cursed by his very name, tried to escape the taint of his father's evil . . . but found himself caught in a bloody web of incest and betrayal . . .

Yet again, lust and bloodshed erupted between black and white . . . and the savagery they bred turned a boy into The Master of Dragonard Hill.

0   552   10420   5   85p.

A SOLDIER ERECT
by Brian W. Aldiss

The Life and hard times of Horatio Stubbs, once THE HAND-REARED BOY and now a soldier at war . . . in India, with the unforgettable forgotten army, and in bloody unspeakable Burma. Horry may have grown up but, underneath that stiff new uniform his most urgent needs haven't changed. Horry needs women and, rather unexpectedly, women seem to need him; all that early practice is beginning to pay dividends. Horry has come of age; a professional soldier among professional women.

0   552   11144   9   95p

A RUDE AWAKENING
by Brian W. Aldiss

The Hilariously grim Black Comedy of Men at War.

Superficially, Sergeant Stubbs is enjoying himself. Plump, sweet Margey has yielded to his repulsive charms and wants to marry him. He may even want to marry her, except that (the world being what it is) she isn't likely to be a lady. Then there's luscious Katie Chae—who's certainly not the marrying kind—not to mention. . . .

Sweet success! But Stubbs has been rudely awakened to the fact that beneath the whoring and drunken parties there's a bitter reality . . . and that on the war-torn island of Sumatra death is as readily available as sex. This is the real, unvarnished world stripped, even in its language, to basics. Horatio can still see the funny side of it all, naturally . . . like a man whistling in the dark.

0   552   11142   2   95p

DRAGONARD BLOOD
by Rupert Gilchrist

Peter Abdee had cast off his father's bloody heritage, and ruled his slaves with humanity. But there were undercurrents at Dragonard Hill plantation of which he knew nothing . . . A conspiracy of fear; blacks tormented by the sadistic lusts of whites—even by his own daughters! For Vicky had special duties for handsome bucks, and Miss Imogen could wield her bull-whip like a man—and meant to run the plantation like one, too. Half-caste babies were born . . . slaves vanished . . . perversion and violence flourished.

Abdee was forced to face the bitter realisation that he could not escape the taint of DRAGONARD BLOOD.

0 552 10710 7   £1.00

DRAGONARD RISING
by Rupert Gilchrist

After the rebellion which drove Richard Abdee from his infamous Dragonard Plantation on St. Kitts, the professional whip-master turned to slave trading to restore his fortune . . . and to satisfy his terrible hunger for power—an unmerciful mastery over those around him: his slaves, his partners, his women . . .

An abandoned Portuguese castle in the Caribbean is the setting for the inhumanity, the barbaric cruelty, and the unhindered lust of Abdee's slaving community. Threatened by forces from within—like the intriguing, malevolent slave Pra and the frenzied jealousy among the women—the community finally tears itself apart, leaving only the mutilated, the dying, and the dead. . . .

0 552 11036 1   95p

MADELAINA, Vols. 1 & 2
by Michaela Morgan

Madelaina meant many things to men . . .

To Peter Duprez . . . she was a breathtakingly beautiful child-woman who blazed a sexuality that roused him till he ached . . .

To her father . . . she was a mystery; she gave up the life of a princess to become a passionate revolutionary and help the poor . . .

To Manuelito Perez . . . she was the woman he made love to in his dreams: for her he would become the greatest matador in the world . . .

To Pancho Villa . . . she was "Little Fox", spirit of the Mexican Revolution. He would have given her all of Mexico as a gift . . .

Fiery freedom fighter, tempestuous lover and loyal friend in one desirable body . . . that was Madelaina.

| 0 | 552 | 10811 | 1 | Vol. 1 | 95p |
| 0 | 552 | 10812 | X | Vol. 2 | 95p |

THE FAN CLUB
by Irving Wallace

'Did you really mean it—what you were saying—about doing anything in the world, even risking your lives, just to make love to Sharon Fields for one night?'

Thus is launched Irving Wallace's powerful new novel about man's ultimate erotic fantasy—and perhaps women's too—the longing and desire for the perfect sexual partner.

THE HAND REARED BOY
by Brian W. Aldiss

It is laid out skilfully, showing a firm and confident narrative gift. It's concerned almost exclusively, with Horace Stubb's sexuality, which is obsessive—and why not? Horry, after all, is at the age when sexuality is obsessive—and with his plunging efforts to satisfy imperious lists. Yet it isn't really pornographic; Aldiss's purposes are manifestly sincere, sometimes serious, sometimes lustily comic. If you think sex is disgusting, or ought not to be described, don't read The Hand Reared Boy. If you can take it you'll like it.

0 552 11143 0   85p

A SELECTED LIST OF FINE FICTION
PUBLISHED BY CORGI

CORGI BOOKS, Cash Sales Department, P.O. Box 11, Falmouth, Cornwall.

Please send cheque or postal order, no currency.

U.K. Please allow 30p for the first book, 15p for the second book and 12p for each additional book ordered to a maximum charge of £1.29.

B.F.P.O. and Eire allow 30p for the first book, 15p for the second book plus 12p per copy for the next 7 books, thereafter 6p per book.

Overseas Customers. Please allow 50p for the first book and 15p per copy for each additional book.

NAME (Block Letters) ....

ADDRESS ....

....